Kristina

For my granddaughter
Cressida

Kristina

ISBN 978-184426-451-3

First published 2007 by
UPFRONT PUBLISHING LTD
Peterborough, England.

Printed by Printondemand-Worldwide Ltd.

Also available from the same author

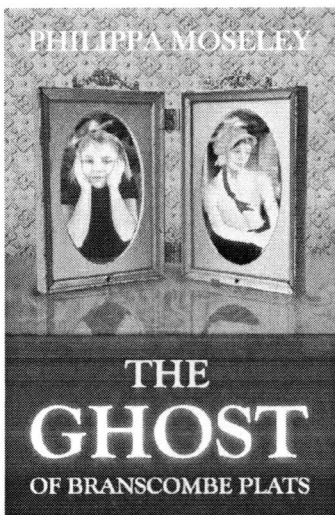

The Ghost of
Branscombe Plats
(2003)

ISBN 9781844262366

Diary of a
Medieval Lady
(2005)

ISBN 9781844263233

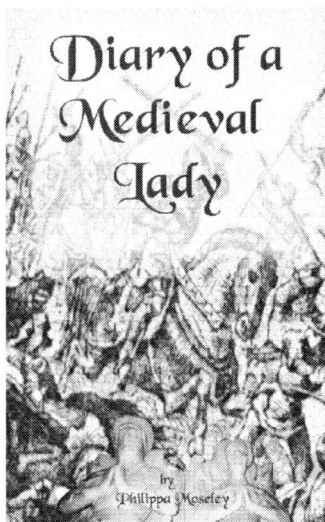

www.upfrontpublishing.com

Also available from the same author

A Free Ride
to the Bridge
(2006)

ISBN 9781844263523

Sir Tristram
And the Great
Commotion
in the West
(2007)

ISBN 9781844264155

www.upfrontpublishing.com

As Kristina rose from the café table she noticed something familiar about the expensively dressed blonde lady at the next table. Was it Miranda? Yes, surely it was – Miranda twenty years on, beautifully made up, dripping with gold and wafting a subtle perfume.

Kristina stared, and their eyes met. Miranda let out a well-remembered bubbly shriek of recognition. 'My God, it's Kristina! How absolutely divine! Come and sit down. We must talk.'

An hour later they were still catching up on the years. 'Poor, poor you!' exclaimed Miranda. 'Married to a struggling actor, and living in a rented two-room flat in Notting Hill! What kind of life is that?'

'I'm perfectly happy now with my career in theatre.'

'But my dear, You could have done so much better for yourself. If only you hadn't been expelled. The Dunbar gives one the best start in life. As Daddy always said, just mentioning you're a Dunbar girl, even if one doesn't make it to Oxbridge, opens all the doors. Rich husbands –' Miranda giggled '– good jobs, super social life, moving in the right circles. Even in the States they've heard of the Dunbar. We were so privileged to be there.'

'Privileged! You used to grumble all the time.'

'Of course, doesn't everyone? But we had some jolly good laughs.'

'Did we?'

'It may sound frightfully silly, but I do actually feel proud to have been a Dunbar girl.'

Kristina

Chapter One

O n the last day of the summer term Mr Morrison picked up his twelve-year-old daughter, Jenny, and her friend Kristina from the Girls' High School in Port of Spain. The girls sat in the back of the car, their legs sticking to the burning leather seat, as he drove slowly down Pembroke Street, edging his way past a honking, overloaded taxi, two cyclists balancing heavy sacks on their handlebars and a vendor pushing a coconut cart.

They breathed in the heavy scent of the red frangipani in the grounds of the buff-coloured Anglican Cathedral before the car emerged into Woodford Square, where a newspaper seller was squatting on a piece of cardboard, munching a roti. On reaching Marine Square they joined the queue leaving the town by the Eastern Main Road.

Kristina detested the hellishly hot first few miles of the traffic-congested road she knew so well. Each Friday afternoon during term time she and Jenny were driven along it between the capital, Port of Spain, and Sangre Grande, where her father, John White, was the Anglican Rector. First came San Juan, a ribbon development of shabby shops, factories and discarded junk, including several smashed cars – the whole overlaid with the stench of copra. On the seaward side, behind the line of Saman trees, a train moved along slowly with several schoolboys clinging dangerously to the outside. Then came shacks made of cardboard and corrugated iron sheets. Filthy gutters overflowed, and rags of washing hung over bare yards. Little houses on stilts poked up behind dusty hibiscus hedges.

After St Joseph the green and white mosque with fretted arches and twin minarets topped by a crescent and star, came into sight. Red and white flags hung on poles in the yards of the Hindus. The car crawled through Tunapuna behind a bullock cart pushing its way through a group of women leaving the stand-pipe balancing buckets on their heads. A couple of mangy, scavenging dogs fought over a bloody bone. Jenny and Kristina held their noses for a few minutes to avoid the smell of dust, dung and rotting mangoes. Sometimes a flamingo or a white egret would appear from the nearby Caroni river. But not that afternoon. All they saw was the familiar line of ugly black corbeaux perched on a tin roof.

After Tacarigua and Arouca the sprawling urban landscape gave way to fields of sugar cane and coconut groves. At last Mr Morrison could drive fast enough to enable a hot breeze to circulate through the car. Kristina fixed her eyes on the road, which seemed to waver in the searing heat, thinking with delight about the two months' holiday ahead.

Recently her father had told her something of the train of events leading to his divorce and to her mother, Tessa's, remarriage. She'd come to Trinidad under the illusion that her husband was to be the Rector of Cascade where friends of hers, Nina and Ted Watson, already lived – a pleasant residential suburb of Port of Spain. Nina had written, eulogising the beaches, parties, picnics, exotic scenery, perpetual sunshine and the cheapness of servants and rum. But on arrival by sea, John White was told that he wouldn't, after all, be working in Port of

Spain. Instead he'd been assigned to take charge of Sangre Grande, some twenty-eight miles from the capital. His wife was bitterly disappointed at the idea of living in a distant small town devoid of white people. John, on the other hand, was relieved to be serving a coloured community in a rural area.

His first impression of Port of Spain on disembarking hadn't been entirely good. The town had struck him as a nightmare of clanging trams, run-down buildings, gaudy milk bars, all-night joints and gum-chewing noisy crowds. Later, however, he grew to love its enormous Savannah, backed by the olive-hued hills of the Northern Range, and shaded on the north side by tall cotton trees. An electric tramline ran round it, and contained within its ample space were a racetrack, a cemetery, a bandstand, clumps of palms, a gigantic monkey-pot tree and numerous pitches for cricket, football and hockey. A bewildering assortment of high-gabled villas overlooked the Savannah, each incorporating different architectural features – pinnacles, domes, fretted spikes, turrets, mosaics, glazed tiles, bow windows, half-timbering, spires, pagodas, cupolas and stained glass. And though John had never been fond of towns, he came to appreciate the extraordinary vitality of its cosmopolitan populace.

By the time they'd reached Sangre Grande, Tessa, who was six months pregnant, was suffering badly from the heat. She had to lie down immediately on the sagging lumpy mattress in the bedroom, while John unpacked their trunks containing clothes and linen, and then the tea-chests full of china, cooking utensils and books.

The Rectory was a large square wooden building with exposed beams inside and fretwork on the shutters and eaves. It had once been the estate house on a small cocoa plantation, but was now dilapidated and still without electricity. The shower room consisted of an evil-smelling rectangular pit of rough concrete over which hung a musty shower-head. The stained tiles were cracked, the toilet bowl discoloured, and the flushing system unreliable. A trickle of brown water emerged from the wash-basin tap. One huge wardrobe and a large chest of ill-fitting drawers had to serve all three bedrooms. The remaining furniture was sparse in the extreme. Rusty clothes hooks protruded from the bedroom walls, and yellowing mosquito nets were hitched up over the beds. The kitchen cupboards were cavernous, but spattered with rat and roach droppings. Cobwebs festooned the rafters, and dead flies clustered on the fly-papers.

A young girl named Clementine, who'd been employed by the previous incumbent, eventually arrived. John smiled, asking many questions, which the maid answered with much shy giggling. Not understanding a word she said, Tessa thought she must be stupid. But John realised it was a question of fathoming the West Indian dialect.

She brought basic provisions – hops bread, Klim milk, porridge oats, tea, sugar, bananas, a pineapple and some hard warty avocados. Also margarine and a packet of lurid orange Kraft cheese, which John put in the icebox. She made up a pint of milk in a jug and boiled water on the calor-gas stove to make tea. She swept the concrete floor and sprinkled white cockroach powder in the cupboards.

Then she departed, saying she'd be back the next day at 6.30 am if required.

John began to feel at home in Sangre Grande immediately, and soon became accustomed to the primitive house in spite of aggressively persistent insects and the horrors of the shower room. His parishioners were welcoming and generous beyond their means, often depositing sacks of grapefruit or sweet potatoes on the doorstep. He'd only to go out of the Rectory by day or night to be entranced by the tropical beauty of the island, with its unusual variety of trees, plants and birds. He liked the feeling of remoteness from civilisation and the deep, unearthly silence which sometimes descended after dark. Living twenty-eight miles from Port of Spain didn't bother him. He drove into town when necessary for diocesan meetings and occasional shopping, but was always glad to return home.

For Tessa, however, Sangre Grande was a nightmare of fear, boredom and loneliness. She was terrified a snake or scorpion might attack. She could hear rats running along the rafters at night. She hated having to keep the heavy legs of the double-bed placed in tins of water to discourage termites from climbing up. As for the shower room, it was a hell-hole. She would never have come to Trinidad had she known what was in store.

Nina and Ted persuaded her to stay in their luxurious modern air-conditioned house in Cascade until the birth of her baby in a maternity clinic, and then to return afterwards to recuperate. Tessa had been a private nurse in England before her marriage, and after Kristina was born, decided she would have to take up nursing in Port of Spain. It had become obvious John's stipend wouldn't be sufficient to support a child. But private nursing meant living in or being within reach of a patient's house for a week or even a month. So John collected their baby and entrusted her to the care of a local widow, Desdemona, whom Kristina christened Dodo. She proved to be an ideal nanny, warm-hearted, loyal and practical, with a raucous voice and picturesque turn of phrase which Kristina loved to imitate.

'I dead soon!' Dodo would groan whenever exerting herself, especially when turning the handle in a bucket of ice to make ice cream. 'I dead soon!' were the first words Kristina repeated as she trailed after her nanny.

Tessa never returned to Sangre Grande; she rented a bed-sitting room, and spent the time between nursing jobs enjoying parties and flirtations. John took Kristina to see her whenever possible, but she showed little interest in her child. When Kristina was four, Tessa caused something of a scandal by asking for a divorce in order to marry Denis, a wealthy British business man she'd met in Port of Spain. His firm was based in Switzerland, and they left Trinidad in 1939 to live in Geneva.

Divorce was unacceptable for an Anglican priest, and John expected to be asked to leave his parish. Had he been a vicar in England he would certainly have had to go. But in Sangre Grande the parishioners were more tolerant, and they petitioned the bishop to allow him to stay. His feeling of failure and disgrace was made easier, however, by the task of bringing up his daughter. Tessa had no wish to take Kristina to Switzerland, even though Britain was on the brink of war with Germany, and civilian travel across the Atlantic might soon become dangerous.

No news came from Switzerland during the war, though John wrote regularly giving news of Kristina's progress. Then in May 1947 he heard from his widowed mother-in-law, Constance Mannering. John had three months' leave owing to him which he hadn't intended to take, but Constance wanted him to bring Kristina to England in September to meet her mother. In the meantime Constance would visit Sangre Grande to discuss her granddaughter's future.

She arrived in July, and within hours had decided that neither Kristina's behaviour nor her manner of speaking came up to standard. She reproved the girl at every opportunity. The more she did so, the more Kristina flaunted her West Indian accent, using all the phrases Dodo and the children at the village primary school had taught her. John ticked her off, but only half-heartedly. Though he'd never picked up the local way of speaking himself, he considered the grammatical faults in the dialect sounded very well in Trinidad. Some sentence constructions even seemed to gain in logic, and certainly in charm.

On the journey home from school, Kristina's mind had been so wrapped up in thoughts of her mother, her grandmother and the uncertain future, that she hadn't noticed they'd passed through the small town of Arima and were now approaching Valencia. Here the road veered south on the last lap to Sangre Grande, with plantation trees rising in ordered ranks on either side – cocoa, citrus and banana. Kristina waited with an excitement which had never abated to catch sight of the immense poui tree growing outside the police station, and having passed that, to see the avenue of royal palms leading to the Rectory.

She got out of the car, drawling, 'So long, Jenny! So long, Mr Morrison!' in imitation of the American soldiers based in Trinidad. She charged up the tree-lined drive to the house, and letting her bulging satchel and holdall fall to the ground, flung off her damp school blouse. Then she leapt joyfully up the four wooden steps onto the rickety balustraded gallery running all round the rectory, over which the eaves extended to protect against driving tropical rain. At the back more steps led down to the yard, in which were situated the washhouse, the hen-coop and various outhouses which had once been servants' quarters.

Dodo, wearing a bright orange and red bandanna, was hanging out her washing as Kristina jumped down the steps, yelling, 'Haul your tail from my yard!' Then she grasped Dodo's ample starched figure, and they swung round in a crazy dance until they collapsed with uninhibited raucous laughter onto the sun-scorched grass, scattering the hens in every direction. This ritual on Kristina's return from school each Friday never altered.

As Kristina heaved Dodo to her feet, a voice came from behind the half-open jalousied door, 'Kristina, do stop using that vulgar phrase. It's high time you stopped behaving like a hooligan.'

'I like being a hooligan!' Kristina retorted rudely, and regretted it immediately, for she'd promised her father not to give cheeky replies, especially to her grandmother. Then she noticed the pink whalebone corset hanging on the washing line, and broke into more laughter. Dodo explained that ladies in England wore such garments to keep themselves looking slim.

Later Kristina overheard her grandmother, whose high-pitched voice penetrated the whole house, trying to persuade her son-in-law that Sangre Grande was no place to bring up his daughter. 'You're letting that girl run wild, John', she said. 'You don't even know where she is half the time. Think of the dangers around here.'

'She's safe enough in Sangre Grande. I'm not her jailer.'

'As for her clothes, out of uniform she looks like a street urchin. She needs a mother to guide her and explain the kind of things men know nothing about. It's time she went to an English boarding school to be taught how to conduct herself properly. The sooner the better, so she can integrate now. When you go home on leave, you and Tessa must find a good school for Kristina.'

'I agree Kristina should meet Tessa. But I don't want her to go to boarding school. This is her home. and the High School is perfectly adequate. The education is based on a British syllabus, and many of the girls go on to university. As for having a woman to explain things, Mrs Morrison, the lady she lodges with during term-time in Port of Spain, is doing a good job.'

Constance's voice became shrill with indignation. 'You don't seem to have any idea about bringing up a child. You can't expect this Mrs Morrison to cope with Kristina all through her teens. And what about the school holidays, what will Kristina do in Sangre Grande? Have you ever thought about that?'

'At the moment she's happy.'

Constance pointed out that John had had Kristina entirely to himself for eight years, and now it was Tessa's turn. There was no denying this, and John was inclined to give in, only adding that post-war Britain wasn't as healthy a place to bring up a child as Trinidad, what with rationing and fuel shortages.

'English children are very healthy', snapped Constance. 'The government issues free milk, orange juice and cod liver oil, and they do very well on it.'

'I'd want her to live with Tessa and go to a day school.'

'That would be impossible. Tessa plans to come to England just for the school holidays, and Kristina can't live in my small flat in Salisbury. I'm prepared to pay the boarding school fees. You and Tessa can share the cost of her holidays. Since Kristina's my only grandchild, I'd like her to have a good education, as Tessa did.'

'I could never understand why you sent Tessa to boarding school.'

'We sent her because she was an only child, and becoming quite a handful. By the age of eleven she needed a more disciplined education, learning to obey rules and concentrate more on her academic work.'

'Most children learn to concentrate and obey rules at a day school?'

'Possibly. But they rarely acquire the manners, consideration for others and team spirit which a boarding school provides. After a year away, Tessa became a different person.'

And later, thought John, freed from the restraints of boarding school and nursing college, she went wild, becoming obsessed with pleasure, material comfort and love affairs. 'D'you really think education consists only in long hours of academic work, team sport and being severely punished if one doesn't obey the petty rules.'

'School rules are devised for a good purpose. You've not been to a boarding school, so you know nothing about it.'

'No, but I read about education. I do admit that recently there have been some interesting experiments in boarding school education, in which children are encouraged to be individuals rather than obedient puppets.'

'If you mean one of those new-fangled mixed progressive schools, run by cranks, then you can be sure Kristina won't be sent to one.'

During the evening meal, sitting at the cedar table with a gleaming pewter pot of enormous dark red impatiens in the middle, Constance expounded her views on the Rectory, 'How do you put up with the conditions here? This house is medieval, especially the shower room. That dreadful brown water, and those dirty cracked tiles! Why doesn't the church replace them?'

'Probably because I don't complain. The diocese is always short of money, and these rural rectories aren't easy to modernise.'

But Constance hadn't finished. 'The food's dreadful, the local shops are grubby, and so are the children. How can you allow Kristina to play with them? That Desdemona does just as she pleases. As for the scorpions, cockroaches and other disgusting insects, words fail me!'

'You haven't actually tried any West Indian cooking, Constance', said John, with that half-patient, half-amused look he kept for difficult parishioners.

'Desdemona isn't used to English recipes. Anyway, I can't afford to buy imported American and Canadian tinned and frozen food. The local fish are delicious, and our own chickens are very tasty made into spicy dishes with home grown vegetables. There's a particularly good dish made with crab, called calaloo, and Desdemona's pumpkin soup's a real treat, but I daresay you…'

'Having inspected your kitchen', interrupted Constance, 'I shudder to think of eating Desdemona's dishes. I shall continue to prepare my own tinned food.'

'You could at least try a mango, or some of these wonderfully sweet miniature bananas we call figs.'

'No thank you. I prefer to avoid tummy trouble.'

'So be it.'

And when they were drinking coffee, even the imported Huntley and Palmer biscuits failed to please, for the tin was running with weevils.

Father and daughter couldn't warm to this thin, pinched-looking woman clad in a grey silk dress, grey stockings and black patent leather lace-ups. Most of the day she would sit upright in the solid mahogany chair, having removed the shabby cushions. If a tangerine butterfly or an iridescent dragonfly flew round her, she would flap agitatedly at it with a palm-frond. Only after her siesta did she venture outside to walk a few times round the gallery. Apart from Dodo's vegetable plot, the Rectory garden was a colourful wilderness of trees, shrubs and wild life. Constance shunned it, partly for fear of snakes, but mainly from fear of the unfamiliar. The first bat of the evening would send her scurrying to her room. John hoped that a rum punch might have mellowed the old lady, but she refused to try one, and every evening ended in unconvivial silence.

That first night of her school holidays, Kristina lay in bed reading Enid Bagnold's *National Velvet*, while jackspaniards dived across the room and huge moths clustered round the gas lamp. Through the window came the intoxicating scent of the Lady of the Night shrub. Her father came to say goodnight as he'd always done, lifting the corner of the much-darned mosquito net, and perching on the edge of the bed.

'Was your mother a nice lady?' asked Kristina.

'She was very kind and understanding.'

'I wish she was here instead of Mrs Mannering.'

'That's not a charitable thought. But I do wish my parents could have seen you.'

'Are you really going to send me to boarding school?' Kristina asked,

'You've been listening to my conversation with your grandmother.'

'I don't want to go away. From what I've heard, England's a dull grey cold wet place. You prefer it here, so why can't I stay?'

'Because it's fair that your mother should have a share in your upbringing.'

'She could have stayed in Sangre Grande and not gone off with that Denis chap!'

'No, Tessa could only have tolerated Trinidad if we'd lived in a house like the Morrisons', with air-conditioning, a swimming pool and lots of white expatriates to socialise with.'

'Why couldn't she socialise with black or brown people?'

'Because they have a different way of enjoying life. I like their way, and I love Sangre Grande. That's partly why your mother and I couldn't live together.'

'How silly to get married then', said Kristina rudely.

Instead of being annoyed, John only said, 'You're right. But people do stupid things – even you, Kristina!'

'I don't want to go to boarding school!'

'No, it's a pity your mother doesn't live permanently in England, so you could attend a day school. Lots of girls have to go to boarding school, and many of them enjoy it. Since you're a clever girl, you'll benefit, as your grandmother puts it, from a proper British education. Trinidad can't provide all the interesting cultural experiences to be had in England. And later, if you want to go to university, I'd prefer you went to one in the UK. It will be easier to gain a place and qualify for a grant if you're already living in England.'

Kristina didn't reply, and he continued, 'We'll be sailing to Southampton in September, with twelve days on the ship. Then you'll have three months to get used to England before going to school.'

Kristina was silent for a while, before bursting out, 'I hate Grandmother! I wish she hadn't come. She doesn't even like being here.'

'At her age it must be strange, even frightening, coming to Sangre Grande.'

'She's lucky to be in the sun in a lovely place where she can swim and eat bananas and coconuts and mangoes every day.'

John laughed. 'The trouble is, she doesn't like West Indian fruit and vegetables.'

'What do they sell in English markets?'

'You won't find avocados, bread fruit, yams, okras or dasheen, for a start.'

'Not any of our vegetables?'

'Marrows'.

Kristina managed a smile before asking, 'When will I see you again?'

'In three years' time I hope to bring you home for the summer holidays.'

'Three years!' exclaimed Kristina. 'I'll be nearly sixteen by then.'

'Your mother won't want to part with you too often, and it's expensive to travel to Trinidad. I'm hoping you might spend some time with my sister, your Aunty Ruth, and her husband, Peter. They've just moved to a seaside town.'

'My mother might not like me.'

'Of course she will.'

'Grandmother doesn't like me.'

'Because she thinks you're cheeky and rather boisterous. As it happens, I received your school report today.' John handed it to his daughter with a grin. 'It would seem that your teachers also think you're loud and boisterous.'

Kristina glanced down the list of subjects and then at the remarks of the Headmistress. *Kristina continues to be a bright, cheerful and helpful girl, but she can be rather boisterous and bossy. She should think before she voices her very definite opinions. And she must learn to control her loud laughter, and conduct herself in a more ladylike manner.*

'You'll have to tone down your voice and your laugh.'

'When will Grandmother be going?'

'Tomorrow.'

Kristina jumped up and down on the bed, shouting, 'De Lord be praised!' and then burst into loud laughter, as one of the bed springs snapped.

'Your grandmother has a point', said John. 'You're too big to jump around like a five-year-old.'

Chapter Two

The summer holidays had always been the best time of year for Kristina. Eight weeks of freedom to roam the land round Sangre Grande on foot or on her bike. She belonged to a group of girls who often swam from the sandy beach at Manzanilla. Her friends were children she'd known at the local primary school, which she'd enjoyed immensely. Most of the lessons had taken place outside, under a ceiba tree, whose huge solid grey trunk and massive roots reminded Kristina of a giant elephant's leg. It was appropriately known as a sacred tree, a tree of wisdom.

This last school holiday in Trinidad would exist for ever in Kristina's memory as the most magical of her youth. The fact that she would soon be going to boarding school didn't at first impinge on her enjoyment. How impossible to believe life was going to change! Yet as the weeks slid by Kristina became aware that time was flying past, and she wouldn't be rejoining her friends at the High School. She even began to get up earlier so as to gain an extra half hour.

The best days were when Kristina's friends, who called themselves the Oropouche Gang, decided to go to Manzanilla. Plantation trucks were always driving the seven-mile stretch from Sangre Grande to the coast, so it was easy to cadge a lift.

At six a.m. Kristina would slip on her swimming costume, a faded cotton dress and the gold ankle-bracelet which had so shocked her grandmother. After gobbling down slices of mango and breadfruit with two spoonfuls of condensed milk, she would stuff hops bread, goat's cheese, a bottle of water and a spoon into her beach bag. Then it was time to dash along the drive to the road, to wait for her best friend, Yvonne Thomas, who was only eleven. Kristina's own age group had left primary school, and could no longer join in day-long expeditions. They were required to assist on the plantations or in the house, hoping to be set free in the late afternoon. Thus, being the oldest that summer, Kristina became the undisputed leader of the Oropouche Gang. They even called her Boss, which pleased her greatly.

The truck would speed along between the citrus trees and the wild tannia with its huge heart-shaped leaves. Then came thickets of tall bamboo, tonka bean and nutmeg – and rows of cocoa trees growing in the shade of other trees. Suddenly the girls would catch a glimpse of vivid blue between the trunks, and a few minutes later the Atlantic ocean would appear, the long waves rolling lazily up and down the strand. They would scramble off the trucks and race to be the first in the water.

Afterwards they would play rounders on the beach. At eleven, one of the girls might produce a bag of soursops, shaped like large pears covered with dark rind, roughened with tiny hooked briars. Kristina adored the soft, snow-white fruit inside tasting like pear drops. Or the girls might share out some pawpaws. These were the same size as soursops, but with smooth, soft rind coloured gold, mottled green and rusty brown. Each pawpaw was halved lengthwise, to reveal the black seeds and the sweet coral-coloured fruit to be scooped out with a spoon.

From midday until about three everyone would alternate between half-standing, half-floating in the sea or lying in the shade of the palm trees backing the beach. Later in the afternoon a few older girls might join the Gang and they would run races along the strand – sprinting, three-legged and hurdle races. Sometimes a group of young boys would appear to taunt them with mild insults.

During this last summer, for the first time one of the boys singled Kristina out as being a stuck-up know-all white girl, and soon they were chanting, 'Kristina think she better than we!' Then they whispered to one another and laughed. They weren't old enough to risk shouting obscenities, for fear the Reverend White might call on their parents to complain. Kristina was put out and puzzled as to why the boys had turned on her in particular, but not unduly bothered. She knew some choice insulting phrases to retaliate with if necessary. And her best friend Yvonne knew even more. Small though she was, she could and did stand up to any gang of boys.

Kristina would often go to Yvonne's house, a small, two-roomed building with a lean-to kitchen and outside toilet. The roof was thatched with palm fronds, and the cracked walls of the house seemed to be held together by a mass of frangipani and a trumpet vine with long orange and red flowers. The garden was a riot of runaway growth and colour – tamarind with pale yellow flowers streaked with red, blue plumbago, yellow pineapple, apricot hibiscus, orange marigolds and pink oleander –

along with two trees producing Julie mangoes, unequalled for juicy sweetness. At the back was a yard laid with an assortment of discarded tiles Mr Thomas had picked up. Here the girls played hopscotch.

Inside, the roof was supported by rafters. Over the years Kristina had been worried by a long sagging, overloaded shelf which threatened to come away from the wall, but somehow seemed to hang on. A bunch of fake orchids in a tin can stood on this shelf.

'Why fake flowers', asked Kristina, 'With all those lovely real ones in the garden?'

Yvonne replied, 'Because they never die, of course.'

Kristina wondered how the Thomas family could live in such cramped conditions. The Rectory was old and dilapidated, with paper peeling off the hessian-covered walls, but at least there was plenty of space in the high airy rooms. The flooring of mora wood was luxurious compared to the baked mud flooring of the Thomases' house. Oddly enough, though, what Yvonne admired most in the Rectory was a large cumbersome wooden coat and hat rack, with large brass hooks, an ornate tarnished mirror and a drawer 'for ladies to put gloves in', so Dodo informed the girls. John couldn't fathom how anyone could have installed this huge monstrosity in the Rectory, since no one in Trinidad wore coats or gloves. Yvonne thought the Whites must be very rich to live in a plantation house with fretwork on the gables and four bedrooms.

Mr Thomas worked on a cocoa plantation, and his wife kept a stall selling oranges and mangoes. Kristina loved her sweet juicy green oranges, mottled with yellow. She couldn't understand why they weren't exported.

'The reason is', said her father, laughing, 'That Europeans don't trust oranges that aren't orange!'

Mrs Thomas seemed to be for ever baking cakes in her mud oven for church soirées. She would always offer Kristina a slab of bright yellow cake and a glass of red sorrel cordial. Her daughter had a poor appetite, she said, and it was a pleasure to feed an ever-hungry girl.

Being an only child, Yvonne was lucky in having a small space to herself, curtained off from her parents' room. Covering every inch of the wall were pictures of tropical birds cut out from newspapers and magazines – parrots and parakeets, honey creepers, humming birds and many others. Obsessed with birds, she declared she was going to be an ornithologist.

John had recently entrusted her with the loan of his binoculars. The bright, dark eyes in her little round black face had lit up with such intense joy as she took them, that Kristina envied her single-minded devotion. Yvonne, who was so excitable and full of movement with her friends, could spend a couple of hours sitting absolutely still and silent waiting for the sight of a particular bird. Kristina eventually asked if she could join a bird-watching session.

'No', said Yvonne firmly, 'You too big and clumsy. You does clump about making so much noise.' But she gave in when Kristina swore to be quiet. In the forest she tried to make herself comfortable on the ground. After half an hour her legs began to ache. She was about to creep away, when Yvonne thrust the binoculars into her hands to watch a humming bird. It was easy to identify, owing to its amazing colours – vibrant ruby throat, green head, and turquoise, light blue and purple body. Seeing it in magnificent close-up was a special experience: its slender bill almost too long for its short body, and its colours like vivid jewels against the dark green tree. Then the girls saw what even Yvonne had never seen before – the humming bird lowered its left wing awkwardly and brought its left leg down over the blade in order to scratch with its claw. As it darted away Yvonne whispered excitedly, 'Did you see how it scratching? Did you see?'

Kristina nodded as she handed back the binoculars.

Yvonne longed to go to South America to see a mocking bird. 'It looks something like a thrush', she said, 'And can imitate the songs of other birds.' Of all the birds she'd seen, the humming bird was her favourite. There used to be many more kinds of birds in Trinidad. Thousands were slaughtered so their feathers could be used for trimming hats and dresses. Even our beautiful humming birds almost disappeared.

'My father told me', said Kristina, 'That the aboriginal Indians called Trinidad *Iere*, which actually means *Land of the Humming Bird.*'

Fired by Yvonne's enthusiasm Kristina began to take an interest in recognising the local birds, such as the yellow, black, white and chestnut coloured *kiskadee*,. Yvonne said this bird was probably from the flycatcher family. It was called the *kiskadee,* since it always seemed to be singing *Qu'est ce qu'il dit – What does he say?*

Soon Kristina recognised the yellow and black corn birds nesting in the eighty-feet-high immortelle, and the blue tanagers, who preferred the mango trees. She accompanied Yvonne on more bird-watching afternoons, learning to sit still comfortably without moving a muscle, while listening to the whirring of insects and watching armies of brown ants marching across her feet. Just when she wanted to scream with boredom, a bird would appear and she'd become riveted. Eventually the fiery red ball of the sun would sink low into the trees. Then the girls had to move quickly, stumbling over tree-roots and getting caught in creepers, for darkness fell swiftly in Trinidad. Yvonne was terrified of spirits, but Kristina was more frightened of wildcats and wild boar, and most of all, snakes.

Every other day the father of one of Kristina's friends, who owned a truck, had to make a trip starting before dawn to Toco, a village on the most northerly point of the island. He would fill the bottom of his vehicle with long ice blocks and cover them with sacking. Quite often he offered to give the local schoolgirls a lift, perched round the edge of his truck with their feet resting inwards on the sacking.

That first week of the holidays, eight girls turned up, including Kristina. The thirty miles to Toco via the villages of Matura, Salibea and Redhead were so bumpy it was a wonder they weren't all sick. When the truck lurched sharply round bends, they had to cling on tight or risk falling off. Kristina became adept at keeping her balance, but joined in the ear-splitting shrieks of the others at each stomach-turning jolt. If another vehicle came up close behind, the girls would make faces at the driver, with much laughter. At Ballandra Bay they passed the white gate of the Morrisons' holiday villa, and the long fence over which hung showers of yellow cassia. Jenny Morrison longed to join the trips, but her parents wouldn't allow her to associate with the local children.

Just before reaching Toco, the girls were told to jump off the truck. In the pink freshness of dawn they walked down into the coastal village of wooden red-roofed houses. St David's, a Gothic revival church, stood beside a school next to a police station adjoining a court house. Naked toddlers were already splashing water over each other under a standpipe, and a white-haired old lady was laying out melons, cucumbers, onions, limes and marrows in front of a mud-plastered shop topped with a thatched roof. A sign standing against the wall read *Opening and closing 6 a.m. to 11 p.m.* The truck had already delivered an ice block to the rum shop, and was now heading along the hazardous North Coast Road to its end at Matelot. Another truck was about to leave from outside the Shell garage, carrying men with cutlasses to work on the plantations.

Kristina and Yvonne led the way to the sea, miraculously flecked with gold in the early sunshine. Wavelets were breaking gently, depositing a fringe of lacy white foam on the pristine sand. As yet there were few flying insects to annoy. This was the time of day when swimming was at its best. Later the sea would seem almost syrupy. Now it felt deliciously cool, and the girls had to swim hard for a few minutes before turning to float on the deep green water.

After their swim, Kristina and Yvonne went off on their own, dawdling in the mounting heat along the twisting track, past a group of king-sized palms with smooth grey trunks to Point Galera. There they sat on a flat rock to share a paper bag of tulum balls, Dodo's speciality – sweets fashioned of molasses, coconut, sugar and spice. A cooling breeze off the sea enabled them to bear the scalding rays of the sun. as they lay on their stomachs to watch a green lizard with blue eyes, and small crabs scurrying along with protruding black eyes on stalks.

'Did you know', said Kristina, 'That years ago when the Spaniards had conquered Trinidad, some of the aboriginal Indians rebelled against being their slaves? The Spaniards chased them to Toco, and rather than be captured and tortured and executed, all the Indians, men, women and children, threw themselves into the sea and drowned.'

Yvonne had not heard of this tragic mass suicide. She looked down at the water crashing against the rocks and shuddered.

'There were two kinds of Indians', continued Kristina. 'The peaceful Arawaks, and the fierce Carib cannibals. In the end the Trinidad Caribs were wiped out.'

'You're wrong. There are some left in Arima', said Yvonne. 'A Carib queen called Mistress Martinez lives there.'

'I know why this place is called "Point Galera"', said Kristina, continuing to show off her knowledge. 'When Columbus came to Trinidad it was a misty moonlit night. He saw the shape of the high rocks, and at first thought they looked like the outline of a galley. So he called it *Punta Galera.*'

When the sun was directly overhead they sought the shade of some trees before walking back to Toco. Several men were listening to a crackling radio in the rum shop, and a tantalising smell of roast wild pig pervaded the village. But the children had to make do with the food they'd brought – vegetable roti with corn bread. Dodo was anxious to provide Kristina with fried chicken, salad, cakes and fruit, but was told it would be so embarrassing to eat such a lavish meal in front of her friends. Outside the rum shop two men were drinking Carib beer as they played draughts with bottle-tops on a home-made board balanced on a crate.

An old woman was taking her siesta in a hammock made of jute bags sewn together and strung between two houses.

While waiting for the truck to take them home they listened to the shrieks of a young boy being beaten in a house down the road.

'D'you get beaten at home?' asked Kristina.

'No, but the boys in the house nearby do.'

'My father says children should never be beaten.'

'Spare the rod, and you does spoil the child', replied Yvonne somewhat smugly.

When Kristina reached home, Dodo was preparing Kristina's favourite meal – grilled pork, rice, peas and okras covered with pepper sauce. The only West Indian dish Kristina disliked was souse, Dodo's favourite – pig's feet in cold brine with cucumber, onion, limes and spices. John would have been content to continue having a plate of food in his study, but when Kristina reached the age of ten he decided they must eat in the dining room, so she could learn table manners. At her request they dined by the light of candles placed in cylindrical hurricane lamps. She loved to watch the flickering light on the walls her father had decorated with black and white family photos and a series of etchings of famous cathedrals. With Constance as their guest, the evening meal had become even more formal, with linen napkins and the Spode dinner plates John and Tessa had received as a wedding present.

Often after dinner John went out with a torch to attend a parish meeting or to visit a nearby family. He rarely drove his car after dark to the surrounding villages. Night in the forest was too black, and the traces badly rutted. Sometimes he would play chess or cards with Kristina for a while before returning to his study. He never ceased to miss the second-hand bookshops he'd frequented in England. His obsession with books had led him to sacrifice many a meal in order to buy a few more cheap Penguins. In Trinidad his books had to be checked constantly to prevent a booklouse from eating its way through page after page. John would read until midnight, and if Kristina woke she would hear him going out to sit on the gallery with his rum and water for a last smoke.

On Sundays John started taking services at 5.30 a.m., before the heat set in. He celebrated Mass at the two small mission chapels in outlying villages, and then returned for Mass at Sangre Grande. The West Indian Christians went to church wearing their best clothes – the men in suits, white shirts and ties, the women in colourful shades of taffeta or silk, with flower-decorated straw hats perched on their heads. Kristina was always amazed at seeing the young children who ran around all week barefoot and grubby, suddenly transformed into well-scrubbed little angels – the boys in dazzling white shirts with bow ties, the girls in pastel-coloured organdie frocks over lace petticoats, the huge bows in their plaited hair matching the sashes round their waists. As a little girl Dodo had put Kristina into such frocks. But she'd always disliked fussy clothes with sleeves and collars, tight sashes and white socks with highly polished shoes.

The congregation liked a long sermon and plenty of hymns sung lustily to an old harmonium. On Sunday afternoons there might be a wedding or a funeral. Such occasions occupied many hours for John, as he was invariably invited to the festive meals or the wakes, and treated royally with food and drink. The very generous hospitality shown by even the poorest of his parishioners never ceased to humble him, and made up for the often tedious speeches.

Dodo always entertained friends or relatives on Sunday evenings in her own private living room. For two or three hours the Rectory would rock with the loud voices and laughter of these ladies. Kristina picked up many of her West Indian phrases from overhearing Dodo's visitors – '*My daughter, she behavin' like a real spoil fish today*' – '*His car mash up again*' – '*That all she good for, having boy friend and making baby*' – '*What she does know can't be licked*' – '*He does be jealous of all my friends*'. For a while Kristina prefixed every statement with '*Is a damn funny thing...*' John laughed in spite of his efforts to make her speak grammatical English without swearing.

The Morrisons, with whom Kristina lodged for four nights a week in Port of Spain during term time, always welcomed her to their weekend villa. Jenny had two younger brothers, Charlie and Ken. Kristina often joined the family on beach picnics and the occasional trek to a deep pool in what they called The Jungle, where some trees rose a hundred and thirty feet into the sky. There were cedars, red sandalwood, nutmeg, divi-divi and an unusual palm, the gri-gri, with a slender white trunk, bearing clusters of shining red nuts.

Kristina loved these expeditions into the darkest depths of the forest where, owing to the lianas, vines and ferns climbing all over the trunks and stretching between the branches, only the tiniest patches of sky could be seen. But the pool in its wide clearing glittered under a large patch of startling blue. If they were lucky they might hear the loud clear notes of a black and chestnut finch, known locally as the chicki-chong. They swam in the greenish-blue water as the sun penetrated the feathery leaves of the acacia trees hanging over it. It was so clear one could see the pebbles and plants on the bottom. Occasionally they heard the distant sound of shooting and the crash of dogs through the undergrowth.

'Hunting for wild pig, goats or monkeys', said Mr Morrison, 'And I'm told there are a kind of small deer as well.'

Jenny was a pretty, good-natured girl, athletic and popular at school. Kristina found her good fun when they were swimming and very game to try climbing trees. Most of all, they shared a love of dancing. Mrs Morrison had been a dancing teacher in England, and she taught the girls all the ballroom dances, including those from Latin America – samba, cha-cha-cha and tango. However, Jenny didn't enjoy reading and had no curiosity beyond her own limited life.

The only excursion she'd ever been taken on was to see the famous pitch lake at La Brea – a hundred and fourteen acres of thick black sticky tar covered with a wrinkled skin, out of which men hacked great chunks, loading them onto miniature railway trucks. She and

Kristina agreed this was the most hellish place they'd ever seen. Otherwise Jenny knew little of Trinidad. It was all swamps and snakes and impenetrable mountains, she said. She had no interest in the extraordinary mix of races in Trinidad. How they had come to be there didn't concern her.

'Why don't your parents let you play with the Sangre Grande kids?' Kristina once asked her.

'Because they're black, and Mummy says they're grubby and might give me a disease. Anyway, I can't understand what some of them say.'

'Your brothers often look grubby. Anyway, what's wrong with being black?'

Jenny was at a loss for a moment, but finally she said, 'Well, black people aren't so clever as us. They're servants and gardeners and work on the plantations.'

Kristina was highly indignant. 'You're talking nonsense! What about Althea, or Michelle, or Cecilia in our class? They get better marks than we do, and my friend, Yvonne, who's just won a scholarship to the High School, is the cleverest girl I know. She's going to be an ornithologist.'

'What's that?'

'An expert on bird life.'

'How boring!'

Jenny did concede there were clever black and brown girls at school, and that Port of Spain was full of educated coloured people, such as doctors, lawyers and journalists. But these people were exceptions, she maintained. They didn't count as black people.

Kristina was baffled by her friend's remarks. 'My father says that soon Trinidad will become independent, and then there won't be any more white doctors or lawyers or priests or teachers or government people or anybody from the UK in charge.'

However, there was no point, Kristina knew, in trying to persuade Jenny. The Morrisons had been very kind, and she couldn't help liking them. They pitied her having no mother at home, and being brought up by a black nanny and an eccentric father who rarely socialised with expatriates and was content to live alone at Sangre Grande. At the beginning of their friendship, Jenny had occasionally come to the Rectory. But the primitive domestic arrangements and Dodo's forthright remarks made her uneasy, and soon the visits ceased.

Kristina sometimes envied the Morrisons their luxurious life, but secretly thought they could be rather stupid. Apart from grapefruit, mangoes and bananas, all their food was imported. They never frequented the nearby market to buy carite and kingfish, or any of the local vegetables. Once when they'd had tapioca pudding for lunch, Kristina told the Morrisons that it was made from the cassava root, which grows in Trinidad. Jenny denied it, saying that the tapioca packet came from the USA.

Kristina loved to listen to Dodo telling stories about Trinidad. She was a Christian, like most of the inhabitants of Sangre Grande. But some of the traditions of the old African religion had persisted, especially among the older generation, some of whom had never even been to Port of Spain. Just once Kristina dared to ask Dodo about *obeah*, a word her friends used to whisper sometimes, without knowing exactly what it entailed.

'It just foolish witch nonsense', said Dodo, but sometimes she too talked mysteriously of certain gods – Shango, the god of thunder, and Eshu the devil, to whom sacrifices were made by the obeah-woman.

'What kind of sacrifices?' Kristina asked, and was told it might be a goat or a chicken, or even a bottle of rum. Dodo always lowered her voice when mentioning Eshu. Only a black hen could be sacrificed to him.

'How sacrificed?'

'De throat cut to let de blood run slowly into de bowl.' She would say no more, but Kristina was left feeling frightened without quite knowing why. For some while afterwards she kept a look-out for a black hen, and considered how she might hide it from the obeah-woman. But who was the obeah-woman? Dodo was more willing to talk about the various Christian sects in the area, such as Moravians, Baptists and especially the Shouters, who were, she said, the strangest people. One could hear them in their chapel hut dancing and banging and shouting as they waited for the Holy Ghost to take possession of them.

As Kristina grew older, Dodo occasionally related thrilling stories she'd heard from her grandfather. In the days when black people were slaves, she said, they were treated badly, and often with great cruelty. But at night in their own compounds in the forest they set up a make-believe world, in which the leaders pretended to be kings and queens, princes and princesses, lords and generals, with the rest of the slaves as their servants. They dressed in fancy clothes, held court and sent secret messages to rival kings on other plantations. They made up songs about killing their masters, which everyone learnt and passed from village to village. For most slaves this was merely an exciting game. However, when several plantation owners were found poisoned, stories began to circulate about what the blacks would do to the whites one day. The slave leaders on each plantation were arrested and tortured. Some were hanged. Dodo didn't stint on the lurid details, and Kristina listened with fascination and mounting horror.

She asked her father about these stories, and he admitted they were true, but Dodo may have exaggerated some of the descriptions. When Kristina started at the High School, John decided to give her a rough outline of Trinidad's history. He knew schoolchildren were not taught much of their own history apart from the arrival of Christopher Columbus in 1498, and the British acquisition of Trinidad in 1797. He himself had been doing some historical research, with a view to writing a book, but it wouldn't be easy to explain what he'd discovered to an eleven-year-old. He wanted Kristina to know how the Spanish, British and French, together with other nationalities and individual adventurers had arrived and settled. Many of the streets in Port of Spain were named after historic characters, such as Chacon, Abercromby and Picton, but few young people knew what they were famous for.

He began by telling her that the Spaniards had seized the island in 1592, bringing a few slaves with them, and gradually wiping out most of the aboriginal tribes. After governing Trinidad for three hundred years, they suddenly abandoned the island. By 1783 the population dwindled to about three hundred poverty-stricken settlers. Then Spain decided to encourage immigration, and all kinds of people arrived.

'Where did the immigrants come from?' asked Kristina.

'Some were adventurers from various countries, including England, but most of them were refugees from the French revolution of 1789. I'll tell you about that revolution some other time. And during this period, new slaves were being brought from Africa.'

'Why did people want to have slaves?'

'Because if you're running a plantation you need plenty of labour, and if you can get workers without having to pay them anything but their keep, you soon become very rich. Black people from Africa were chosen in particular because they were already used to working in a hot climate.

'In 1797 Britain captured Trinidad, and years of harsh rule followed, particularly under Governor Picton, and later under Chief Justice Smith and Governor Woodford.' John had found the record of those years made very depressing reading, and he refrained from describing the details. He himself shuddered every time he passed the high ochre-coloured walls of the gaol in Port of Spain, even though it wasn't the original building. 'The British settlers were only interested in making lots of money from tobacco, cacao and sugar, and they saw nothing wrong in having slaves, whom they considered to be inferior human beings. On some of the plantations the slaves resorted to sorcery and poisoning, and were arrested, as Dodo has already told you.

'In 1834 the slaves were finally emancipated – that means set free – and persuaded to become Christian and adopt Christian names, but it didn't make life much easier for them. Understandably they refused to continue working on the plantations, so East Indians were brought in as paid labour. They were Hindus and Muslims, which made for religious problems.'

'Just to think', Kristina exclaimed, 'That Dodo's ancestors were treated so cruelly, and yet she's so kind to us.'

'I should point out that trading in slaves was abolished ten years after Trinidad became British. So, although the French brought some slaves with them, most of the black families here hadn't been slaves for very long, and they escaped the results of centuries of slavery. Not being so cowed and hopeless as slaves in other islands, they preserved enough spirit to rebel and to keep up their flamboyant life style.'

'Perhaps the owner of this house kept slaves?'

'Probably.'

'How horrible!'

'Well, those years are over, and we have to be glad now to live among such interesting, generous people.'

All too soon September came, and Yvonne had to rise early to catch the train from Sangre Grande to Port of Spain to start at the High School. Kristina longed to go with her instead of having to help her father prepare for England. She visited familiar places and climbed her favourite trees for the last time. She said goodbye to Yvonne, who was envious of her going to England. 'Think of all the new birds you'll see', she said. But that was no consolation. At night she couldn't sleep, and took to wandering in the garden or sitting on her childhood swing in the velvety soft darkness, watching the fireflies and listening to the frogs.

Dodo had become unusually silent and when Kristina voiced her fears about boarding school, she said glumly, 'What you fussin' so for? You'll get accustom.'

'No, I'll never get accustom!' Kristina shouted, wishing Dodo would say how much she would miss her. Years later she realised that Dodo must have suffered at the thought of parting, and dogged silence was her way of showing it.

One night in bed, Kristina realised with dismay that she'd miss Carnival, the most exciting event of the year, which took place during the three days prior to Ash Wednesday. Since the age of five her father had taken her to Port of Spain to enjoy the last day of Carnival. Dodo had described in colourful detail what she could expect to see on the never-ending floats which would cross Queens Park Savannah in front of the grandstand together with the numerous steel bands.

'Everybody does have such a good time, jus' you wait and see.' Dodo, who had a cousin living in Port of Spain, had never missed Carnival, and would remind Kristina every year how as a child she used to lie awake all night in wild excitement, 'Jus' waitin' for that bell on J'Ouvert mornin'!'

Over the years John had taken his daughter to visit several calypso tents based in the forest round Sangre Grande. These tents consisted of open sheds on wooden supports roofed over with palm fronds and lit by flambeaux –kerosene-soaked rags stuffed in bottles. From the time Kristina first heard the sound of a steel band in the distance, she became hooked on the music, and later on the calypsos. These were mostly satirical or scurrilous songs made up each year about politics, local and foreign scandal and love affairs. Kristina would listen avidly to these calypsos, snatches of which she would sing continually, though not always understanding the references.

John, who knew some of the musicians in a particular tent, had had the various instruments of the steel band described to him. The Tock-tock consisted of the sawn-off base of a kerosene tin hammered into fourteen different sized triangles, each one producing a different note when struck with an iron bar. Another tin, called Belly, was divided into seven lower notes. Then there was the Bass-kettle, a large tin drum, and the Bass-bum, made from a biscuit container. Kristina was particularly fascinated by the rattling Shack-shack, a cylinder of bamboo filled with pebbles or large seeds.

Soon, like all West Indian children, she knew the name of every steel band going back to the Desperadoes and the Crusaders, and the intriguing names of calypso singers such as Attila the Hun, Mighty Spoiler, the Iron Duke and Lord Kitchener.

For the last two years Kristina had taken part in the three-day carnival festivities with the Morrisons, dancing in the streets (known as *Jumpin' Up*, and *Playin' Mas'*) to the mesmerising rhythm of the steel bands all night long. She and Jenny would stare wide-eyed at the authentic, beautifully made costumes of the people on the floats in brilliantly lit tableaux, depicting historical and current events. Some costumes had thousands of paste pearls and coloured sequins sewn on them. The young black men on the streets were also intriguing to watch. They had the perfect physique to carry off their flamboyant clothes – long jackets, beautifully cut shirts patterned with anything from palm trees to skeletons, two-toned shoes, multicoloured ties and broad-brimmed hats.

It was intoxicating to be amongst so many swirling, uninhibited crowds of young and old people, residents and tourists alike, all moving as one to the ear-shattering rhythms.

'I could jump up all night, couldn't you?' Jenny would shout breathlessly.

'Yes', Kristina shouted back. 'But is a damn' awful thing, we have school tomorrow!'

Kristina wanted Carnival to go on for ever, but the magic was the greater for its brevity. Many of the people who planned and created the great event would go home and immediately start working on the next carnival. There was nothing like it in England, said John, and if there had been, the war would have ended it. Anyway, carnivals wouldn't be much fun in cold weather. *Grey and drab, cold and wet*, was how expatriates talked of England. They forgot the beauty of an English spring, and wished to end their days in Trinidad.

On September 18th Kristina had to forego her thirteenth birthday party. Her father was too busy organising his affairs before going on leave, and Desdemona was plunged in gloom. John's sister in England had warned him to bring plenty of clothes, including warm pyjamas, dressing gown and slippers for Kristina, since the clothing coupons would barely cover the school uniform she'd need. He hated shopping, and only replaced his own shorts and shirt when Dodo could darn them no more. So it was arranged that Mrs

Morrison would take his daughter shopping. Already she'd been buying material for her own dressmaker to run up simple dresses for Kristina.

They went to a shop specialising in warm clothing for people returning to the UK. It was air-conditioned, but even so, trying on woollen garments was most unpleasant. Long mirrors covered three sides of the changing room walls, and Kristina hardly recognised herself in a navy blue winter coat, one size too large, so it would last. The gym mistress at school had written in her report that she was athletic and fearless, but must try to be more graceful. It was true, thought Kristina, regarding herself critically when she'd taken off the coat. Her limbs did look rather uncoordinated, and the mass of long curly auburn hair sticking out from her head made her look wild. Her facial features – high, prominent forehead, large nose, wide mouth and determined chin, didn't please her either. 'I'm so damn' ugly!' she said aloud.

'No, you're not', said Mrs Morrison.

'Yes, I am!' She made a face at herself and laughed. Then her large brown eyes sparkled, and her teeth were even and very white against her tanned skin.

When they finally emerged from the changing room, Mrs Morrison said, 'You can't wear that ankle bracelet in England'.

'Why not?' said Kristina.

'Because most of the time you'll be wearing socks or stockings and lace-up shoes. I suggest you leave it with your father till you come back.'

With Dodo chivvying them along, they were more or less packed and ready two days before the sailing date. On the last day John drove Kristina to Manzanilla before dawn for a swim. There were rainbow jellyfish in the water, but they'd learnt how to avoid them. They sat on the beach until sunrise, when the sky became streaked with dramatic mauve, crimson and peach.

'This time next year you'll be here and I won't', said Kristina.

'Three years will pass very quickly, and then you'll be back.'

'Yes, but only for a holiday.'

'When you're grown up you can come back to live here, but by then you may not want to.'

'Of course I'll want to. I want to live here for ever.'

For supper they ate oysters with pepper sauce, roast corn cobs and yams. Dodo had made Kristina's favourite ice cream flavoured with guava syrup.

In the morning she was up at five o'clock. She stood looking at the familiar bedroom, feeling sick with misery. Years before, her father had lined one wall with shelves, similar to the ones he'd put in the study to hold his many books – narrow lengths of polished wood laid across red bricks. On these stood all kinds of objects she'd found or been given – shells, pebbles, a bunch of dried immortelle flowers, driftwood, carved animals, cones, pottery, a miniature Indian doll and her books. Sisal mats covered the floor. Dodo had sewn bright yellow and red curtains with bed cover to match. A faded Indian tapestry with a pattern of elephants hung above the bed, and a brilliant green and scarlet cardboard parrot made at primary school dangled on a string from a rafter. In two large baskets were heaped a mixture of clothes and discarded toys. This was her very own space, and a decorated notice saying *No entry on pain of death without permission* had been stuck outside the door.

Dodo was in the yard feeding the hens. Kristina stared at her from the gallery for a moment before leaping down the steps, shouting, 'Haul your tail from my yard!' in her best Trinidadian accent. She went into the old ritual, but instead of collapsing on the grass with laughter she burst into loud childish tears which wouldn't stop. Dodo sat up and rocked the girl in her arms.

The taxi arrived, and as they drove out of Sangre Grande, Kristina glanced up to see a boy she knew cutting coconuts at the top of a palm. He grinned and waved, and she waved back. They passed the poui tree, and then they were on the road to Valencia.

Sangre Grande and Kristina's childhood were left behind.

Chapter Three

O n reaching Port of Spain they drove along South
Quay to St Vincent jetty behind a great buffalo cart
laden with sugar cane. John recalled his initial dismay on
arrival in 1935, at seeing the dreary dockland of dirty red-
brick barracks and rusting iron enveloped in a sweltering
evil-smelling humidity. Thirteen years on, and nothing
had changed. He wished the town with its romantic
name could have had an attractive harbour to welcome
newcomers.

Kristina barely noticed the docks. She was more
interested in the French ship they were to board after the
tedious formalities at the customs office. She spent some
while exploring the decks, and when, deep within the
vessel, the engines began to judder, and they moved
slowly away from the land, her sadness was tempered
with sudden excitement.

The ship sailed west past pale green islands, which
seemed to have broken off in small pieces from the
mainland, ending with Chacachacare, the leper colony.
Kristina had heard about the terrible ravages of leprosy,
and the enforced isolation the sufferers had to endure.
Beyond Chacachacare, at the Dragon's Mouth, could be
seen the distant coastline of Venezuela, fifteen miles
across sea discoloured by the Orinoco estuary. Here the
ship turned north to travel up the long crescent of the
Windward Isles. By the time they started across the

Atlantic, Kristina had acquired a hazy impression of three ports of call, Barbados, Martinique and Guadaloupe.

Compared to the mountains and hills of Trinidad, British Barbados had presented a strangely flat skyline of fields of sugar cane beyond the neat little port of Bridgetown. In contrast, the French colony of Martinique was mountainous, the highest point being the volcano, Mont Pelée, which erupted from time to time causing much destruction. At Fort de France Kristina was astonished to hear everyone speaking French. She could hardly conceive of a West Indian speaking anything but Trinidadian.

The last port of call had been the sheltered harbour of Pointe-à-Pitre at Guadaloupe, another French colony, consisting of two islands, Bas-Terre and Grande-Terre, separated by a river spanned by a drawbridge. The cranes and warehouses on the quay were backed by palms and picturesque stone houses with their wooden upper storeys and balconies painted in bright colours.

They could have disembarked at all three islands, but John decided against. He'd always disliked the idea of being what he called a dash-in-and-dash-out tourist.

During the rest of the voyage Kristina swam in the small pool and enjoyed the meals, which as one might expect on a French boat, were excellent. She shared a cabin with a pleasant young teacher from Barbados, but would have preferred someone nearer her own age. As the weather grew colder, she was obliged to wear a jumper, woollen skirt and thick socks. She hated this heavy clothing, and complained constantly about the wool irritating her skin. The recent summer in Britain had been one of the warmest on record, but John feared that October would prove too cold for his daughter, and even for himself after the long absence in Trinidad.

As they sailed up the English Channel in mist and rain, John said, 'Don't be too disappointed when we reach Southampton, Kristina. It was badly bombed during the war. They built ugly fortifications along the south coast, so maybe one still can't use the beaches. But in Devon, where your Aunty Ruth lives, you'll see some beautiful countryside.'

They docked at midday on a Friday. John had been hoping the weather would be clear, but it was not to be. Kristina couldn't have had her first sight of England in more dismal conditions – mist, a chilly wind, driving rain, and gulls shrieking as they circled up above. She looked out eagerly from the deck, listening to the sirens in Southampton Water, but nothing she saw in the gloom gave her encouragement. The predominant colour was grey, every shade of grey with splashes of dirty green and brown.

By the time they'd disembarked it seemed to be getting darker, and all along the docks dismal lights glimmered between ugly concrete and dirty brick. They waited for their luggage in a drab shed with peeling brown paint on the walls and disintegrating linoleum on the floor, and then queued endlessly to go through customs. Kristina noted how tanned and healthy-looking were her fellow passengers compared with the greenish-white faces of the dock officials under the naked light bulbs.

'I hate this country!' stated Kristina. 'I want to go home.'

'Have patience', said her father. 'England's not all like this.' But he himself wondered about the rest of the country, and felt vaguely guilty for having missed the ravages of wartime Britain.

He looked round for his sister, Ruth, hoping he'd recognise her. But it was she who picked him out first, though he was as brown as an Indian and had lost his boyish looks. Kristina, regarding the slender, smiling woman in a shabby tweed coat and hat, suddenly felt reassured. Ruth embraced her warmly, asking questions with such interest and sympathy that she knew here was someone she could trust. This feeling was in some measure due to her aunt's great resemblance to her brother. She had the same gentle slightly amused voice and similar kind brown eyes. However, Kristina was soon to discover Ruth possessed a strong, practical streak which John lacked.

When the luggage had been loaded into the back of the express bus and they'd taken their seats, Ruth put an arm round her shivering niece. 'I'm afraid it's quite a long journey to Seaton. I should have brought a rug. It's quite warm for October, but the rain makes it seem chilly. Never mind, I've brought hot soup in a flask and some sandwiches.'

The rain continued without a break, slanting against the windows, making it difficult to see the countryside clearly. After drinking some soup, Kristina dozed on and off, now and again waking to hear her father and Ruth talking.

'What made you choose Seaton?' asked John.

'We wanted to be on the coast, and Seaton's cheaper than other seaside places in East Devon. The town does look rather drab after the war. But we found an old cottage halfway up the cliff with a large garden and a fantastic view across Seaton Bay towards Portland. The house needs renovating, and the garden's a wilderness. We're gradually knocking it into shape, but be warned, it lacks all mod cons.'

'Don't worry, Kristina and I aren't used to mod cons. Tessa and her mother were horrified when they saw the Rectory at Sangre Grande.'

The bus stopped briefly at Dorchester, and later at Lyme Regis on the sea front, where waves were lashing the promenade in the wind. Ruth led a very bleary-eyed girl to the public toilet in the pouring rain. What an introduction to England for the poor kid, she thought. She could only find one penny piece to put in the slot. Kristina had to wait for Ruth to come out in order to let her into the same cubicle.

'We're getting a taxi from here to Seaton', said Ruth. 'It's only twenty minutes. Peter will have supper ready, and a good log fire going. The twins, Penny and Anne, are dying to meet you. Then you can forget about this horrid journey.'

It was after eight when the taxi deposited them halfway up a steep lane at the west end of the town, known as Seaton Hole. The rain had ceased at last, and using a powerful torch Ruth led the way through a wooden gate set in a high stone wall and up uneven stone steps to the house. Kristina just had time to note a profusion of trees and shrubs smelling freshly of rain, stars in a patch of clear sky, and the sound of the sea far below, before being ushered into the cottage. Her Uncle Peter welcomed her warmly, but Kristina's attention was fixed on the ten-year-old twins standing on the stairs in their pyjamas. They weren't identical, Penny being dark-haired with pigtails, and Anne being the taller of the two with short fair hair.

'You girls could show Kristina her bedroom and the bathroom', said Ruth.

Partly because she was tired, Kristina felt shy for the first time in her life. But the twins sprang up the stairs eagerly. 'It's a tiny loft bedroom', said Penny, 'But we've tried to make it pretty, and you'll see the sea from the window.'

There were floral curtains and matching bedspread, and a lamp casting a pink glow over a pile of books on the bedside table.

'We chose the books, so I hope you haven't read them', said Anne.

'No', said Kristina, as she glanced at titles by Arthur Ransome, Elizabeth Goudge and Violet Needham.

'We saved our pocket money and bought you a little welcome present', said Penny, thrusting a tiny parcel at Kristina, who was overwhelmed.

In a small box lay an elephant and a giraffe in delicate blue glass lying on cotton wool. England was not so bad after all, she thought, with such generous cousins as these.

'There's a shop in Fore Street, called Smith's, which sells glass animals. You can save your pocket money and add to your collection if you like', said Penny. Anne pointed out a shelf on which she could put ornaments.

It was ten o'clock by the time Kristina had finished her apple pie and tried a mug of Horlicks, which was strange but not unpleasant. She went to sleep with the box of glass animals under her pillow, and slept soundly through the night for the first time since leaving Trinidad.

On Saturday morning she was woken by Penny and Anne jumping on her bed and demanding she get up to look at the sky. They'd drawn back the curtains at the little window, which looked out across the wide crescent of Seaton Bay. The long dark back of Haven Ball above the valley ended at Haven Cliff and then dropped gradually down to the dark shingly beach.

'You must watch the sun rise over the sea', said Penny. 'We don't often see it rise at this time of year. But when we do it's better than in the summer, when it rises over the land.'

Kristina was amazed at the transformation of the sea from the day before. The extensive sweep of the bay, in contrast to the dark cliff and shingle, glowed with a pinkish-orange light. The deep purple crests of the choppy little waves shimmered and danced on the mauve and lilac water. Above stretched a sky of the palest bird-egg blue, slashed horizontally with bands of crimson, softest peach, green and yellow. *It's just like Manzanilla,* thought Kristina in surprised delight. *The day's going to be hot and sunny, and I'll be able to go swimming.* But as the sun rose, dispersing the colours, the sky turned grey, and disappointment set in. The rust red of the cliffs partially covered with green vegetation looked sadly muted, compared to the vibrant green of palm trees, white sand and vivid blue sea in the West Indies.

'That high land on the other side of the bay, sloping down to the beach, reminds me of a sleeping crocodile', said Kristina.

'Have you seen a wild crocodile?' asked Anne.

'Of course I have, lots', she replied airily, though in fact she'd only seen two alligators in Trinidad, and one had been dead.

'If we're lucky, it might be dry today. But usually a lovely sunrise means rain later', said Penny. 'Let's hurry up with breakfast and then we'll show you the rest of the house and garden and all our favourite places.'

An interesting feature of the cottage for Kristina was the carpeted front staircase and an uncarpeted rickety one at the back. It was fun going up one and clumping down the other. She also enjoyed sitting on a stool close to the fire in the inglenook fireplace.

In spite of the weather that first weekend in Devon was so enjoyable Kristina almost forgot the reason for coming to England. The wilderness of the garden was all she could desire. There was even a monkey puzzle tree and three small palms amongst the camellia, fuchsia, laburnum and other flowering shrubs.

Secret overgrown paths led to a shrubbery, a grassy hollow and a summer house. Best of all, there was a seventy-feet-high holm oak with lower branches almost sweeping the ground, which looked perfect for climbing,. A long zigzagging path alternating with stone steps plunged down the cliff-side to the beach.

'This is where we swim in the summer', said Penny.

Kristina walked over pebbles for the first time, and putting her fingers in the water withdrew them hastily, gasping, 'It's freezing! No one could swim in that.'

'It's freezing even in August, but you soon get used to it.'

The girls trudged a mile and a half along the shingle to the little harbour full of yachts, where the wide estuary of the River Axe joined the sea. Kristina had borrowed an old windcheater with a warm hood belonging to her aunt. But she still shivered as they sat on the beach watching the waves rolling in and receding with a great sucking up of pebbles.

'When there's a really bad storm', said Anne, 'The sea throws these pebbles right up onto the road against the houses, piles and piles of them.'

A large flock of small black birds suddenly swooped across the sky, and then glided up in spirals. 'What are those birds?' asked Kristina.

'Jackdaws', said Penny. 'A kind of crow.'

'We have huge crows in Trinidad.'

They crossed the bridge and walked along the estuary. In the distance could be seen flocks of white birds standing on long sandbanks in the shallow water.

'What are those birds called?' asked Kristina.

'From here they all look the same, but if we had Dad's binoculars you'd see there are different kinds – herons and oyster-catchers and shelducks, and lots of others', said Anne.

'Someone told me birds in England are white, black or brown.'

'Not all of them', said Penny indignantly, 'There's the pheasant, and the kingfisher and the woodpecker, for a start.'

'Blue tits and robins and goldfinches and bullfinches', added Anne. 'You have to watch some birds in flight to see their wing colours.'

'I bet they're not like the ones in Trinidad', insisted Kristina, and she felt a sudden surge of homesickness as she thought of Yvonne and their bird-watching afternoons in the forest.'

While the twins were at school, John gave his daughter lessons in English, history, geography, Latin and maths until lunchtime. Kristina enjoyed these sessions, for her father was a good teacher and could be relied on to deviate from the subject.

They spent the afternoons following the cliff paths past yellow-lichened gorse, blackthorn scrub, stunted sycamores and hazel catkins. It was pleasant because it wasn't too hot to walk, and the coast was so different from Trinidad. The sky was constantly changing. Once they saw a thick inky blue line marking the horizon below which a band of luminous green merged into a motionless pale grey sea. Up above, pillows of ominous black cloud were moving slowly across the sky.

'Is there ever a clear blue sky in England?' asked Kristina.

'Oh yes', said John. 'Even in the autumn and winter. The coldest days often have the clearest skies.'

On their walks, he would discuss current affairs with Kristina. 'Of course, if we'd been living here during the war we'd have worried about being bombed. Even if it hadn't happened to us, we'd have shared in the sadness of hearing about people being killed, mostly in the big towns. The allies won the war, as we know, but every war brings a host of new problems. There's fighting just now, between India and Pakistan – and in the Middle East between the Jews and the Palestinians.'

'Our history teacher at the High School told us the Jews had all been murdered in German concentration camps.'

'Most of the European Jews were. But some escaped and went to Palestine. They planned to establish a state just for Jews, which they would call Israel. It sounded like a good idea. Unfortunately, to do this they forced most of the Palestinian Arabs, who'd lived there for centuries, to flee, leaving behind their homes and land.'

'Why couldn't they all live together like we lived in Trinidad?'

'Because there would have been too many people living in a small country, and the Jews wanted it to themselves. You have to remember, as I told you not long ago, that the same kind of thing took place in Trinidad. The Europeans came and wiped out the original inhabitants. It's happened all through history. But now we ought to be civilised enough not to kill or drive people out of their country.'

'Aren't the Jews civilised?'

'No country is truly civilised. We all want more than we need, and we think up all kinds of excuses for taking over a country and making life intolerable for the people who already live there. Britain's been one of the worst offenders, though we have moved out of some of the countries we occupied for years.'

'Which countries?'

'Australia, Canada, India and large parts of Africa for a start. Once we even ruled over the United States. I expect you'll learn all the details at school.'

'So the Jews aren't as greedy as us?'

'Maybe, but what they're doing is still wrong. There have always been individual people in the world who think it's wrong to grab another country and ill-treat or even kill its inhabitants. I hope you'll be one of the people who stand against such injustice.'

John had procured ration books, which he gave to Ruth. She worked wonders in providing nourishing meals on meagre amounts of meat, dairy produce and bread. Yet Kristina found English food tasteless without the spices she was so used to.

'Don't you ever have curried shrimps?' she asked.

'Peter and I like curry, but the girls don't. In any case you can only buy very bland curry powder. Chillis and spices are quite unavailable. And shrimps are very expensive.'

The only food Kristina took to straight away was piping hot fish and chips, straight out of the newspaper it was wrapped in.

Peter's vegetable plot produced very little at this time of year, and one had to rely on old potatoes and other root vegetables. Ruth bought bottles of concentrated orange designated by the government for children, and jars of cod liver oil and malt, which Kristina hated but was persuaded to take. The cold weather and the daily walks gave her a great appetite, and she devoured far too many sweet wrinkled apples from the store in the loft. She longed for all the fruits of Trinidad, especially mangoes and grapefruit. So many foodstuffs were rationed in England, even bread and jam. Gradually Kristina realised just how hard it had been for her aunt during the war, and now in these post-war years, to feed and clothe her family.

It did occur to John that if Tessa were to agree to Kristina's living with Ruth during term time, his sister might find it difficult to keep pace with her appetite. He'd heard that sugar might well be rationed for some time. Tessa wrote that Kristina would be better fed at boarding school, since it was easier to eke out rations in an institution. John replied, suggesting they choose a school in the country which grew its own fruit and vegetables.

John went to London to deal with his business affairs. In his absence Kristina began to explore on her own, even going on short bus trips. Riding on top of a double-decker was a great novelty. The bus conductors were very friendly and always warned her where to get off.

Many trees were still ablaze with autumn colours, but each day the wind grew colder, the leaves fell, and the countryside took on a strange hazy greyish-brown colour – or was it a greenish-mauve? – only relieved by sudden bright spells when the sun gilded the sea on the horizon. Kristina kept her bedroom curtains open at night so she could watch the sky on waking. Slowly she began to appreciate the swift changes in the English weather. She would have been hard put to it to give a name to all the shades of colour in the sea and sky. And she'd never before seen such wicked-looking black clouds, occasionally outlined with a thin band of silver. She became aware of the strange, almost sinister, calm of a grey dawn before a wind came up and whipped the sea into a fury, throwing high waves against the red cliffs.

It was almost dark when the twins returned from school, and after tea they would settle down in front of the fire to play board games or cards. Sometimes Kristina would regale the twins with her stories of Trinidad. To begin with she boasted about how much more exciting life was in the West Indies. But the twins hotly defended their own life. Gradually Kristina admitted to herself she was enjoying England in spite of the weather and rationing. She particularly looked forward, as did her cousins, to the day each week when they could buy their sweet ration. Penny always chose dolly mixture – tiny sweets which tasted of nothing, but lasted a lot longer than chocolate, which Kristina craved, and usually devoured in a few mouthfuls.

When John returned to Seaton he was glad to see how well his daughter had settled down with his sister's family. She had become deeply attached to Ruth, but this only gave him much foreboding about her future, knowing how intense were all her loves and hates. It wouldn't be easy to prise her away from his motherly sister.

One afternoon he and Kristina walked to the local grammar school, where the twins were still in the lower school. Peter, who was the deputy head of the upper school, had invited him to have a look round. It was impossible, of course, to judge a school merely on a quick visit, but John liked what he heard and saw. It had high academic standards and sporting achievements, but also found time for music, art and drama. The twins were a good advertisement for the school, being polite, lively, well-informed children, who admitted when pressed that it wasn't a bad place.

One evening after the children were in bed Ruth suggested that since Tessa lived in Switzerland, why not let Kristina live in Seaton and go to the grammar school.

She could join Tessa in London for the holidays. John was still hesitant at the idea of foisting a teenage girl onto his sister, but she insisted she could cope, and a settled home background with the twins as companions would do her good. The more John thought about it, the more attractive the prospect became. But he was sure Tessa wouldn't agree, even allowing that she'd still have Kristina for the school holidays.

Chapter Four

T essa returned to England in mid-November, and asked John to meet her at the Royal Hotel in Bristol, where she wanted to inspect a famous boarding school called the Dunbar Academy. She had no other school in mind. Ruth had suggested John should visit Dartington Hall in South Devon if Kristina must board. It was a progressive school set in acres of beautiful country, where the pupils were encouraged to develop their particular skills, whatever they might be, in their own time. Discipline was maintained on democratic lines and all the arts and outdoor activities were well provided for. John had sent for a prospectus, and felt it might well be more suited to Kristina than a rigidly disciplined desk-oriented boarding school. If Tessa was determined on conventional education, Peter recommended a small school set in parkland near Newton Abbot. It had a name for encouraging the arts, giving the children a fair amount of freedom, and creating a homely atmosphere. But the chance of Tessa and her mother accepting a small, unheard-of school with no academic reputation, was non-existent.

They travelled by bus and train to Bristol. Kristina felt a mixture of apprehension and curiosity combined with resentment at the thought of meeting her mother. John himself was nervous. He could no longer picture Tessa's face clearly, and wondered if he'd recognise her.

The Royal Hotel in the centre of Bristol was an old-fashioned comfortable establishment, providing accommodation John wouldn't normally have been able to afford. They sat on a deep leather sofa in the empty lounge until the door opened, and in a waft of expensive perfume Tessa entered. Kristina saw a small, slender woman with neatly permed blonde hair, made up and fashionably dressed in a well-cut navy suit with white trimmings. She was wearing high-heeled shoes and sheer nylon stockings. In contrast, John, in an old grey coat smelling of mothballs, which Ruth had stored for him during the war, looked decidedly shabby.

'Well, here she is, your long-lost daughter!' said John with false joviality. 'She's just about getting used to the English weather.'

Tessa had never been given to effusive greetings, and now she seemed almost frigid. She brushed her lips against Kristina's cheek, saying, 'I'd no idea you'd be quite so big.'

The way her mother emphasised the words "so big" made Kristina colour with shame. Her father had sent Tessa a few small snapshots, giving no impression of Kristina's height. Her daughter's looks were a disappointment. Kristina, on her part, was just as disappointed, for different reasons. It wasn't the meeting she'd imagined. Her mother wasn't only a stranger, she was also ill at ease with children. John, too, felt constrained, and it was a relief when Tessa announced, 'We have an appointment in half an hour at the Dunbar Academy. You may remember it's on the Downs near Stoke Bishop.'

'I don't remember', said John. 'I didn't know Bristol as well as you. But of course I've heard of it.'

'It's the best academic school in the country, and you'll be glad to know it's an Anglican foundation. The main building is Victorian gothic of the better sort, with a quad in the middle, rather like an Oxford college. The girls live in various houses round the Downs or in Redland, each one run by a house mother. There are a couple of houses just for sixth formers, which sounds a sensible idea.'

'How many girls?'

'About nine hundred. I do hope Kristina's up to the entrance exam. There's a Latin paper as well as the usual maths, English and general knowledge.'

They took a taxi up Whiteladies Road and Blackboy Hill onto the beautiful grassy Downs, criss-crossed by roads and paths, and overlooking the deep Avon Gorge, spanned at Clifton by the famous suspension bridge. They drove along Stoke Road until they reached the school on their right, situated in a small park near the elite residential area of Stoke Bishop. They were directed to the Headmistress's private apartment above the porter's lodge overlooking the large quadrangle garden, where the girls walked at break.

Miss Craig, a tall, angular figure with a parchment complexion and a tight grey bun, fixed penetrating grey eyes over the top of her pince-nez on the family trio and wasn't impressed. Too much make-up on the mother, a distinctly shabby father, and the daughter untidy and ungainly. All that wild-looking hair needed thinning and cropping. Kristina sensed immediately that here was an implacable enemy. However, Miss Craig had interviewed an infinite variety of parents and their offspring, and her fears were concealed hastily behind an encouraging smile and some brisk questioning.

John would like to have asked a good many questions himself, but Tessa spoke first and it quickly became clear that she'd already decided on the Dunbar Academy, should Kristina pass the entrance exam. As the interview proceeded Miss Craig kept referring to a long printed form which Tessa had filled in, but which John hadn't seen. This infuriated him so much that he made little attempt to join the conversation. Eventually Miss Craig rose saying a prefect would show them round the school. She hadn't spoken a word to Kristina.

Kristina was bored by the tour of laboratories, gymnasium, assembly hall, library, prefects' study and one or two classrooms which they viewed through glass-topped doors. She'd have been more interested in seeing one of the boarding houses, but this wasn't suggested. They were handed some sample entrance papers, and it was arranged she should sit the examination the following week.

They caught a bus back to the Royal Hotel, and over tea and toasted tea-cakes John reminded Tessa they had an appointment at Dartington Hall the following day.

Tessa was scathing. 'Now we've seen the Dunbar Academy we could cancel it. We can't send Kristina to a progressive school. They sound completely undisciplined. Anyway, I don't agree with mixed schools. Besides, Dartington is stuck away in the country, too far from London. Bristol is a more suitable place for a school.

'Nevertheless, Tessa, I'd be glad if you came to Dartington. Friends of my sister who've sent their daughters there, speak very highly of the school.'

Finally, with a bad grace, Tessa agreed they should travel by train to Totnes and then by bus to Dartington. At dinner that evening, Tessa told John and Kristina a little about her life in Geneva, describing the small luxury apartment she and Denis lived in. Her husband had also retained a small two-bedroomed flat in London, and they'd decided Tessa and Kristina should live there during the school holidays. Denis would join them for Christmas and for a short period in the summer.

'It's a most convenient flat', Tessa informed Kristina, 'In Harley Street, right in the West End, within easy distance of all the best shops, parks and theatres. You could even walk to Buckingham Palace.'

Kristina wasn't encouraged by this information. She wanted to live in the country.

Early next day they travelled by train in cold, sunny weather to the small town of Totnes. On the way, Kristina could see the dark purple hills of Dartmoor stretching into the far distance. It was surprising to see so many bare hills after the thick jungle covering the Trinidad mountains.

'Dartmoor looks a bit forbidding in winter', said John, 'But in the summer it's lovely. If you go to Dartington you'll get a chance of walking on the moors'.

From Totnes it was a short bus ride to Dartington Hall. The Headmaster was very welcoming, and spent more time during the interview talking to Kristina than to her parents. She gathered there was a farm on the premises, where pupils could participate if they wished in farming activities. There were horses to ride and canoeing on the River Dart. Music and drama were much to the fore. All kinds of sports were available. By the time Kristina was on her way back to Exeter, she'd decided that, if she must go to boarding school, she desperately wanted to go to Dartington.

Tessa, however, hadn't been impressed. On entering the main building, they'd been confronted by a beautiful wide staircase sweeping down to the gracious hallway. She'd almost been knocked over by a young boy sliding rapidly backwards down the polished banister, and leaping off at the bottom. With a cheerful 'So sorry, didn't realise you were there', he ran off.

'Do you always allow your children to behave so rudely?' Tessa demanded when the headmaster appeared.

'Just high spirits, I'm afraid. No harm done, I hope', came the reply.

In the train going home, Tessa said, 'You do realise, John, don't you, that those Dartington children aren't obliged to attend any lessons. They call teachers by their Christian names! Did you see the clothes they were wearing – some of the girls in slacks? Imagine, having no uniform!'

'It would make it a lot easier if we didn't have to buy Kristina a uniform. As for the freedom to miss lessons, Ruth says 99% of the children do eventually attend classes regularly, if only because they get bored drifting around doing nothing. And you heard the headmaster saying that the few children who miss lessons are the ones who become totally absorbed in farming or other physical or artistic skills. The school does insist on all the children knowing the three Rs. Frankly, if Kristina desperately wanted to be a farmer, then I'd be happy for her to opt out of some lessons..'

'Well, I wouldn't. We're paying for her to have a proper academic education, not to be feeding hens or milking cows.'

'I wouldn't be feeding hens or milking cows', said Kristina. 'I'd go to all the lessons, and after school I could go to drama and art classes.'

'After school I would hope you'd have plenty of homework to prepare', replied Tessa.

'The headmaster said there wouldn't be any homework until the School Certificate year.'

'There you are, John, how can children pass exams without doing homework?'

'It seems that at Dartington they do. Being out in the fresh country air, doing things that really interest them is more stimulating than hours of homework every evening. I'm all for giving Dartington a try.'

'I can't agree. Kristina's done well at school so far, but I noticed in her reports that she tends to daydream in class, and doesn't always give in her homework on time. She obviously needs a structured conventional education if she's ever to get into university.'

'Why do I have to go to university?' asked Kristina.

Tessa stared at her daughter in surprise. 'These days anyone who's got any brains should take the opportunity of higher education of some sort. You can't get an interesting well-paid job otherwise.'

'That's not quite true', said John. 'Plenty of people without college qualifications run enterprising and lucrative businesses.'

'Maybe, but I want to send Kristina to the Dunbar, and so does my mother. She is, after all, paying the fees. You've made all the decisions in Kristina's life so far. It's my turn now.'

She's not interested in my opinion, Kristina thought. She doesn't care whether I like the Dunbar Academy or not. And now I've got to live with her, Dad won't be able to change what she's decided about anything in my life. Already she recognised a certain look on her mother's face which said, "My decision is final". Her father had never adhered rigidly to rules. He'd always discussed the rights and wrongs and pros and cons of an action. 'Let's be reasonable about this, Kristina', was his favourite phrase. There would be no discussion with her mother.

John was due to return to Trinidad in early January, after spending Christmas with Ruth. Tessa had reluctantly agreed to forego Christmas with Kristina this year in order to let her spend it at Seaton with her cousins.

John spent the next four days going over the sample entrance papers with his daughter.

'If I refuse to answer the questions they won't accept me. Then I could go to Dartington', said Kristina.

'No, you wouldn't', said John. 'Your grandmother would find another conventional boarding school where the standard wasn't so high..'

There was no evading the exam, and John put a rebellious Kristina on the Bristol train at Taunton. Tessa stood waiting at Temple Meads station, unenthusiastic about spending nearly three days with such an unsatisfactory daughter, but determined to undo the damage John had done. Alone together for the first time, they had dinner in the high-ceilinged dining room of the Royal Hotel, where the other guests spoke in hushed tones.

'What kind of soup is this?' asked Kristina, when a bowl of thin brown-coloured liquid was set before her.

'I'm not sure', replied her mother, 'They have to make soup out of whatever scraps they can get.'

'It tastes absolutely horrible. I can't eat it.' Kristina's voice echoed round the room, eliciting disapproving stares from the other tables.

'Don't speak so loudly, Kristina. Just leave it. Of course, if you were really hungry you'd eat it.'

'I am, very hungry.'

'Then eat it up.' Tessa sighed, and her mouth set in a hard line. The main course of roast chicken, mashed potato and carrots, was more appetising, though the gravy looked suspiciously like the soup. Prunes and a watery custard followed, which Kristina made no attempt to eat. Tessa ate her own prunes and Kristina's without saying a word. She then rose, and Kristina followed her into the lounge.

Two elderly ladies reclined on a settee in one corner reading, and a young man in a smart suit sat at the writing desk, checking figures in a file. Tessa walked to a sofa as far away as possible from these guests, since she had much to say to her daughter. 'You may not like England, Kristina, but it's time you learnt to tolerate it politely. You've been very lucky living in Trinidad and not having to suffer wartime Britain. I was lucky too, being in Switzerland. But when I'm in England I don't grumble or waste my food, and nor should you. They won't put up with your attitude at school. So you might as well decide right now to stop complaining and try and look more pleasant.'

'I don't want to go to the Dunbar Academy. I hate that headmistress.' Kristina intended to speak quietly, but the words came out loud and challenging.

The elderly ladies peered from behind their novels with shocked expressions, and even the young man glanced round. Tessa, however, kept her voice low and quite determined. 'I suggest you go up to your room and do some Latin revision, and then go to sleep early. The exam starts at nine, and they hope to give us the results by four o'clock. The day after tomorrow we can go to Merchants, the school outfitters, to buy your uniform.'

'I don't like that sludgy green uniform. Even the hat is that horrible colour. Why do we have to wear hats at all?'

'To wear to church, and of course to walk to the main school each day.'

When the first paper was placed on the desk, Kristina was told to complete it in forty minutes. She had a sudden urge to tear it up and rush out of the room. But pride made her start, and by one o'clock she'd completed all the papers with comparative ease. The invigilator, a small spidery woman, thanked her without smiling, and said nothing more, other than at half past two a prefect would show them round the boarding house she might be living in.

After having a drink and a currant bun in a café at the top of Whiteladies Road, Tessa and Kristina were shown round the red brick boarding house in Belvedere Road called Cabot House.

'Why is it called Cabot?' asked Kristina.

'John Cabot was an Italian who settled in Bristol and became a merchant seaman. He discovered Newfoundland', explained the prefect. 'All the boarding houses are called after famous people connected with the city.'

They weren't able to see Miss Deacon, the House Mother, who was occupied teaching, or the girls, who were still at lessons in the main building. Cabot House had once been a large Victorian family residence including an attic and basement. The drawing room, with large bay windows and a faded floral carpet, contained two armchairs, a tall bookcase, two wooden chairs and an upright piano. Otherwise, worn dark green linoleum covered all the floors of the house. The woodwork was varnished in dark brown. Kristina hadn't been expecting beauty or much comfort in a school, but she was chilled by the dank atmosphere of Cabot House and the pervading smell of boiled cabbage, fish and disinfectant.

'It's a horrible house', declared Kristina, as she and Tessa walked down Claypit Road, across Durdham Down and back to the main school building.

'It is rather bleak, I do agree. It's surprising they still have blackout curtains so long after the war. But the drawing room is quite pleasant, and I suppose you can sit there when you've done your homework.'

'Thirty-five girls can't sit in two armchairs at once.'

'The house will feel more friendly when the girls are there. And I noticed a large garden at the back.'

They sat in a little waiting room adjacent to the porter's lodge until Miss Craig appeared with the news that Kristina had passed the exam. 'In a moment Miss

Deacon will be coming to meet you. In the meantime, here's the uniform list. Several items, such as the scarf and the blazer, have been marked as not being compulsory until clothing coupons come to an end. And this is a list of rules and dates for the coming year. There's no weekend half term break in the spring term, but you may take Kristina out twice a term on a Saturday from twelve till six.'

'Unfortunately', said Tessa, 'I'll be in Switzerland, and therefore unable to take Kristina out.'

'But my Aunty Ruth could come', said Kristina.

Tessa was saved a reply by the arrival of Miss Deacon, who seemed even less prepossessing than Miss Craig. She was an extraordinarily plain, even repellent, middle-aged woman, with oddly bulbous ice-blue eyes. Her rough-textured iron-grey hair was cut in a severe mannish bob, and her complexion had a yellowish tinge. Kristina had come across plain and even eccentric-looking teachers in Trinidad, but all of them pleasant and kindly. It was the lack of humanity in Miss Deacon's protruding eyes which was so disconcerting. Could this person really be called a House Mother? And yet there was her own mother smiling and saying that Mr White would be bringing Kristina to Bristol on the first day of term.

'By then', said Miss Deacon, 'You will either have to have Kristina's hair cut short or provide her with green ribbons and elastic bands to tie it back. She certainly can't wear it loose.'

Then the interview was over, and they were on a draughty bus again, crawling down Whiteladies Road and

Park Street. 'Couldn't you ask Aunty Ruth to come and take me out during the term?' said Kristina hopefully.

'No. You can't possibly expect her to come all that way, especially on a Saturday, when her own children are at home.'

'They could come too.'

'It would be much too expensive. I expect when you make a special friend, you might be invited out by her parents.'

'But I wouldn't be able to ask her back.'

'Don't argue, Kristina. It's difficult having parents living abroad, but lots of girls at boarding school are in the same position. So you won't feel different.'

'I shall hate every minute at the Dunbar Academy.'

'You can't know until you've tried it.'

'Will you let me leave after a term if I hate it?'

'I refuse to discuss it any further.'

The following morning Tessa bought a regulation winter coat and mackintosh, indoor and outdoor shoes, a velour hat with the house band in yellow and black, a yellow and black tie, a plain green tie, gym skirts and blouses, three pairs of cotton underpants and three pairs of thick green knickers, a cardigan, lisle stockings, a suspender belt and a dozen white handkerchiefs. She arranged for the parcels of uniform to be sent to Seaton. 'Your father will have to buy name tapes', she said to Kristina. 'I hope you've learnt how to sew. It'll take you quite a long time naming the clothes and a dozen hankies. I'm flying back to Geneva in a few days, so I can't help.'

Thus her future was decided, and nothing could be done to prevent it. However, as they waited for the train to Taunton, Kristina became excited at the thought of returning to Seaton, and put school out of her mind. Tessa was acutely aware that this meeting with her daughter had been a failure. She'd had no direct experience of children, and until recently hadn't thought much about Kristina. But now that her daughter had materialised and she was taking on the role of mother, she craved her whole-hearted affection and respect.

When the train drew up at the platform, Kristina kissed her mother hurriedly and climbed eagerly into an empty carriage. Tessa followed, and helped to heave her case onto the luggage rack. She handed Kristina a small parcel wrapped in red and green paper. 'This is your Christmas present, so keep it safe until Christmas day.'

Kristina suddenly felt a twinge of shame for wanting to depart as soon as possible. She searched her mother's face, but Tessa's expression betrayed nothing.

'I'll see you just before Easter, and of course I'll write. You must write back and tell me all about school.'

Until the local school holidays began, John planned to take Kristina on day trips to places of interest, hoping to instil in her a liking for Devon and Somerset. He wanted her to be happy in the country he'd put behind him, but of which he had fond memories from his youth. But the days were too short and the weather not conducive to visiting outdoor beauty spots. So he took her to see Exeter Cathedral and Sherborne Abbey and several village churches and manor houses. She became used to cold wind, pouring rain and sudden changes in the weather. When they got off a bus and trudged over fields and up green lanes or through woodland, she didn't complain. She liked having John to herself. The exercise made her so ravenous that she even enjoyed the spam and margarine sandwiches with tepid cocoa they consumed on the bus going home.

He himself, after so long an absence, found the English winter depressing and strangely exhausting. He felt increasingly guilty at the thought of leaving his daughter behind. It struck him forcibly how much time and effort in England was taken up with lighting fires and cleaning grates, putting on and taking off layers of warm clothing, struggling to get boots on over thick socks and finding hats and scarves. The weekly washing in Ruth's old copper seemed to take all day. After pushing clothes, linen and towels through a mangle, the drying, followed by hours of ironing, posed a marathon task for his overworked sister. How much easier and more pleasant was the simple life he'd adopted for himself at Sangre Grande – shorts, shirts and sandals, basic furniture and no curtains, upholstery or blankets. His books, his pictures, one or two floor rugs, a scattering of cushions and the lush plants which grew indoors and out provided all the colour and interest he required.

As the days went by, he was glad to see Kristina adapting well to English life. When the twins were at home they would clamber up and down the cliff paths and jump with ease across the rough-surfaced rocks when the tide was out. They were for ever devising new games to play. The main reason for his daughter's great contentment was the happy family life he'd not been able to give her.

Kristina's still a child enjoying herself with uninhibited enthusiasm, thought John. But she's also on the brink of adolescence, with all its attendant problems.

How will she cope on her own? Some days he felt like taking her back to Trinidad and going through the courts to try and gain custody. But should he be successful, he could still visualise difficulties with having a teenage girl in Sangre Grande. She'd want to be in Port of Spain, not only for school, but also at weekends to attend social events. And then there was the question of nationality. Did he want her to feel British or West Indian? He contemplated giving up his vocation as a parish priest and returning to England to teach; but it would be some time before he'd be able to afford accommodation suitable for Kristina. She needed a family, and neither he nor Tessa could provide it. It was even possible Tessa might tire of her daughter and be glad to hand him back the responsibility for her. But how would Kristina feel? Would she take it all in her stride and learn to adapt? It was impossible to predict.

John sent away for name tapes, and when they arrived Ruth suggested getting the job over straight away. With much grumbling the twins were dragooned into doing half a dozen hankies each.

'I've made you two shoe bags', said Ruth, 'They'll also need name tapes.' By the time Kristina had completed the task, her fingers were sore and her temper short, for Penny couldn't stop giggling at the idea of having to wear thick green knickers on top of underpants.

In mid-December Kristina began to feel discouraged by the English weather. She'd always spent as much time as possible out of doors, and she continued this habit in Seaton, clad in an old mac, woolly scarf and hat of Peter's. Most afternoons at three she'd walk up a narrow lane to meet her cousins coming home from school. The fallen leaves lay in sodden heaps underfoot, and the tall elms in the hedgerows made the lane seem very dark as daylight slowly drained from the sky. A shivery dampness hung in the air, and she felt the strange melancholy of late autumn merging into winter. But as soon as she saw the twins running down the lane, her mood lifted, and they made their way home talking cheerfully of Christmas.

This first Christmas in England turned out to be the best Kristina had ever experienced. Her father and Dodo had done their best to make Christmas a magical time, and so it had been. At primary school she'd always joined a group of children dressed up incongruously in red coats and bonnets trimmed with white fur, all carrying candles as they went round Sangre Grande carol-singing. It had been fun, but it couldn't be compared to being with her Aunty Ruth's family. Cutting holly, ivy and mistletoe to deck the cottage, making cards and paper chains, joining the carol singers, decorating the tree, baking gingerbread men and hanging up stockings – all these traditional activities became infinitely more exciting shared with the twins. They devised a nativity play and several of the twins' friends participated. The day before Christmas eve the play was performed with Ruth at the piano and Peter, John and half a dozen parents as audience.

The excitement on Christmas day started with the stockings filled with oranges, nuts and useful little gifts, and rose to a crescendo in the early evening with the family ritual of processing up one staircase and down the other, banging pots and pans, a tambourine and a toy drum, and playing recorders. The day ended with Monopoly by the fire and a bowl of Uncle Peter's special chocolate fudge made with condensed milk. On Boxing Day they spent the evening singing, accompanied by Ruth at the piano.

For John too it was a new experience spending Christmas with his sister's family. He realised how good she was with children, and how eagerly they responded to her pleasant, sympathetic character. With her knack of teasing persuasion rather than strict commands, any activity she suggested became interesting, even if it was only washing up. Kristina had fallen entirely under Ruth's spell and in the easy family atmosphere her own vitality and capacity for enjoyment expanded. Seaton Hole Cottage rocked with her laughter and the twins' shrieks of excitement. Future holidays with Tessa and her stepfather, Denis, might be bleak in comparison.

On new year's day, when John went up to say goodnight to Kristina, he found her in a paroxysm of tears. She hated the Dunbar, she hated him for agreeing to let her go, and above all she hated Tessa who'd ruined her life for ever. He stroked her hair, but there was nothing he could say. He hated himself.

Kristina packed the uniform into the trunk Ruth had lent her, together with sheets, pillow cases and towels, all duly marked with Cash's name tapes. Ruth provided a tin containing biscuits and boiled sweets for Kristina, promising she'd send more tuck, including the sweet ration, every fortnight. The trunk was sent ahead to the school two days before term started. Only then did Kristina bother to scrutinise the list of school rules Miss Craig had given her. They covered a large sheet in small typescript. Some she didn't quite understand. But there were a few which struck her as extraordinary. There was to be no talking in the corridors and no running anywhere, inside or out. Ruth agreed it was restrictive, but added that there would be plenty of running on the playing field. The rule preventing girls other than sixth formers from leaving the school premises without a teacher or parent also made Kristina indignant.

'I want to explore the Downs and the town.'

'I daresay there will be occasions when the girls get taken out on walks', said Ruth.

'That's not the same. I like looking at places by myself.'

The night before they left Seaton, John presented Kristina with an illustrated book published in the USA, entitled *Growing Up.* 'I know Dodo's told you about sex and having babies, and we have talked a little about such things in the past. But I thought it would be instructive to have this book to refer to. You'll find it's quite humorous. You don't have to read it all at once.'

John had no idea how Tessa would approach the adolescent problems of her daughter. He suspected the Dunbar Academy wouldn't be addressing these at all. The book he was giving Kristina dealt in a sympathetic and sensible way with all the questions a teenager might ask.

On Wednesday, January 7th, John delivered his daughter to Cabot House at 4 pm, as it was getting dark. He carried her case up to the dormitory where three girls were unpacking. One of them approached Kristina, saying briskly, 'My name's Rosemary Tyson. You must be Kristina White. Your bed's nearest the window, and that's your trunk. Your case has to be taken down to the basement when it's empty. Trunks are left in the corridor to be taken down later. We're not allowed to put anything on top of our chest of drawers. You'll have to make the bed when your sheets are unpacked.'

As the girl was speaking, John looked round the room, noting the naked dim bulb hanging from the ceiling, five iron bedsteads, five wooden chairs, rough grey blankets, cracked linoleum, stark chests of drawers, a large, hideous wardrobe and thick black curtains, presumably left over from wartime blackout. Not a single touch of colour or comfort. A penitentiary couldn't have been more dismal.

Kristina followed her father down to the waiting taxi. Her expression was set in such grim misery he could hardly bear it. He kissed her stiffly, not daring to show much emotion, only saying, 'I'll write tomorrow'. As the taxi drove away, he didn't turn to look at Kristina for fear of weeping.

Chapter Five

The next few days turned out to be as confused and difficult a time as Kristina could have imagined, made worse by the fact that everyone around her, staff and pupils alike, seemed to be moving as though through an efficient factory, with relentless machine-like precision. She felt like a lost screw which had fallen out of the works.

When she returned to the dormitory after her father's departure, Miss Kelvin, the house matron, was waiting for her.

'You must hurry, Kristina, if you're to be ready in time for tea at five thirty. First I'll check your uniform list.'

This was done so hurriedly that Matron omitted to ask if she'd brought any books. Kristina was handed a small bible, a Bible Reading Fellowship pamphlet, a sheet of house rules, a laundry book and pocket-sized notebook. Matron beckoned to a dumpy, earnest-looking girl with mousy plaits and eager eyes behind ugly horn-rimmed spectacles.

'This is Mary Grant. She'll explain all you need to know for the time being.'

Mary smiled at Kristina. 'I'll help you make the bed, and then show you the bathroom.'

This room, smelling strongly of disinfectant, comprised four curtained cubicles, each containing a bath and a stool. There were four smaller cubicles with wash-basins. On the door was pinned a rota for bathing, washing and hair washing. 'Two baths a week', said Mary, 'Strip wash on other days. Hair washing once a fortnight. The 'aunts' are next door.'

'What are they?' Kristina asked.

'It's what the toilets are called here.'

After depositing Kristina's case in what was known as the dump, Mary went through to the cloakroom. A stench of hockey boots, gym shoes, linseed oil and damp mackintoshes filled the large room. Each girl had a locker in which to keep outdoor shoes, together with a bag to carry indoor button-up shoes to the main school. Kristina was then conducted up the stairs to the Middle Common Room, furnished with a table, desks, another row of lockers and the inevitable black curtains. In the wide hallway stood a large padlocked cupboard.

'Our tuck's kept in there. It's only opened after lunch for ten minutes', said Mary. There was also a large notice board on the wall. On one side was posted a seating plan of the dining tables. 'Today we can sit anywhere. Tomorrow you'll be on table one for the rest of the week. Miss Deacon sits at the head, and at least once you have to sit next to her and make interesting conversation.'

'But I don't know her', said Kristina.

'You soon will.'

On the other side of the board were lists dividing the girls into groups. 'Those are the deportment groups. You're in Group D. We're marked out of ten each week for neatness, good manners, conversation at table, deportment and collect. You have to learn a collect each week, and recite it to the prefect in charge of your group on Saturday evening. Mirabel Levett is your group leader.'

'Why do we have to learn it?'

'To make us better Christians.'

Back in the dormitory, Mary explained how to use the laundry book – green knickers only sent once a fortnight; the BRF pamphlet –'There's a short passage to read each day before breakfast' ; and the notebook – 'You have to walk to school with a partner, preferably not always the same person. You write down the girl you booked in the notebook.'

'How can I book someone when I don't know anyone?'

'As you're new, you'll get asked. I'll go with you tomorrow.'

'It sounds crazy to me.'

'The point is, they don't trust us walking alone. Only sixth formers can walk alone.'

'And if there's an extra person?'

'They just have to tag along behind a couple.'

The clanging of a bell sounded downstairs. 'Bring your notebook', said Mary.

Swept along by the tide of girls, Kristina lost sight of Mary and found herself in the dining room. School tea was more like a light supper – sardines on two thin slices of toast, followed by a slice of bread, margarine and jam, with a cup of tea. Since Miss Deacon didn't appear at this meal, the excited chatter was deafening. It was most unusual for Kristina to be silent in the company of other girls, but for once she could only listen to the unfamiliar schoolgirl jargon. This was delivered in a high-pitched precise English, with words such as *super, wizard, jolly-dee, ripping,* being bandied to and fro. A pretty and vociferous girl at her table was holding forth in an extreme upper class accent on the subject of her Christmas holiday. Her voice would drop suddenly as she whispered in giggling confidence to the girl beside her. It was the first time Kristina had ever felt completely excluded from her contemporaries.

After tea she climbed up the narrow creaking stairs from the basement to the middle common room, whose monitor, Hilary Dane, informed Kristina which locker she could have. Then she found herself surrounded with girls all asking questions. She explained that her home was in Trinidad, but her mother lived in Switzerland.

'Divorced?' asked an attractive brown-eyed girl with blonde hair called Miranda.

'Yes.'

'How awful for poor, poor you! Have you got a wicked stepmother?'

'No, only a stepfather, but I've never met him.'

'Stepfathers can be wicked too. What form are you in?'

'Lower 4b.'

'That's Miss Rayburn. She teaches biology and she's a real stinker!'

Someone else said, 'It must be hot in Trinidad. You'll find Lower 4b absolutely freezing. The pipes never seem to work.'

Then several girls booked Kristina for walking to school: Rosemary Tyson and Jacqueline Biggs from her dormitory, Mary Grant for two days, and Miranda Lane, the brown-eyed blonde girl who always looked on the brink of laughter, the last two.

'Do we go to school on Saturday, then', asked Kristina.

'Oh, yes', said Miranda, 'Can't have us idling around Cabot House all morning! Saturdays till twelve, with an afternoon off during the week.'

'To do what?'

'To finish essays, or read if you like. Naturally, no chattering! If you're a gamesy type aiming for a hockey team you'll probably have extra practice.'

'I hate hockey!' said Kristina.

'So do I', whispered Miranda. 'But don't admit it. Cabot House is top of the league.'

Kristina's impression of the girls so far had been a sea of faces and a constant hubbub of voices. Miranda was the first to stand out as someone she might like. It was a relief to hear that she was also in Lower 4b.

'Who's in your dorm?' asked Miranda.

'Mary Grant, Rosemary Tyson and Jacqueline Biggs. I don't know the other two.'

'Rosemary and Jacky are frightfully brainy and completely barmy. They're in Lower 4a and spend most of their time quoting Greek at each other. Mary's all set for sainthood, and sucks up to authority. She latches on to new girls, so watch out.'

'Why does she?'

'Looking for a bosom pal, I suppose. It's rather sad, really. The trouble is, she's always trying to convert people.'

Kristina thought of her father. Presumably he was always trying to convert people. Yet the way Miranda spoke of Mary and mimicked her voice made her sound tedious and annoying.

Conversation with Miranda was interrupted by the sound of another bell, summoning the house to prayers in the cold, draughty drawing room. A feeble coal fire was burning in the small grate, giving warmth only to those close to it. The girls stood in a wide, double semicircle around Miss Deacon, whose voice was dry and monotonous. Heads were bent, eyes shut and hands clasped, but now and then Kristina opened her eyes and caught Miranda grinning at someone. As they piled out of the drawing room, Miss Deacon addressed Kristina for the first time.

'I hope you're settling in and finding out how we operate at Cabot House. Let Matron know if you have any difficulties.'

Mary informed Kristina 'Cocoa' was at eight, and bedtime at eight-thirty. 'We get biscuits with the cocoa. Sometimes it's Ovaltine or Bovril. Lights out at nine-fifteen.'

Until eight, Kristina followed Mary up and down the stairs, putting things in her lockers and drawers and onto hooks. Cocoa was taken standing around in the dining room – three plain biscuits each and a mug of weak, watery cocoa. The eight-thirty bell went and Kristina took off the uniform she hated so much, especially the thick brown lisle stockings held up by a suspender belt that cut into her midriff. Leaving her clothes in a heap on the chair she joined the queue for the wash basins. The water was tepid, and the bathroom cold. In the dismal black-curtained dormitory, anticipating the icy sheets she got into bed with her dressing gown on. Matron appeared and told her to get up and fold her clothes neatly on the chair. 'We must start as we mean to go on, mustn't we?' she said.

For the few minutes before 'lights out' she was able to observe her roommates more closely – Kit Taylor, asking if she was good at hockey, athletics or swimming; Rosemary Tyson and Jacky Biggs discussing the Madrigal Society; Fiona Kirk-Davis enthusing over a sixth-former at Marlborough who danced with her twice on new year's eve; Mary Grant reading her Bible.

When the light went out there was silence for a moment, and then Rosemary spoke. 'Kristina?'

'Yes?'

'It's not much fun being new, especially starting in the second term. If you can stick out a week you'll find that it's not so bad.'

'If you're clever, that is', muttered Fiona.

'You've got a funny accent', said Jacky,

'It's West Indian. I didn't know it was funny.'

'I had an accent when we came home from India. But it soon went.'

I don't want my accent to go, thought Kristina. I don't want to speak like these girls.

'What does your father do in Trinidad?'

'He's an Anglican clergyman.'

'D'you mean a missionary?'

'No, an ordinary Rector of a place called Sangre Grande.'

'But doesn't he have to convert the Negro tribes?'

Kristina laughed loudly before she could restrain herself, and was quickly shushed to be quiet, or Matron would descend.

'Black West Indians are mostly Christian already, and don't live in tribes. You're thinking of Africa.'

'You're such an ignoramus, Fiona', said Rosemary.

The last words Kristina heard before falling asleep were, 'Don't forget you're first wash.'

Kristina awoke abruptly, still wearing her dressing gown, to the sound of the ubiquitous bell, and leapt out of bed. It was still dark, and very cold. She sat on the bed thinking, *This time yesterday I woke up in Seaton, and now I'm here. It's like waking up in prison.*

'That's just the six-twenty warning bell', said Mary, whose bed was the nearest.

At the second bell the light was switched on. 'Time to rise, girls, for first wash'.

Kristina was slow at putting on the uniform and combing her tangled hair. Mary, who was quick and neat at everything she did, stripped Kristina's bed, showing her how the bedclothes must be folded in three and hung over the chair. By now everyone was reading the Bible passage and the notes to go with it. Kristina stared at the words in a daze until the breakfast bell. Prefects sat at the head of the tables, pouring out cups of weak tea from huge tin teapots. A sliver of bacon, an anaemic fried egg and a triangle of fried bread arrived at each place. A slice of bread and indeterminate jam was available. Then came the charge upstairs to make the beds.

'Hospital corners', said Mary, showing Kristina how to tuck in the sheets. 'I forgot to tell you yesterday that at break we go into the quad if it isn't raining. You have to book a partner for that too. I'll be your partner for the rest of the week. Before we leave for school, Matron checks that shoes and nails are clean, and uniform correct. Macs and hood on grey days, coat and hat on sunny days. Some girls do slip out without being noticed, but in the main school cloakroom the pre's can pounce at random.'

'And what do they do?'

'Tell our head of house, who tells your group leader.'

'Who is our head of house?'

'Lucy Richmond.'

It was a clear day with the sun just risen. The grassy Downs sparkling with frost looked so inviting that Kristina longed to go for a walk. But Mary kept up a fast pace along the pavement, saying she must bag a desk near the window. They entered the school by a side door and went down some steps into a very large basement cloakroom. Kristina was shown the Cabot House rail of hooks, with a hollow bench under each rail to park shoes. Mary led the way to the dark panelled entry hall, and up a wide polished staircase. There were two floors, with classrooms on either side of long dark panelled corridors. Lower 4b overlooked the quadrangle with shrubs, small patches of grass, walkways and two seats. Kristina took the desk next to Mary, and then watched her classmates filling up the half-panelled room. Heavy wooden seats were attached to ancient, much-carved desks. The initials PC were etched deeply inside the lid of Kristina's desk.

There followed the usual tedious school procedure with Miss Rayburn checking the register of twenty names, filling in timetables and giving out notices. Finally she turned her attention to the new girl. 'Kristina, you must to go to the stock-room at break to collect textbooks and exercise books. Will someone show Kristina the way? Thank you, Mary. Line up for assembly, girls.'

From each classroom a silent and orderly procession moved towards the assembly hall, a vast gothic-style space with arched windows, a stage and four side galleries. Miss Craig, behind a massive carved table, presided over a psalm, a hymn and prayers, before admonishing the girls to work hard, behave with quiet courtesy and never forget the team spirit which had made the Dunbar Academy such a great establishment. Kristina wasn't listening, she was thinking of the High School in Port of Spain, where there'd been no hall and no assembly, only a couple of prayers in each classroom and a few notices given out before lessons began.

The silent processions moved out of the hall. Once again Kristina had to rely on Mary to show her the classroom for the double maths lesson. For maths and languages the pupils were divided into three sets in order of ability. Biology was taught in the science wing, and art in the studio. Only history, geography, RE and English were taught in the Lower 4b classroom.

Miss Trench, clad entirely in brown with wispy grey hair, taught set B for maths, and was obviously irritated by Kristina's temporary lack of books. 'I suppose you'll have to share a textbook this morning', she said, handing Kristina two sheets of squared paper. 'We'll start with the usual ten minutes of mental arithmetic.'

A groan ran round the class, none more heartfelt than Kristina's. She wasn't a natural mathematician, and needed time to think. Perhaps Miss Trench sensed this, for she announced with grim satisfaction, 'We'll start with you, Kristina.'

The questions came quick-fire up and down the rows, and each time drew a confused blank from Kristina. At the sixth time someone tittered faintly, and she flushed with shame and anger. 'You don't give me time to think', she complained.

Miss Trench glared at Kristina over her rimless spectacles with astonishment, as if to say, *At this school we don't answer back.* 'No one gets time to think. That's the whole point of mental arithmetic. They're very simple questions. Any first former could answer them.'

At break Mary directed Kristina to the stockroom, and then hurried away.

'Oh, dear', said the lady in charge, 'Your starting in January does make it difficult.' She laid exercise books of various colours on a table, but then had to spend some time rummaging in cupboards for textbooks. 'You'll have to make a couple of journeys with all these.'

Carrying half the books, Kristina turned down the wrong corridor, and by the time she retraced her steps and found Lower 4b she became aware that the next lesson had commenced. She laid the books outside the door, bounded up the stairs and ran to the stockroom, only to bump into Miss Trench emerging from there herself.

'Your first day, and already breaking the rules, Kristina White. I suggest you walk to your classroom and then walk back.' Kristina gave an impatient sigh. 'And you'll do it with a good grace, my girl.'

The French lesson was well-nigh over when Kristina opened the door and staggered in, her arms piled high with books, two of which slithered onto the floor. By this time it was nearly midday. She was hungry and thirsty and not inclined to concentrate on the rest of the French lesson or the geography lesson that followed. At twelve-forty the lunch bell rang and Mary, pointing out that the thick exercise book was for noting down prep, helped her sort the books out. Then it was a rush to change into outdoor shoes to return to Cabot House. Lunch consisted of fish pie and cabbage, followed by a small square of ginger pudding with the inevitable watery custard. Kristina could have devoured three squares, but there were no second helpings. Miss Deacon, sitting bolt upright, an example to the girls of a perfect ramrod back, was at the head of her table. Several times Kristina felt herself scrutinised by the bulbous eyes.

'We call her The Toad', Miranda whispered in her ear, and Kristina guffawed loudly, partly from nerves. A sudden hush descended as everyone turned to stare at Table One.

'Maybe we could all share the joke', said Miss Deacon.

'There was no joke', said Kristina.

'We do not expect inane laughter from Cabot House girls, particularly if there was no joke.' Thus in her first twenty-four hours at the Dunbar Academy, Kristina had already made an enemy – one who would always have the upper hand. But there was no going back.

After lunch came the scramble at the tuck cupboard. Kristina only just resisted the temptation to eat most of her biscuits, remembering her aunt wouldn't be sending a parcel for a fortnight. Then came the rush in the cloakroom to get ready to join Mary, who was waiting neatly at the door.

'Sorry you missed the milk and bun at break', she said.

'How did you manage without a partner?'

'A new girl in year three from Penn House was looking lost. I teamed up with her.'

'Can't anyone ever go outside alone?' asked Kristina.

'Not until the sixth form. I forgot to mention, you've also got to go to church with a partner.'

'How far is the church?'

'About half a mile. We go to the eleven o'clock service, and once a month to Evensong. When you get confirmed you have to go to early Communion as well.'

Afternoon school brought more difficulties. RE and Latin passed off without reprimand, but to Kristina's horror, English Literature, her favourite subject, was taught by Miss Deacon. The set books for the term were *The Trumpet Major*, by Thomas Hardy, *An Anthology of Modern Poetry,* Shakespeare's *As You Like It* and a book of nineteenth century essays. All her copies were well thumbed, with words underlined and covers disintegrating, but she was pleased to see in tiny letters on the back inside cover of the poetry book, *Down with Toad!* The girls were set to read a chapter of *The Trumpet Major*, after which there would be questions. They were to look up words they didn't understand.

Kristina read the chapter quickly and then glanced through the rest of the book. She suspected the story would prove to be rather long-winded, and the description of the heroine, Anne Garland, didn't appeal. So disappointing, since starting an interesting novel had always been something of an adventure. Her father's shelves contained several Hardy novels, and she'd almost finished *Tess of the D'Urbervilles* just before leaving Trinidad. She was thinking about this when Miss Deacon asked her the meaning of 'sanguine'.

'I don't know.'

'You've been daydreaming instead of using your dictionary. Look it up now, and write it out in your prep book ten times this evening. Homework will be to read to the end of chapter three. Be prepared to read an extract aloud next week.'

By the time Kristina and Mary left the main school in the dusk, their satchels hanging heavy on their shoulders, a wind had arisen, blowing across the Downs in icy gusts.

'What happens next?' asked Kristina glumly.

'First we change into mufti. Tea is at five fifteen, then prep for two hours till seven forty-five, when we have prayers like last night. Then Cocoa and bed.'

'What's the point of wearing mufti just to do prep?'

'Some girls like to change. It gives Fiona a chance to show off. Her rich American relations send her clothes, including gorgeous nylon stockings.'

Kristina thought of her own limited wardrobe of two jumpers and a skirt. In Trinidad she'd never felt the desire for many clothes. Keeping cool was all that mattered, and three sleeveless faded short cotton frocks had been quite sufficient for wearing at home.

The thought of the dreary evening ahead filled her with gloom. In Port of Spain after school she and Jenny and several of their friends had walked home together to Cascade, dawdling on the way. There was always something to look at on the Savannah, or one could wait for the boys to come out of Queen's College. There was never any hurry. They would drop in to each other's houses for a drink, or Jenny might ask everyone for a dip in the Morrisons' pool. Later they could play tennis. Homework had to be done, of course, but it could if necessary wait till dinner was over. It was cooler working late. Kristina and Jenny had often worked or read a novel till one in the morning, and still woken up refreshed.

After tea at Cabot House Kristina caught sight of a notice pinned on the wall beside the hatch into the kitchen. It was a washing up and laying table rota for Saturday and Sunday, to enable the kitchen staff to have time off.

'Oh, God, not another rota!' exclaimed Kristina loudly.

Behind her someone giggled, intoning, 'At Cabot House, Kristina, we expect our girls to help out with humdrum tasks. In addition, we do not expect them to take the name of God in vain.' It was Miranda, who'd perfected the art of mimicking The Toad. She continued in her normal voice. 'Yes, isn't it ghastly! All the money our parents are paying for this five-star establishment, and we have to do the chores! Lucy Richmond of course will tell you privation is character-building.'

During the prep period no one was permitted to talk without the monitor's permission. Kristina had constant need to ask Mary to explain the homework, but after three interruptions she dared not ask again. She could feel the disapproval all round.

At Cocoa Mary reminded Kristina it was her bath night. 'Be quick and bag a cubicle, and don't be long. You're not allowed more than four inches of water. Matron often pops in to check.'

After lights out Kristina lay thinking about her first day. Nothing about it gave her hope, unless it was the slight hint of rebellion she'd detected in Miranda. Without Mary's vigilant guidance she could hardly have survived the day, yet she didn't warm to the girl. There was no laughter in her, barely even a smile. If there was one thing Kristina thrived on, it was a good joke and uninhibited laughter. Dodo, Yvonne and Jenny – how she missed them!

Kristina's second day brought no improvement. She was slow at rising and performing the early morning tasks and was late thereafter for each appointment. Miss Trench had quickly judged Kristina to be a fool at maths. Having no patience with fools she determined to be rid of her. Geometry, which Kristina had always enjoyed when it was explained carefully, turned into a nightmare under Miss Trench's sadistic eye. At the end of the lesson she suggested Kristina remove herself to Set C with Miss Pollock in Room 6.

Kristina fell asleep in the RE lesson. This was conducted by an emaciated, vague-looking deaconess in dove grey with a large cross dangling over her flat chest, who fortunately didn't notice. She'd been reading and explaining the *Acts of the Apostles,* and had given the class an essay to write for homework. Yet again Kristina would have to ask Mary for the details, but when? It wasn't going to be possible to keep disturbing people in the common room during prep period.

In her first history lesson Miss Hodgson said, 'We started the reign of Queen Elizabeth last term, Kristina. Do you know anything about her?'

Kristina rose and said enthusiastically, 'Yes, she sent her courtier, Walter Raleigh, to the West Indies to look for gold. He landed in Trinidad and fought against the Spaniards who'd got there first. He used pitch from the Pitch Lake to mend his boats, and then, after burning the capital, St Joseph, he left. He was just an adventurer.'

'So, where did you read all that?'

'I didn't read it. My father told me. But I did read a novel called *Young Bess,* about Elizabeth's first love affair.'

Several girls giggled as Miss Hodgson said sternly, 'That's not history, it's just rubbishy romance and has no place in our lessons.'

During the prep period that evening, Mirabel Levett appeared at the door and beckoned to Kristina. 'I'm your deportment group leader. You may come now and recite the collect.'

Kristina confessed she'd forgotten to learn it.

'You've not made the best start, have you? I'll hear it on Sunday evening. Deportment marks start on Sunday. I want everyone to aim at ten out of ten.' She surveyed Kristina with disapproval. 'At this moment you wouldn't get one out of ten for tidiness. Can't you do something about your hair?'

Kristina's attempt to tame her springy mass of wavy hair with an elastic band and a ribbon was doomed to failure. The ribbon slipped off and the band snapped. Already she'd lost two ribbons and only one band remained in her drawer. She'd have to ask Ruth to send some more. Mary had told her that each girl had a pound pocket money deposited with Miss Deacon to cover the cost of stamps, writing materials, cough sweets, reels of cotton, church collection and so on. Should a girl run out of such necessities, Matron would do the shopping for her. But on Kristina's return from school that afternoon, she'd found the contents of her drawers on the bed, with a note on top telling her to tidy her clothes. So she didn't dare ask Matron that evening to buy her some rubber bands.

'I warned you to keep your drawers tidy', said Mary primly. 'Matron goes through them quite often.'

'Poking around among our things!' said Kristina angrily. 'I suppose she looks in our lockers too?'

'It does happen sometimes. Miranda left some torrid love letters in her locker last term. Her parents were told to prevent the boy from writing again. Miss Deacon keeps a very close eye on Miranda's post.'

After lunch on Saturday, a pale sun suddenly lightened up the large lawn at the back of Cabot House, and a robin alighted on a bare branch. Kristina, who'd been wanting to explore the garden, went out of the basement door and bounded up the steps onto the grass. On inspection it proved to be an uninteresting place. However, at least for the first time she was alone. But not for long. Miss Deacon was soon tapping on the drawing room window and beckoning. 'The rule is, you don't go into the garden without permission, and no one is allowed to walk on the lawn', she said when Kristina came in.

'Why not? I won't spoil it.'

'Don't question me in that insolent manner. Just see it doesn't happen again.'

Mary explained that the garden couldn't be used except by prefects, because there were too many girls for one garden. The lawn would be trampled on, and if the juniors were allowed to play noisy games it would annoy the elderly neighbours.

On Saturday afternoon Kristina wrote an emotional letter to her father. *This is an absolutely dreadful school. It's freezing, as the radiators are luke-warm. We have no privacy and no freedom, and no place to be alone except the toilet, and the weekends are just as awful as the weekdays. We have lessons on Saturday morning, and after lunch there's shoe cleaning, and anyone who doesn't have hockey team practice, has to go on a run twice round the boring playing field. Before tea comes letter writing and mending quietly. Only after tea are we free to talk in our common room till prayers. After that it's just cocoa and bed time. This is the most miserable Saturday I've ever spent.*

It was a relief telling her father how she felt, but there was no hope of his interfering with her mother's choice of school. She'd have to resign herself to staying at the Dunbar, even if she didn't resign herself to the system.

Sunday was as dreary a day as Saturday. Kristina had been used to going to church, but attending church at school was irksome in the extreme. There was the task of getting clean and tidy, and putting on hats and gloves to join the crocodile which marched sedately along, often running the gauntlet of a few lads who jeered or wolf-whistled. In the large church, full of ugly Victorian stained glass and huge marble memorials, the girls occupied a block of side pews. Miss Deacon, wearing her Sunday suit of beige and brown tweed with a shapeless felt hat, sat in the front pew of the main block, to keep an eye on her girls. The Reverend Kenneth Speare, after welcoming the girls back, preached at length in a soft monotone which made no impression. Miss Deacon had an unnerving habit of asking the person sitting next to her at Sunday lunch what the sermon was about. Kristina's thoughts all through the service were far away and she couldn't even remember the text being read out.

The girls paraded back to Sunday lunch – a thin slice of roast beef, lumpy gravy, two roast potatoes and a heap of yellowish sprouts. Sour apple pie with watery custard followed. For the first time however, the food tasted wonderful, and Kristina longed for a second helping. Already, because her appetite was rarely satisfied, her standards had dropped, and she was prepared to eat everything on offer, except lumps of fat and black fish-skin.

Kristina's first experience of washing up came after lunch. A giant-sized sink was filled with tepid water, which quickly turned cold as blobs of food floated round in it. The drying-up cloths became sodden long before all the plates and cutlery were wiped. Such was the haste in which the girls rushed through this distasteful job that most plates were put away moist and greasy.

To Kristina's dismay everyone other than the prefects was expected to spend an hour and a half on her bed on Sunday afternoon, reading in silence. It seemed to her that during the four days she'd been at the school she'd hardly been able to talk to anyone. She longed for Dodo's amusing chatter, the hours of intimate exchanges with her Trinidad friends, and the long talks she'd had with her father. Frustration and resentment festered within her, and sooner or later she knew she wouldn't be able to contain these feelings.

Chapter Six

Children the world over are placed in boarding establishments, and quickly learn to knuckle under to the relentless routine, the weight of tradition, the lack of leisure, space and privacy, the uniformity and discipline necessary to keep the wheels turning smoothly, and the pressure to put the good of the school (whatever it may be) above all else. Kristina, however, was not made for such institutional rigour.

After a few weeks she'd still not organised her life sufficiently to avoid constant trouble. And having missed the first term of the school year, she hadn't caught up on each subject. Mary did her best to help, but unfortunately she herself found the work difficult. It was only by dint of intense hard work that she managed to acquire reasonable marks. One of Kristina's problems was trying to concentrate while always feeling cold. She needed a thick jumper under the regulation cardigan.

Kristina was mystified by the snobbery of many of the girls. In Trinidad, white snobbery had been directed against the various coloured races, something she'd never understood. At the Dunbar she began to discover the gradations of the British class system. Miranda's great friend, Kate Benson, whose father was a greengrocer, was eternally grateful for Miranda's protection against snobbish contempt. Fiona told Kristina in the dormitory that Kate's mother was a vulgar-looking woman with peroxide hair and a Lancashire accent. They lived in an ugly yellow brick semi-detached house. What would Fiona have thought of the Rectory at Sangre Grande? Fortunately, being a clergy daughter was acceptable enough at the Dunbar; but to Kristina's amazement she found she was expected to be rather serious and not given to gaiety. It was thought quite natural that she should team up with Mary as a special friend.

Mary soon took it for granted, and began to confide her aspirations to Kristina. Her father was a GP in Clevedon, a small town on the Severn Estuary near Bristol. Her mother was an Anglican, but Dr Grant was an atheist, much to his daughter's chagrin. She wanted to become medically qualified in some way to enable her to go as a useful missionary to Africa. During the summer holidays she'd attended a Christian youth camp for a fortnight. With shining eyes she said she'd committed her life to Jesus, and wondered whether Kristina might be interested in accompanying her to the camp the following summer. Kristina thought of her father. His life was definitely committed to Jesus, but he seemed totally different from Mary, who exhibited a reproachful air, even a superior attitude, to pleasure. Kristina's father, in contrast, had always seemed to be enjoying life and encouraging others to do so. His attitude towards his parishioners, even the malefactors, was one of understanding and hope, never outright condemnation. She recalled his saying in one of his sermons that if Christians were to be rigidly intolerant and unforgiving in Jesus' name, then they were in effect making Him out to be as mean-minded and cruel as themselves.

Everyone except Miranda assumed that Kristina was glad to be Mary's best friend, and kept their distance, for no one relished being lectured on religion. Initially Kristina felt sorry for Mary. She'd been flattered by the girl's attention and grateful for her help. But after a month it became irksome.

'I'm not good like you', she told Mary, 'I can't seem to keep tidy or quiet or do my homework in time or remember to learn the collect.'

'With my help you can. It's just a question of thinking ahead. By the end of term it will seem easy.'

'I don't want to spend all my time worrying about stupid rules.'

Kristina realised that for this first term there could be no getting away from the relationship. Mary had even cleaned her muddy shoes and sewn on a button for her when she'd been trying to get some homework finished on Saturday. Next term she determined to avoid walking to school and spending every break with Mary. She missed having a friend with whom she could be in tune. She'd even yearned for the kind of friendship which went beyond getting up to mischief and having forbidden adventures. She needed someone to talk to about serious subjects. Yvonne Thomas might have fulfilled these desires, and the familiarity of Jenny Morrison, whom she'd known since babyhood, would have provided security. But at Cabot House she could see no possibility of close friendship.

Having all started at the Dunbar in year one, the fourth form girls had settled into their relationships long ago. Rosemary and Jacky, for instance, were bound together through being especially 'brainy'. They even borrowed musty tomes out of a section of the library which most fourth formers would never dream of entering. At the same time they continued to share a childish game which they had begun at the age of ten. Rosemary had brought a teddy bear replica of A.A. Milne's Pooh Bear to school. The second term Jacky had come with the Piglet character made in pink satin by her mother. Thereafter the girls called each other Pooh and Piglet.

They swiftly became proficient in classics, and decided it would be a lark to translate certain incidents from *Winnie the Pooh* into Latin. Regularly each morning they would greet each other. 'Salve, Winnie Ille Pooh!' 'Salve Porcelle!' Then Jacky might look out of the window and say, 'Pluviae impendent, Pooh. Vis me umbellam expandere?'

One night as Kristina returned from the bathroom Jacky jumped out at her from behind the door, shouting, 'Heus!' And when Kristina dropped her sponge-bag, 'Jocus, ha ha!' Then she and Rosemary did a little ritual dance round her.

'Take no notice!' said Kit. 'They're both crazy.' Kristina soon became used to their eccentricities and the way they were always declaring gloomily that everything at the Dunbar was absolutely *patheticum*. She envied them the make-believe world they had created, which distanced them from the monstrous tedium of the Dunbar regime.

Fiona had arrived at the Dunbar as an adorable blue-eyed blonde beauty whom everyone wanted to protect and to forgive. Rosemary wondered how she'd passed the entrance, until she discovered Miss Craig was a distant cousin of Fiona's father, who was in the diplomatic service. The girls at Cabot House, immersed in trying to keep abreast of the heavy load of academic work, all found Fiona's beauty and stylish clothes, her pastel-coloured sheets and lace-edged pillow-cases, her copies of *Vogue* and *Harper's Bazaar,* her endless descriptions of 'Mummy's parties' and her elder sister's love affairs, a relief from the grindstone. Everyone laughed at her, but she was too sure of her superior social position to care. She was always at the centre of an animated circle to whom she often dispensed hunks of gorgeous pink Turkish delight or walnut fudge sent regularly from her godfather in Cairo.

Kristina could see no place for herself among the sporty group, of which Kit Taylor was the leader. These girls were all in some team or other. They were the darlings of the sports staff, who could sometimes be seen marching briskly along the school corridor wearing navy gym shoes, green aertex shirts with whistles round their necks and long green shorts above their muscular calves. Kristina had spent some hours standing blue with cold on the wind-and-rain-swept playing field. Hockey in England was a miserable affair. She bitterly resented being ordered by the games mistress in a booming military voice, to 'Take off that cardigan this instant. This is a sports field, not an old folks' home.' A roar of laughter went up and for the first time in her life Kristina experienced a white-hot, murderous hatred.

Miranda and Kate were especially pleasant to Kristina, but she knew it could never be a satisfactory threesome. Miranda was quick to offer sympathy, but Kristina sensed she'd never had to face adversity herself, and couldn't entirely empathise with anyone who had.

Kristina lived for the days when she received a letter connecting her briefly with the outside world. Her father had written a short consoling letter before returning to Trinidad. *Give it a chance*, had been his message. *It might just turn out better than you think.* Some weeks later came a long letter from Trinidad giving her news of everything she might conceivably be interested in. Yet here she was, so miserable in Bristol, while her friends continued to live their happy life. They sent their love, but did they really care if they never saw her again?

Ruth included a letter each fortnight with the tuck parcel. Not wishing to rub in too strongly that family life was pleasant, it was hard to know what to write. She was worried about her niece, and felt it necessary to tell Kristina they were thinking of her all the time and looking forward to seeing her again.

Tessa had written too, admonishing her to work hard and obey the rules. She hoped Kristina had made some friends. She and Denis had been doing a lot of entertaining. The weather in Geneva had turned rather cold. She was looking forward to seeing Kristina in London. Would she please write to tell her how things were going. Tessa had asked to be called Mummy, but Kristina couldn't bring herself to do so when she forced herself to reply. The word 'Mummy' was so intimate, so much bound up with childhood, security and dependence. It was almost as awkward as thinking of Miss Deacon as a house mother. *Dear Mother,* she wrote, *Thank you for your letter. I'm trying to work hard and to obey the rules. I've made lots of nice friends. I'm looking forward to the end of term. Love from Kristina.*

Hardly realising what was happening to her, Kristina began to suffer from debilitating anxiety, with no let-up between one hurdle and the next. For several of her essays she needed books from the library, a vast, silent place with small gothic windows. Section upon section of dark volumes stood on dark shelves up to the ceiling. Unsmiling staff and girls seemed to move about on tiptoe, filling Kristina with awe and trepidation. There had been no library at the High School. The few books she'd needed were borrowed from the adequate public library, a cheerful sunny building looking out onto a garden, where the librarians behind the desk had been especially kind and helpful to children. Mary had told Kristina she must go to the desk at the entry to join the library, and to be shown how the system worked. 'We all had to join in the third year', she said, 'And then we had a special tour of the library. It takes a while to get the hang of it.'

But when Kristina approached the librarian on a Friday, she was greeted with impatience. 'It's after four. You should have come earlier.'

'How could I, when I've had lessons all day?'

'Well, I haven't time just now to explain the procedure. You'll have to come back next week. You should have been here last term, when you could have joined the third years for their tour of the library.'

'But I must borrow a particular book to write an essay this weekend', protested Kristina loudly.

Immediately everyone nearby hushed her and the librarian said, 'You must learn how to behave in a library before you join.'

By the time Kristina was ready to walk back to Cabot House it was pouring with rain. Mary was waiting with her usual long-suffering patience. The few people in sight on the Downs were dashing along under umbrellas. 'Let's run', said Kristina, who was very cold, and she set off on a steady jog. Since Mary wouldn't join her she arrived at Cabot House alone, and was seen by Lucy Richmond entering the cloakroom.

Another few marks gone, she thought, *And I haven't learned the collect.* She decided to miss tea, and sat in the corner of the freezing cloakroom in her damp clothes struggling to learn the prayer. Luck was with her, for no one remarked on her absence, and she recited it with only two mistakes.

By Cocoa time Kristina was extremely hungry, and her stomach felt hollow. Having eaten her ration of three small biscuits, she longed for something more substantial. She was the last person in the dining room when she noticed a lone biscuit on the platter. Like a starving beggar she pounced on it, cramming it into her mouth as she fled up the stairs.

The following morning she woke feeling unusually hot, with a sore throat and a headache. She got up only to start shivering violently. 'You feel absolutely boiling', said Mary. 'You'd better go back to bed. I'll fetch Matron.'

By ten o'clock it had been decided, in view of her high temperature, that Kristina should be conveyed to the sanatorium. She'd heard girls referring to 'the San', and had gathered that this was a house outside Bristol where girls were sent when they were ill. Several of her year, including Miranda, had spent time there in year two with chickenpox. 'After a few days it was quite fun', Miranda said. 'We were in a dorm for eight. Parents were allowed to visit, and they brought masses of much-needed food which we shared. The Matron there is even worse than the one here, but she couldn't easily bully eight of us. She's known as the Hairless Wonder.'

Kristina was vaguely aware of being wrapped in blankets and bundled into the back of a taxi. At the sanatorium she was carried upstairs by the driver to a single room. There was no heating, but there were two hot water bottles in the bed. Kristina dozed off for an hour and then woke to complete silence. The room was just big enough to contain the narrow iron bedstead, a bedside cupboard and a chair. Black curtains hung limply at the sash windows. She could see her dressing gown on a hook on the back of the closed door. The bare walls were painted in pale grey, and dark maroon lino covered the floor. A smell of disinfectant pervaded the room. Her head was still throbbing, and now her nose was bunged up, forcing her to breathe through cracked lips. She desperately wanted to blow her nose, but there was no hanky in sight. On attempting to sit up she was sick over the stiffly starched white sheets. In a panic she shouted 'I've been sick!' but her words emerged as a croak. Her head fell back in exhaustion on the flat pillow, and there she remained until lunchtime, when the door opened and a young woman in an overall and cap entered carrying a tray.

Seeing the state of the bed she put down the tray and hurried away. Within minutes she returned with an older stout woman dressed in a blue nurse's uniform. Sparse strands of mousey hair barely covered her reddish skull.

'Why didn't you call me?' reproved the matron, as she and the maid sat Kristina on the chair wrapped in a blanket. Then, with swift expertise, they whisked away the dirty sheets and remade the bed.

Tears were trickling down Kristina's face, combining with the mucus from her running nose.

'For goodness' sake, child, where's your hanky?' said the matron with distaste.

'I haven't got one.'

'They should have sent some with you.' And she dashed away, returning with a couple of large hankies and a flannel in a bowl of water.

Putting Kristina back to bed, she asked, 'D'you want your soup?' The liquid had congealed in its bowl.

'No, thank you.'

'Better not to eat much today. I'll leave you the glass of water.'

The tray was removed, the door closed and silence descended once more. The hours passed while Kristina slept fitfully, half waking at times to feel the oppression of her surroundings and the lack of humanity in every sense. Eventually it grew dark and Matron returned with a thermometer, followed by the maid with a bowl of hot water, towels and soap.

'You've still got a temperature', said Matron. 'D'you want any supper?'

'No', said Kristina, who dreaded the ignominy of being sick again.

'Very well. The toilet's next door, but there's a chamber pot in your cupboard if you feel too weak. I'll see you in the morning.' She closed the curtains and was gone.

Kristina had no idea what time it was. Her watch was still in the drawer at Cabot House. She tossed and turned for a while in the dark, and then pulled the string above the bed to switch on the shadeless ceiling light which hung dazzling into her aching, watering eyes. Turning it off quickly she lay back on the flat limp pillow, which made breathing harder.

For a week she remained wretchedly ill with a severe attack of flu. She was visited three times a day, either by the matron or by her part-time assistant, a taciturn woman who spoke gently but who looked so unhappy herself she was no consolation. The maid who brought the food had nothing to say. By the third day, in addition to feeling feverish, bunged up and headachy, she was still weak in her legs. She developed a chest infection, and for three nights coughed herself into exhaustion. Matron produced an evil-tasting mixture, saying she should make an effort to control her coughing fits. Mrs Morrison had told Kristina in Trinidad that with a bad cough it was better to prop one's head on several pillows. But Matron was not willing to produce more pillows. 'We can't be washing pillow cases all the time. It's bad enough having to provide you with so many hankies.'

As she began a slow recovery she became bored – not mildly bored, as she'd very occasionally been in the past, but crushingly bored by the solitary confinement – a grim blankness of slow-moving minutes and hours which made her mind cry out for some kind of diversion.

The only relief came in the form of two notes from Cabot House – one from Mary saying, *I'm so sorry you're ill. Get better quickly. I'm praying for you every night.* The other, from Miranda, said, *Poor, poor, poor you, falling into the hands of that heartless Hairless Wonder. You can flush the Friday fish down the 'aunt', but make sure you cut it into small pieces, or the pipe will get blocked, and the firing squad will be after you. We all miss you. The Toad mentioned you at prayers but I bet she didn't mean it. Did you know she used to be housemistress at a boys' school. Apparently she much prefers boys. So why did she leave? Perhaps she was caught in flagrante delicto with a sixth former. Can't you just imagine it!! Tear this note up immediately.*

Eventually Kristina began to feel hungry, but the food was uneatable. A tepid chunk of grey boiled fish might appear, with two slices of hot beetroot and a splodge of lumpy mashed potato; or a pale heap of watery scrambled egg on soggy toast; or a sour baked apple with a dribble of custard. Worst of all was suet pudding, scattered with hard black currants embedded in a glistening gluey whitish-grey mass. Salt and pepper and sugar were never offered. Drink consisted of water or warm milk covered with a skin. Cough sweets were unknown. She'd lost over half a stone of weight, so Matron insisted she ate her meals. She followed Miranda's advice and secreted the most disgusting bits of food into toilet paper to flush away. Inevitably she was discovered, and made to feel like a criminal. She asked for books to read and was brought *The Broad Highway*, by Jeffrey Farnol, and *Alan Quatermain,* by Rider Haggard, both of which she'd read.

'Well, read them again', said Matron.

Kristina burst into angry tears, shouting, 'I hate you. I hate this horrible place and everything in it. You're nasty and mean, and I'm going to write to my father and tell him all about the miserable time I've had here.'

Matron was quite unmoved by her outburst. 'Hysterics will get you nowhere. I'm surprised at a big girl like you making such a fuss. You're not the only person in the world to have flu. You'll soon be back at school, so in the meantime, pull yourself together. You wouldn't want us to tell your parents that you're a crybaby.'

During Kristina's last three days at the sanatorium, Matron took her temperature in the morning, and after that only the maid entered the room. Her uniform was brought on the last day, and she was led down the stairs to the waiting taxi. She noticed with a start of surprise that the house was surrounded with lawns and trees, and birds were flying in the sky. The sight of them suddenly made her feel glad to be alive, like a prisoner released from a long incarceration.

Miss Deacon hadn't notified either John or Tessa of Kristina's illness. Since a letter sent to foreign destinations might not be received until the patient was back at school, it wasn't considered necessary to write unless an illness was very serious, in which case a telegram would be sent.

News of Kristina's outburst at the sanatorium had reached Miss Deacon. She'd already been told by one of the kitchen staff that the evening before Kristina was taken ill she'd pinched a spare biscuit at cocoa time. Thus Kristina's return was marked with icy disapproval. It was left to Miranda's warm-hearted nature to bestow an affectionate hug and to insist that she accept a large slice of chocolate cake from her recent tuck parcel. 'Poor, poor you!' she said. 'The Hairless Wonder's turned you into a skeleton!'

Two days later Kristina had to sit next to Miss Deacon, who started a conversation with Jacky on her other side about Jane Austen's *Northanger Abbey*. Kristina had read *Pride and Prejudice,* but dared not mention it. Jacky had visited Bath where *Northanger Abbey* was set, and she conversed with animation about its historical buildings. Three spare slices of treacle tart were left on the serving plate in front of Miss Deacon. Kristina hoped for a second helping, since it was usual for the girls sitting on either side of Miss Deacon to be asked first. But Miss Deacon rose, deliberately leaving the tempting treacle tart uneaten.

Friday came, and yet again Kristina had forgotten to learn the collect. Mirabel was angry and became even more annoyed when Kristina protested loudly. She'd been catching up on homework, there wasn't time to learn the stupid collect, and she wasn't going to! On Saturday she saw she had 0 out of 10 for collect, conversation and manners, and 2 out of 10 for deportment and neatness. Mirabel informed her they were the lowest set of marks anyone had ever had. She was a disgrace to the House, and quite frankly, didn't deserve to be at the Dunbar Academy.

'I don't care!' shouted Kristina. 'I never wanted to come to this prison, and I wish I could leave.'

The door of the senior common room had opened slightly, and giggles could be heard inside. Mirabel had never been confronted with rebellion before. 'I shall report you to Miss Deacon', she said, and retired to the prefects' study.

Miss Deacon announced at the end of prayers that Kristina should remain behind. She then left the room herself for ten minutes, leaving Kristina waiting. 'You've only been back a few days' she said, 'And already your behaviour is a disgrace. While you were at the sanatorium I heard that you'd taken more than your share of biscuits at Cocoa.'

'I was starving', said Kristina.

'Starving is hardly the word. I should have said downright greedy.' And Miss Deacon's hostile eyes seemed to bulge more than usual. 'As for your rudeness to Matron at the sanatorium, and to Mirabel here, it is quite unacceptable. This means a Conduct Mark, which will be read out at school assembly. I expect you know three Conduct Marks in a term means expulsion.'

By the time Kristina was dismissed, Cocoa was over. She was sure Miss Deacon had deliberately made her miss it. Mary was sympathetic, but seemed as always to be primly exasperated by Kristina's outbursts. 'You shouldn't argue with Mirabel, or any of the prefects, and certainly not with the teachers or Matron. Just say you're very sorry, and that you'll try harder. The more you argue and shout, the more they'll want to punish you. Can't you see that?'

'No, I can't. Why should I be sorry when people are being so unfair?'

'And you could learn to be more tidy', went on Mary. 'Why don't you mend that hole in your stocking?'

'Because I've never darned a stocking.'

'I suppose I'll have to teach you.'

When Miranda heard about the Conduct Mark, she was indignant. 'Oh,. poor, poor you! But don't lose any sleep over it. People are always getting them. Miss Craig saves them up and reads out half a dozen at a time. No one really listens.'

'Have you ever had one?'

'Not so far, touch wood.'

'Has anyone in Cabot House been expelled?'

'Yes, Anita Rigby, last year. She got her third conduct mark for washing her hair at midnight. Poor girl, she had that kind of limp hair which goes greasy in a couple of days. It was announced very solemnly – *Expelled for persistent gross disobedience.* Miss Craig loves to make a ghastly ritual in assembly, making it sound as though it's a sentence of execution!'

On Sunday afternoon during rest time Kristina wrote a despairing letter to Ruth, hoping that her aunt would come just once to take her out. And a fortnight later Ruth did come, on a clear sunny day early in March, after some difficulty in proving to Miss Deacon that she was a responsible relative.

She was disturbed to see how thin her niece looked, with an unhealthy-looking complexion and a slight blotchiness round her eyes. They walked across the Downs and down Blackboy Hill to Whiteladies Road, to find a café. In the next hour Kristina put her case for leaving the Dunbar well enough, but Ruth doubted whether her mother would take any notice. She was sure Tessa relished being able to boast about her clever daughter at the Dunbar. She'd no doubt decided that the girl was too rebellious, too emotional and unlikely to gain academic honours without regular coercion. If she were to hear Kristina's story, it would only confirm this opinion. A few more terms, and Kristina would be brought to heel. It was common knowledge that discipline was character-building. John had told Ruth he thought Kristina should stick it out until the summer before he confronted Tessa. It was just possible that if she'd made some close friends, she might find the Spartan routine and petty rules bearable.

It was a dilemma for Ruth, but she promised to write to John with Kristina's complaints. The most disquieting aspect of it all, she thought, was Kristina's hunger. Surely a school charging such high fees should be able to satisfy the appetite of growing young girls in spite of rationing. There would have been no such problem at Dartington, with its farm produce. The Dunbar should have converted some of its gardens into vegetable plots.

After a substantial meal Kristina asked if they might cross the suspension bridge and have a walk in the vast expanse of woodland she'd seen on the other side of the Avon Gorge.

'I'm sorry, my dear, we haven't time. I mustn't miss my train to Taunton.'

It was disappointing, but after a walk around the edge of the Downs in the spring sunshine, she felt more cheerful. Ruth pointed out some daffodils, flowers Kristina had only read about. Then she asked whether any school trips were planned into the countryside where she might see other wild spring flowers.

'Not this term. Next term we're going to Wells to see the cathedral and the Bishop's palace.'

'That's where your father went to Theological College. It's a lovely place.'

They returned to Cabot House, and Ruth promised to include more food in future tuck parcels.

For the rest of term Kristina struggled to keep up with her work and to obey the rules. Mary was constantly at her side, helping, warning and advising, subconsciously aware that their friendship might not last. Miranda and the rest of the Middle Common Room were shocked yet amused by Kristina's outspoken pronouncements, and the loud guffaw of laughter which authority could not tolerate. She became the centre of gossip in Cabot House.

Then out of the blue, two weeks before the end of term, came a miraculous reprieve. Tessa wrote to say that unfortunately she was to have an urgent (though not life-threatening) operation, which would require a lengthy recuperation period. It would be impossible to come to London for the Easter holidays, and she'd arranged for Ruth to have Kristina. She could travel by train to Taunton, where her aunt would meet her.

Kristina felt it was the most wonderful thing that had ever happened to her. The horrors of school melted away, and the allure of Ruth's family life at Seaton mounted steadily in her mind, even rivalling her memories of Sangre Grande. She could now look forward to the holidays with the same excitement as the other girls. Ruth wrote saying how pleased the twins were, and how good it would be to show her the Devon countryside in the spring. She would be able to see primroses and possibly bluebells for the first time.

On the last day of term Miranda announced she was bringing a gramophone to school, so they could dance on Saturday evenings.

'You'll never get permission', said Mary primly.

'Ha, ha! I've already got it. Daddy rang up the Toad. He can get round anyone.' *Daddy*, everyone knew, was someone high up in banking. 'So don't forget, everyone, if you've got any dance records, bring them next term.'

Kristina was delighted. She adored any kind of dancing. She didn't know it, but her sense of rhythm was the only good thing she'd inherited from her mother.

Chapter Seven

Waking up at Seaton was wonderfully unreal. Kristina had been so conditioned to bells, rigid routine and the sound of someone chiding her at every turn, that she could hardly take in her freedom. Looking out of the bedroom window at Seaton Bay, she thought, *It seems like a year since I saw the sea. I could walk along the coast to Beer and Branscombe, and no one would give me a conduct mark for being out of bounds.*

And as though to confirm this freedom, Penny bounced in, saying it was going to be a heavenly spring day. They were planning to take a picnic to the top of Haven Cliff, and then to go down into the 'jungle' on the Landslip.

'A real jungle?' asked Kristina.

'No, not like a tropical jungle. We just call it the jungle, because everything's left to grow as it likes, and no one's allowed to dig up the rare plants. It's a seven-mile-long strip of land which came away from the cliff in a storm during the last century.'

'Mum says you've been starved at school', said Anne, 'So she's going to put in an extra sandwich for you.'

During her first evening at Seaton, Kristina had said very little. She'd been told so often to stop chattering, stop laughing, and stop being silly, that she'd fallen at last into the habit of being quiet. But soon Kristina regained her voice, and began relating her experiences in horrific detail to the wide-eyed twins. The second night Ruth and

Peter heard the three of them chattering and giggling in Kristina's room until midnight.

Ruth suggested sending Tessa a get well card. 'She's sure to be feeling very weak and also upset that she couldn't have you for the holidays. Do write and say how sorry you are, and how much you're looking forward to seeing her in the summer.' Kristina dutifully sent a card. The notion of Tessa being her mother still had no reality, and had she to choose between Tessa and Ruth she would have chosen Ruth.

Ruth was worried about Kristina's lack of interest in her mother, and particularly about a sudden outburst of hostility one night in her room. 'She won't even consider moving me to Dartington. Or best of all, she could let me live here and go to day school. Doesn't she like you?'

'We only met once, at the wedding. Perhaps after leaving your father she didn't want to have anything to do with his family.'

'How could Dad have married someone who doesn't share any of his interests? How *could* he have made such a mistake?'

'You're old enough to understand, and it might help you to know now why he married Tessa. You must promise to keep it to yourself, and not to mention what I say to your father. He'll tell you in his own good time.'

'I promise not to say anything.'

'Your mother had just finished her training, and had started work as a private nurse in Bristol when she met your father at a party. He'd come over from Bath, where he was a curate, to visit a friend of his. She was, and still is, I expect, very beautiful and lively. She was attracted to him for, as you probably know, although he's usually rather quiet and studious, he can be very good fun in the right company. He fell in love with Tessa, and they met a few times. Possibly she thought it was just an affair that would end, but he desperately wanted to marry her. When you first fall in love you don't consider things like not having much money, and not sharing the same interests and outlook on life. And your father is a bit eccentric and unworldly.

'Anyway, they went on seeing each other. Eventually your father wrote to tell me that after all, he wasn't sure they should marry, especially as he was intending to work in Trinidad. But then came the news that Tessa was pregnant. Her parents would have been horrified if they'd known, and so would the Bishop of Trinidad. And, of course, they didn't want you to be illegitimate. There was no other solution but to get married quickly.'

'Without even loving each other?' said Kristina.

'Yes, but you can see they had to. In most people's eyes, to be illegitimate is a disgrace. Tessa's parents might have refused to see her again, and your father would have had to give up his vocation. He intended to try and make the marriage work. It might have done if he'd had a parish in Port of Spain. However, it's too late now. At least you're very much loved by your father, and your mother wants to have a good relationship with you too. Do give her a chance, and try not to condemn either of your parents. They made a big mistake, but young people in love often do make mistakes.'

'I don't condemn them for getting married', said Kristina. 'But if my mother cares about me, she'd want me to be happy at school. I shan't forgive her or my grandmother for keeping me at the Dunbar.'

'Another thing', said Ruth, 'Your father's worried because he hasn't heard from you lately. I wrote and told him you'd had flu, and were catching up with your work. As it happens, it might be better when you next write not to mention how horrible you found the sanatorium. It would upset him because he can't help you, and...'

'I know that', interrupted Kristina. 'I don't tell him the worst things.' But inwardly she thought he could have done something to have her removed from the Dunbar.

'If life gets really bad, then write to me, and I'll reply straight away.'

A letter came from Tessa, thanking Kristina for the card, and going on to say she'd just read her school report. Miss Craig conceded that missing the first term of the school year, and then being ill for a fortnight, had made it difficult for Kristina to keep abreast of her studies. But her teachers felt that if she hadn't caught up by the end of the summer term, it would be wiser to have her repeat the year. Tessa exhorted her daughter to make every effort to catch up. Repeating a year, she wrote, would be very expensive and quite unnecessary. Kristina must try very hard to pass the end of year exams. For entirely different reasons, Kristina too was horrified at the idea of repeating Lower 4b and increasing her five years to six. It was essential to pass those exams.

Tessa also included a note for her aunt, asking if she'd mind ordering two regulation dresses, a pair of shorts, aertex shirts and white socks from Merchants for the summer term. Ruth would have to send Kristina's measurements. When the dresses arrived, Kristina was aghast. They were shapeless garments in a dull green and yellow check cotton with floppy elbow-length sleeves and wide collars.

'What dingy dresses!' said Kristina. 'The prettiest girl in the school must look a fright in these.'

Recalling what Miranda had said about dancing, Kristina asked her aunt whether she possessed any dance records.

'There are some scratchy old things in the attic, and a gramophone too. When we moved last year we never got round to unpacking them.'

The girls lost no time in bringing down the gramophone, finding the tin of needles and dusting off the dozen records. They rolled back the carpet in the dining room, and under Kristina's expert guidance, Penny and Anne were given their first dance lesson. It became a craze, and every evening, and often early in the morning, Seaton Hole Cottage was filled with the sound of waltzes, quicksteps, foxtrots, tangos and rumbas – all the dances Kristina had been taught by Mrs Morrison in Trinidad. The twins learned fast and soon invited one of their friends to make up a foursome. Kristina kept the twins enthralled when she danced the rumba on her own, a performance which would have surprised the Cabot House prefects.

Ruth said Kristina could take away the records and she'd buy some more for the twins.

Back at Cabot House Kristina had no sooner unpacked than her troubles started again. She'd forgotten to include her indoor shoes, still lying under the bed at Seaton. Until Ruth sent them – and how embarrassing it would be to have to ask her – she'd be obliged to wear outdoor shoes with all the explanations it would involve.

And sure enough, while walking along the corridors at school, there was always some officious teacher or prefect ready to pounce on spotting a pair of heavy lace-up shoes among the shiny button-ups marching along in line. Outdoor shoes looked particularly conspicuous with the summer dresses.

Kristina booked to walk to school with several friends, but since Mary took it for granted they would spend every break together, she thought it would be churlish to refuse. Miranda's gramophone had arrived, and a number of girls were keen to start a dance session on Saturday afternoons. The monitor of the senior common room offered to ask Miss Deacon if they might roll back the carpet and use the living room. She consented reluctantly, saying the noise might be disturbing to those girls who wanted to work. But they could have permission for the following Saturday.

On Friday Miranda and Kate set up the gramophone and tried out a record. The catchy tune reverberated round the house, causing great excitement. Most of the girls could dance the quickstep and the slow waltz, and the first Saturday they stuck to these two dances. Miranda, Kate and Kristina took turns in winding up the gramophone and changing the record.

Mary was no longer in the same dormitory as Kristina. For a few days the bed remained empty. Matron said they were awaiting an Indian girl, who would be in the third form. Fiona had found out that Gita Rau was the daughter of an important, wealthy Hindu family from Madras in southern India. Kristina was curious as to whether she'd resemble the Hindu girls she'd met at school in Trinidad. It was hard to imagine a foreigner putting up with all the rules, the strict uniform and the bland food at the Dunbar. As there were no other coloured girls in the school, she would feel very strange. Fiona commented sniffily that it was surprising an Indian girl had been accepted.

'Why shouldn't an Indian be accepted?' asked Kristina.

'Because this is an Anglican school for white Christians.'

'Who says so?'

'It's obvious. They've never had Indians before.'

'Well, I think it's a good idea.'

When Gita arrived on Sunday evening she reminded Kristina of several Indian girls at the High School – small and slender, with waist-length black hair and dark almond-shaped eyes. She had a shy smile, a soft meek voice and graceful movements. The girls were astonished when, instead of arriving in uniform, Gita was wearing a sari, delicate embroidered sandals, gold earrings and a jangle of thin gold bracelets. In no time the news had spread around that the Indian girl even had painted toenails.

Matron was speechless for a moment, as she sat down to check Gita's uniform. 'Next term make sure you arrive in uniform', she said.

Gita replied sweetly but firmly, 'When I'm travelling by plane from India, I certainly can't wear this ugly uniform. Everyone would laugh.' She omitted to mention that she'd spent a night in London before travelling to school.

'Well, you'll have to change before you reach Bristol. The rule is, you don't arrive in mufti.'

Kristina was astonished, and not a little envious, at how, from the start, Gita got away with ignoring many of the rules. Her meek demeanour and innocent wide-eyed look excused her all the time. Even Miss Deacon gave up with an exasperated sigh as though the girl came from a tribe of idiots who knew no better. But Gita was far from being an idiot. She got her own way by calculated intelligence, and since she had an excellent memory, she quickly excelled in most subjects. The teachers were willing to give her extra tuition, or to let her off an essay when she explained so reasonably that she'd have to read up in the holidays what she'd missed during the year.

Gita was not shy, nor did she feel uncomfortably different from the white girls. She'd already been to a British school in India. She seemed older than her thirteen years, and full of self-possession. Yet she was reserved, answering questions politely, but never expanding. Since she was in the junior common room, Kristina couldn't see much of her during the day, but in the dormitory she wished they could talk privately. There were so many questions she wanted to ask. India was very large, she knew, but was it hot all the time with jungle and mountains and palm-fringed beaches like Trinidad? What kind of food did they eat? Were there any black people or Chinese living there?

'What language do you speak at home?' asked Kit.

'Tamil, but there are many, many languages in India.'

'I thought Indians all spoke Hindustani.'

'Hindustani isn't a proper language. It is how the British speak to us. There are about fourteen languages in India, and two hundred and eighty dialects.'

'Say something in Tamil', said Fiona.

The words sounded exotic, and as far removed from the world of Cabot House as one could imagine. As Kristina listened to Gita, or watched her unplaiting her glossy black hair or pulling on a lacy white nightdress over her smooth brown skin, she felt they must surely become friends.

Since Gita hadn't brought pyjamas she had to wear the exquisite nightdresses they all coveted. And when it came to making out the weekly laundry list, Gita insisted that on no account could her nightdresses be sent. She'd brought some special liquid soap, and she asked Matron to have them washed by hand. Everyone collapsed with laughter and disbelief, but Gita got her way, and the nightdresses were hung in the kitchen to dry. Gita remained adamant on other aspects of the uniform. Instead of regulation underpants, she wore what she referred to as silk panties, which she washed herself and dried on a towel rail. She also refused to wear the green knickers. Only on gym days did she stuff a pair into her satchel. Matron made no comment.

She won the battle too over washing-up. Never in her life had she washed dishes. She pointed out that her father wasn't paying huge sums to send her to the Dunbar Academy just to wash up. Her name never again appeared on the rota. Kristina was indignant about this, but said nothing. Gita mightn't have understood about English fair play.

At the next dancing session, Gita appeared in the living room with two other third formers.

'D'you want to learn?' asked Kristina kindly.

'I know all the dances', replied Gita.

'Oh, well, come on then, let's try a foxtrot.'

Being tall, Kristina took the lead. She realised with delight that her partner could follow with perfect timing and graceful movement. When the tune ended, Kristina said, 'Do put it on again, Kate. Gita and I will show you how the foxtrot should be danced. Then we'll try a tango.'

Everyone backed up against the wall, and for the first time school Kristina was able to demonstrate that she could do something better than anyone else, excepting Gita. For the rest of the session they were given the floor, and the girls watched with fascination as they performed the more complicated steps of each dance, ending with a quick waltz. They swirled around to the exacting pace of *Tales from the Vienna Woods,* never losing their balance, and laughing all the while. At the end clapping and a few cheers broke out. Then there was the rush to right the room for prayers. Kristina was euphoric and hot. Gita looked cool and collected.

It was arranged that Kristina and Gita should teach various steps for half of each dance session, and then everyone would practise them. Miss Deacon ordered there to be no more clapping or cheering. During prayers Kristina, imagining Miss Deacon dancing the tango with a handsome South American in tight satin trousers, couldn't suppress a giggle. She was sternly warned that one more giggle in prayers would mean no more dancing.

Kristina and Gita became firm friends. As they whispered to each other after lights out, Kristina complained of the lack of privacy. Gita replied she'd never had any privacy. At home in India the house was always full of relatives, visitors and servants. Crowds filled all the public places, especially the railway stations. Beggars followed one everywhere.

Kristina said Port of Spain was crowded, but at Sangre Grande, away from the main road she could walk or cycle and see very few people. 'My father says that in England he used to walk all day on the moors without seeing anyone. I shall do that one day.'

'A girl walking alone would be much too dangerous.'

'No, not in England it wouldn't.'

They compared the flora growing in India and in Trinidad. Gita loved the flame tree best, Kristina the poui. They checked through a list of fruit and vegetables, and were delighted when the two countries grew something in common, such as avocados, pomegranates, limes, oranges, plantains and coffee.

'What about mangoes?' — 'Yes.' — 'And sugar cane?' — 'Yes.' — 'And rice?' — 'Of course.' They also coincided on crocodiles, vultures, snakes and monkeys. 'But we have tigers', said Gita triumphantly.

'Oh, do shut up, you two', said Rosemary. 'You sound like a geography lesson.'

'My father shot a tiger in India, and had a rug made out of its skin', said Jacky.

'Did you live in India?' asked Gita.

'Yes, but I was only eight when we came home.'

'Is India still ruled by us?' asked Kristina.

'No, of course not. Don't you remember all the fighting last August when it became two independent states, India and Pakistan? It was all over the newspapers, and on the wireless.'

'I do remember my father mentioning it.'

Mary had no interest in learning to dance, and didn't care for Miranda or Kate, and certainly not for Gita. It was only at break that she could speak seriously to Kristina. 'The school doesn't approve of close friendships between different years', she warned. 'You and Gita sometimes walk to school arm in arm. It might get you into trouble.'

'What a crazy idea. I was thirteen in September, and Gita was thirteen in April. I've walked arm in arm or hand in hand with my best friends all my life.'

They got on well, partly because they were opposites, but mainly because they shared a healthy disregard for officious authority. But while Gita continued to win most of her battles, Kristina was for ever in detention or condemned to extra washing up. Yet they remained friends. It gave Mary great pain that a promising friendship with a girl from a religious background was coming to an end. She became jealous, and Kristina felt guilty. She'd been willing to talk seriously about religion with Mary, but couldn't tolerate the way she condemned many of the pleasures of life. Mary even condemned her own father for being an atheist.

When Mary's parents came to take her out one Saturday to their home in Clevedon, Kristina was invited. The rooms in the large grey pebble-dashed house were high-ceilinged, shabby and without comfort. Dr Grant looked a most unhappy man, thought Kristina, as he greeted her with a grim face. Mrs Grant was an older replica of her daughter. Surprisingly at lunch there was a bottle of white wine and two glasses on the table. Even more surprising, after Dr Grant had poured a glass and drunk it, he winked at Kristina and offered her half a glass. Mrs Grant gasped, saying, 'George! How could you?'

But her husband had already half filled the other glass, and he pushed it towards Kristina. 'For heaven's sake, Janet, it won't kill her. The kids in France are all brought up on wine.'

Kristina had tried a mouthful of rum in Trinidad, which she disliked, though a little cold white wine mixed with orange juice on special occasions had been delicious. However, it was impossible to enjoy the wine at the Grants' house.

After lunch Mary and Mrs Grant went to the kitchen to make coffee. Dr Grant, who'd finished off the bottle of wine, told Kristina to take a seat in the living room, adding with a smile, 'Can't you do something about Mary? You look like a sensible, fun-loving girl.'

'She's helped me a lot at school', said Kristina.

'Yes, that's the trouble. She'll help you become an earnest kill-joy Christian if you don't watch out. Don't let her, my girl. Go back to school and wash your hands of her. She and her mother have ruined my life. Don't let Mary ruin yours.'

Kristina was too astounded to reply.

Back at school, Mary apologised for her father.

'I didn't mind', said Kristina. 'He seemed a rather sad man.'

'He's a wicked unbeliever, and he drinks too much!'

'You can't make yourself believe.'

'If you turn to God, He'll help you believe.'

'How can you turn to someone you don't believe in? Your father probably doesn't want to be helped.'

'That's right. He won't even try. He just laughs at my mother and me. He'll burn in hell!'

'How d'you know there's fire in hell?'

'Because the Bible says so.'

'My father says hell isn't like that. Hell is probably what your conscience suffers when you realise you've been wicked and it's too late to do anything about it, and you don't deserve to be forgiven.'

But there was no arguing with Mary.

It was a relief this term to be able to play tennis instead of hockey. Kristina was a competent player, but the games mistress assumed she'd be as hopeless at tennis as she seemed to be at hockey. She was put down to play with girls who had little idea of the game. There was no coaching, so none of them improved. Kristina tried to get into one of the house teams, but when Mirabel came to watch her play, she said that apart from a few good shots, Kristina was far too erratic.

'How can I learn to be better when I'm always put with poor players?' she fumed at Gita. 'No one will give me a chance to do anything. Everyone's against me. I loathe this school.'

'Don't get so upset', said Gita. 'They're stupid teachers with their stupid rules. We should just laugh at them.'

'You put up with them because they don't go on at you.'

'I know I'm lucky. I hate it here as much as you, but my family imposed just as many stupid rules at home. Coming here is my chance to have a good career and to be free of my family. When we leave, we can boast we went to the Dunbar Academy, and everyone will be impressed.'

'Why should they be'

'Because it's such a famous school.'

Kristina was not consoled. She wondered if Gita was being serious. She wasn't sure how she herself would define a good education, but the Dunbar wasn't providing it.

A letter came from John, saying he hoped by now she'd found a friend to give her moral support. Kristina replied, giving an enthusiastic description of Gita. *...I do wish she was in my year* she wrote, *But luckily Miranda is in my form. We sit at the back and write notes about the teachers to each other, in code, of course. You'll be angry to hear I play around in class. The trouble is the lessons are so boring, especially Miss Deacon's. We're studying modern poems from an anthology. A few are OK, if only she'd read them properly. Yesterday it was The Hound of Heaven, by Francis Thompson. We all detest the poem, except Mary. By the time we've paraphrased every line for homework we shall hate it even more. I did find several good poems in our anthology, and asked if we could read them aloud. One was The Song of Wandering Aengus, by W.B. Yeats, and another was Beeny Cliff, by Thomas Hardy. But The Toad said we could only read the set poems. As You Like It is also boring. If we could act the scenes it might make it more interesting, but The Toad said we'd make too much noise. Being quiet is all that matters.*

The Latin mistress must be at least 100 years old. We call her Granny Gregg. She has a wispy white bun, and always wears black. She has a walking stick, which is used to poke anyone who isn't concentrating. When she comes in she shouts "Aut vincere, aut mori, girls", and then sets us a horrible unseen. After that we have to translate the Virgil we're meant to have prepared. She always keeps us after the bell, and shouts "Vade in pace!" as we're having to dash along the corridor to the next lesson. She's crazy like hell...

Few girls lived near enough to make it worth going home for the half-term break, and relatives were obliged to stay near the school. Gita's aunt and uncle from London were coming, and suggested she invite Kristina to their hotel.

'Won't it be very expensive?' asked Kristina.

'Maybe, but my Uncle Billy's very wealthy. He'll think nothing of it, and it means I'll have someone to swim and play tennis with.'

On Miss Craig's recommendation, Gita's relatives had chosen The Cedars, an opulent hotel just outside Bristol, much frequented by parents, with a swimming pool, tennis and squash courts, large garden and sun lounge. Kristina was thrilled at the idea of swimming, since the school pool had been closed during the war and wasn't due to reopen till 1949.

At five o'clock on Friday, Gita's aunt and uncle arrived by taxi to take them to The Cedars. Uncle Billy was an Englishman who'd lived in India for many years. Gita's aunt, Renouka, was Indian, but spoke English with an almost perfect accent. She was wearing a silky ultramarine sari with plenty of gold jewellery.

'Gita, my darling!' she said, hugging and kissing her niece, and then kissing Kristina. 'We've come to take you out of prison!' She regarded the dirty red brick façade of Cabot House with the few greyish-green shrubs on either side of the steps, with distaste. 'It looks very drab, doesn't it, Billy? Never mind, the Downs are most attractive, and we shall be crossing the famous suspension bridge.'

Billy had ginger mustachios and a gingery-red face. 'My goodness, you are a tall girl!' he said genially, fingering the gold pin glinting on his silk tie. 'You could put our little Gita in your pocket.'

Kristina tried to smile, hating the way everyone commented on her height.

The girls were most impressed with the bridge, which the driver traversed slowly so they could take in the view. Once over the bridge, the houses were left behind, and they drove with Leigh Woods on their right and the vast Ashton Park Estate on their left before turning up the drive of The Cedars, a large villa-style building with yellow shuttered windows under wide eaves and a trellised veranda running round three sides. At the back was an immense conservatory full of comfortably cushioned cane chairs and flowering pot plants. Two great cedars of Lebanon dominated the front lawn.

Several shiny cars drove up behind them, and soon the foyer, furnished with sofas and flower arrangements, became crowded with parents and schoolgirls who gradually dispersed up the wide staircase. Kristina had never entered such a grand building before. On the way up to the room she was to share with Gita, they met Fiona and her parents and younger brother coming down. Fiona whispered to her mother, 'That's the Indian girl I told you about.' But the whisper was so loud Kristina and Gita heard it. The Kirk-Davis family stared, barely smiling, and Kristina, who'd been about to say something to Fiona, felt embarrassed and kept silent.

This incident set the tone for the whole weekend. The parents of the Dunbar girls all seemed to know one another, and some of them sat together at the same table for luncheon and dinner, talking in the loud, confident voices Kristina had become used to hearing from Fiona. There was much complaint about the recently introduced free National Health Service, the number of squatters in empty houses in London, and the appallingly ugly prefabricated huts being put up everywhere to house the homeless. None of them uttered more than a polite 'Good Morning' to Gita's aunt and uncle.

The only other Cabot House girls staying at The Cedars were fifth and sixth formers who studiously avoided noticing the fourth formers. By Sunday evening Kristina and Gita felt the half term had been spoilt by the unfriendly atmosphere. Kristina had enjoyed the luxurious bedroom and bathroom, the food, the swimming pool and the gardens, but she felt sorry for Gita's aunt and uncle, and she detested the waiter, who spoke obsequiously but showed contempt in his eyes. She wouldn't have wanted any of her own family to stay at The Cedars.

For the next two weeks Kristina had to concentrate on the forthcoming exams. She'd copied out Mary's notes from the autumn term, and with the copious notes she'd taken from the blackboard she had whole exercise books to learn by heart. Unlike Gita, who could memorise anything, even if she didn't understand it, Kristina's memory was more selective. She only remembered clearly what interested her and she wasn't interested in her notes. Gita would pass; most likely she herself would not. Another year in the lower 4th would mean being with Gita. But six more years! It was unthinkable. She revised by torchlight in bed almost all night before each exam, and just managed to retain what she learned long enough to sit the following day's papers, whereupon she immediately forgot everything. However, she scraped through and was told she would be in Upper 4b in September.

Chapter Eight

On the last day of term Kristina almost missed the train from Bristol to Paddington, where she was to meet her mother. Her hat was missing. Matron said there could be no leaving without it. 'Go and look again!' she kept repeating. The taxi arrived. The driver loaded the suitcases, and still the hat was missing. Kristina dashed past Matron and clambered into the car, only to find Mirabel was one of the passengers. All the way to the station she was harangued for being a disgrace to Cabot House. Only an utter nincompoop could have lost her hat.

Kristina sat glumly in the train, wondering what her mother would say, and wishing Gita, who'd left a day early to catch a plane to India, had been with her.

Tessa greeted her daughter fondly, but she considered two terms at boarding school had done nothing to improve Kristina's appearance. Her hair still looked a mess, and she'd lost a button from her dress. Tessa had brought a pair of sandals and four cotton frocks from Switzerland. But even in these she still looked ungainly. *How can she be my daughter?* thought Tessa. *Perhaps a visit to the hairdresser would help.*

The living/dining room in the upstairs flat at Harley Street was tastefully furnished with two deep armchairs, tasselled silk cushions, Persian rugs, water-colours and delicate ornamental china. A circular table stood in the bay window, with four upholstered chairs. Kristina felt like a giant in it after the large rooms at school.

Her bedroom contained white furniture and a pale blue bedspread and eiderdown. A picture of lilies on a pond hung above the bed. She unpacked, but when she'd put her clothes in the drawers and hung the new frocks in the wardrobe, the room still looked as impersonal as the hotel room at The Cedars. Recalling her room in Trinidad brought tears of angry misery to her eyes. What was she doing in this large alien town, sitting in this unfamiliar flat, when she should have been in the Morrisons' car heading for Sangre Grande and all the pleasures of the long summer holiday.

'There aren't any books in this flat', said Kristina, as she and her mother were having tea.

'No, I'm afraid not, we only use the flat for the short visits we make to London. Otherwise we let it, so it isn't like our home in Switzerland', explained Tessa. 'But we can go to Boots' library tomorrow. I've got a couple of Agatha Christie thrillers you might like to try tonight.'

Tessa suggested they take a stroll to Oxford Street to look at the shops, but this didn't appeal to Kristina. 'Isn't there a park near here?'

'Yes, Regents Park, just up the road.'

They started up Harley Street, Kristina striding along and Tessa endeavouring to keep up in high-heeled sandals and tight linen skirt. The park was full of people enjoying the early evening sunshine. Kristina wanted to walk all round the perimeter, but her mother sat on the nearest bench, saying she wasn't used to long walks. 'Now you know the way you can come and explore the park on your own.' After a pause Tessa enquired hopefully, 'I do hope you passed your exams?'

'Yes. I'll be in Upper 4b next term.'

'What a relief. Are you beginning to enjoy school now?'

'No! I hate it.'

'But you did say you'd made some friends. That's the important thing.'

'There are a few decent girls. My best friend is Gita Rau. She's Indian.'

'Indian! How surprising. Do her parents live in England?'

'No, but she has an aunt and uncle in London. They invited me to stay in a posh hotel at half term.'

'And does Gita like school?'

'No. She puts up with it because her father told her the Dunbar provides the best academic education in England. It will help her to get into Oxford, where he went.'

'He's quite right. It might help you too if you work hard.'

They walked back to the flat and Tessa prepared supper. Kristina enjoyed the mushroom omelette and the gooseberry fool. But the small helpings didn't satisfy her hunger, and she asked for more bread. Tessa realised she'd have to stock up on currant buns from the nearby bakery to satisfy her daughter's appetite. She'd brought some Swiss chocolate from Geneva, and offered Kristina a bar as they sat in the armchairs after the meal.

A silence descended on the room. Kristina had answered all her mother's immediate questions, but she wasn't inclined to chatter on to this unfamiliar person who smiled but hadn't as yet laughed. Tessa was thinking as she looked at Kristina's long legs stretched out across the hearthrug, *How she seems to fill the room. Denis will be irritated if he finds her sprawled in his armchair.*

'Did you have a nice holiday with your Auntie Ruth?' ventured Tessa at last.

Kristina's face brightened as she plunged into a glowing description of her time at Seaton. She wished the twins were her sisters. 'Couldn't we go and see them this holidays?' she begged.

'I'm afraid not. Our summer's already planned. Denis arrives in two weeks' time, and we're going to stay in a hotel in Torquay for a fortnight. Then we'll go down to Salisbury to see your grandmother.'

'Couldn't we call in at Seaton on the way to Torquay?'

'No, we're travelling to Torquay with two friends of ours, in their car.'

'Will we be able to go for walks on Dartmoor?'

'Our friends aren't the walking sort. We might drive across the moor.'

The next fortnight turned out to be a frustrating time for Tessa. On the first day they looked at Buckingham Palace, visited the Tower of London and took a boat trip on the Thames. Tessa had never enjoyed sightseeing. The walking exhausted her, though she could always find the energy to traipse round the shops, finishing up in a café for tea. But Kristina had no interest in shops other than bookshops, which her mother rarely entered. Tessa dutifully took her to several museums, but was bored after ten minutes. By the time they'd moved slowly from room to room her feet ached so much she wanted to scream. For a few days she refused to do any sightseeing. Then reluctantly she agreed to visit the National Gallery.

Kristina had never entered an art gallery before. She was overwhelmed by the vast size of some of the oils in enormous gilt frames. Most of these depicted religious or classical subjects crammed with people, gods and angels. It was impossible to take in more than a fraction of all the masterpieces.

She did, however, stop for some while in front of a painting by Velásquez, in which a woman was pounding garlic in a mortar on a table. It reminded her of Dodo, who'd always been preparing garlic dishes. On the table lay a bowl of silver fish, looking uncannily slippery and alive, and two white eggs on a plate looking so real one could have picked them up. She noted two other Velásquez paintings, one of Philip IV of Spain in a rather ridiculous glittering frilly outfit, and the other of the back view of a ravishing nude Venus lying on a couch. Kristina was familiar with sculptures and paintings of Venus in one of her father's books, some of which she considered quite ugly. The beauty of Velásquez's Venus, and the way the sinuous white body seemed to jump out of the picture, was a revelation.

Among the modern works Kristina was surprised to find paintings of mundane objects – a pot on a stove, or a kitchen chair with a rush seat. Finally she was delighted to identify a painting by Renoir of two ladies boating on a river, which she'd seen in a book entitled *French Impressionists.*

'Can we go to the National Gallery again tomorrow?' she asked

'Not tomorrow', replied Tessa. 'You have to realise, Kristina, that work has to be done in the flat. Sheets and towels go to a laundry, but everything else has to be washed at home, and hung in the yard at the back, which we share with the lady downstairs. It's time you learnt to do some washing and ironing, and how to prepare a simple meal. I don't suppose you've ever made a pot of tea.'

'I have to do washing up at school.'

Tessa was surprised. 'How much washing up?'

'There's a rota for the weekends.'

'Well, I suppose it's good for girls to do some chores.'

'Couldn't I go to the National Gallery on my own?'

'No, you're too young to go wandering around London alone. You can only go to Regents Park, because it's so near and you can be home at a definite time.'

'Dad let me go on walks and bus trips alone in Devon.'

'He wouldn't have let you in London.'

Kristina hadn't realised she would be restricted in this manner. On the way home they passed a bookshop, and Kristina asked if they could buy a map of London. Back at the flat she opened it out on her bed, and was amazed to see how big a city it was. Her mother had already shown her how the underground tube trains functioned, and she longed to try them on her own.

When they weren't going out shopping, and the housework was done, Kristina would bury herself in library books from Boots. She was working through Daphne du Maurier, Mazo de la Roche and Dickens. Tessa was glad Kristina could occupy herself reading, yet she herself found the evenings tediously long with no one to chat to. What had she expected of a thirteen-year-old – no longer a child, but certainly not an adult? Unlike Ruth, Tessa was inhibited about discussing such subjects as divorce, sex, marriage, death or religion with her daughter. Only once did Kristina talk freely to her mother, and that was of Trinidad. Listening to her daughter's description of the place she loved so much, Tessa saw how Kristina's face lit up, and felt jealous.

A letter came from John. Tessa wondered how he could write so much. Kristina read and re-read this letter. Her father assumed she'd be visiting a number of interesting places. He particularly recommended the Tate Gallery. She must look at Turner's paintings, and he mentioned in passing that Turner had had a house in Harley Street. *I've written to a bookshop',* he wrote, *Asking them to send you a useful guide to London, and a book called "The Story of Art'.*

After a fortnight mother and daughter weren't much closer than they'd been at the start. Kristina had livened up when taken to see the films, *Oliver Twist* and *Great Expectations,* and to a stage production of *Pygmalion.* Tessa considered her head was too full of romantic ideas about actors and actresses, and her enthusiastic talk of working in theatre was not to be taken seriously. 'It's hardly a respectable career. Few people can earn a decent salary.'

Then Denis arrived. When the doorbell rang, Tessa ran down the stairs to greet him while Kristina remained in the flat, apprehensive about meeting her stepfather. She could hear his hearty, cheerful voice before he appeared at the door, a tall man, expensively dressed, with bushy blond eyebrows and a neat blond moustache. He walked with a slight limp, using a stick with a silver handle. Shaking hands with her, he said, 'Well, well! So you're Kristina. Keeping your mother in order, I hope.' He laughed rather too loudly, and Kristina smiled weakly.

Tessa went to the kitchen to make tea, while Denis sat in his armchair. 'London hasn't changed', he continued, 'Still pretty drab after the war. Your mother been showing you the sights, has she? – Tower of London, Madame Tussaud's and all that?'

'We haven't been to Madame Tussaud's.'

'It's not far. We'll have to drop in sometime.'

After these few remarks Denis spoke to Tessa of the things he'd been doing and the friends he'd seen in Geneva. Then they talked of the condition of the flat, of their neighbours and of the people they must see in London. By the time Tessa put supper on the table and Denis had opened a bottle of wine, they were still talking. For the first time Kristina heard Tessa laughing. When the coffee was brought and Denis had poured two large glasses of brandy, Kristina got up, saying she was going to read in her bedroom.

'What about helping your mother wash up?' said Denis.

'I'll let you off tonight', said Tessa.

From her room, Kristina could hear the conversation going on and on, without actually hearing all the words. Once or twice she caught her name. What could they be discussing so avidly? The line between the adults' and the child's world had been firmly drawn, and Kristina felt very much in the way. Denis and Tessa invited her to accompany them whenever they went out to shop or to call on a friend, but she knew they were relieved when she declined. She would walk up to Regents Park every afternoon, merely to get out of the house. There were tennis courts where young people were playing, but watching them only made her envious. She desperately wanted someone to talk to, and felt bitter resentment one evening when Denis said, 'Can we leave Kristina on her own if we go to a show?' and Tessa replied, 'No, I think she has to be fourteen.'

'Couldn't we ask Mrs Greenfield below to keep an eye?'

'I suppose we could.'

'Why can't I come with you?' said Kristina.

'I promise to take you next time. But just this evening we want to be on our own.'

At six-thirty, Tessa said, 'There's cold ham and potato salad in the fridge, darling, and some ice cream. If anything goes wrong, just knock on Mrs Greenfield's door. We'll be back by eleven.'

When Tessa and Denis had gone, Kristina became so enraged she seriously considered going out herself. But where could she go? Most places would be shut, and she'd still be alone. *Tomorrow,* she decided, *I'll go to the Tate. I don't care what they say.* She ate her supper, but left the dishes in the sink as a protest.

At breakfast Tessa announced that since they were leaving for Torquay early the following morning, the packing would have to be done that day. There was also some ironing Kristina could do. It wasn't going to be easy to go to the Tate, but she was determined to try, should the opportunity arise. Eventually Tessa went out to the chemist, while Denis sat reading the newspapers. Kristina left a note in the kitchen and slipped quietly out of the flat.

After studying the wall map at the tube station she had no trouble finding her way. Fortunately, Oxford Circus to Westminster involved only one change, at Charing Cross. Then it was an interesting walk along the river from Westminster, past the Houses of Parliament and along Millbank to the Tate, where the rooms seemed lighter and more airy than those at the National Gallery. It would be impossible to see the whole gallery in one morning, so Kristina decided to concentrate on the Turners.

To begin with, most of the paintings struck her as a messy blur of colour. All the swirls and sprays and indeterminate contours behind smoke or fog or mist puzzled her. She did find a realistic painting of Venice, and then one of a house and trees beside a river with a rowing boat, which she liked.

Her father had written that Turner started a completely new way of painting land or sea. People in England hadn't liked his work at first, any more than people in France had liked the French impressionists in later years. Kristina walked past the paintings a second time, standing well back from each one. Suddenly she began to appreciate the amazing movement in the pictures. In *The Shipwreck* she could feel the force and terror of the storm. The vibrant colour of some of the skies reminded her of sunrise and sunset in Trinidad. She'd experienced enough days of rain, wind and mist in Devon to see how wonderfully Turner had depicted light shining through them in his paintings. She stood for a long time in front of the picture entitled *Norham Castle,*

Sunrise. At first this had seemed merely a few vague blobs seen through fog. Then she began to make out the castle with the sun rising behind it. A russet smudge turned out to be a cow drinking at the edge of a river which joined the sky. *I must look at a real sunrise again,* thought Kristina. The pictures had made such an impression on her mind that she would never fail in the future to recognise a Turner.

Kristina was glad she'd been to the Tate. She could now write to her father and tell him her views on Turner. But first, her mother had to be faced. 'Dad said I ought to visit the Tate', she said. 'I was perfectly safe.'

'That's not the point', said Tessa. 'I told you not to go out alone.'

'What am I supposed to do if I can't go out?'

'You can come out with us.'

'I hate shops, and I don't know your friends.' Kristina retired to her bedroom, banging the door.

'Kristina, come back!'

'Oh, never mind', said Denis. 'Let her be.'

That evening Tessa warned Kristina to behave politely and cheerfully on holiday. 'Our friends, Michael and Rowena Atkinson, won't want to share their holiday with a sullen girl.'

'I'm not sullen.'

'Denis thinks you are. I don't want the Atkinsons to think badly of you.'

'Have they got any children?'

'No.'

Kristina had a premonition that these Atkinsons, once they'd been introduced, would ignore her. This turned out to be true. During the long journey to Torquay

Kristina sat at the back of the Humber with her nose against the window pane, half-listening to the adults' boring conversation.

They stopped at Salisbury for a snack, and then Denis took over the driving, cursing every time they got held up by a charabanc or a lorry. The countryside looked serene as they travelled across the south of England to Exeter. They passed wide open plains, fields of golden crops ready for harvesting, woodland, isolated groups of majestic trees and rolling green hills dotted with white farms. Summer in the countryside was very different from the winter. Kristina wished they could stop and take a walk.

Kristina had dozed off when she heard Denis say, 'Here we are, the Cliff Hotel, overlooking Babbacombe Bay.'

They piled out of the car with stiff legs. Kristina was shown into a single room overlooking the sea and a terraced garden with a path leading down a steep cliff. The sea and gardens in the evening sunshine looked very tempting, and without bothering to wash or unpack she ran down the stairs. Finding an open door out of the sun lounge, she made her way down to the small private cove at the foot of the cliff. But it was disappointing to find that there was no possibility of going beyond the beach at either end. After a whole day in the car she was desperate to go for a walk. Instead she climbed back to the hotel and met her mother coming down the stairs.

'For goodness' sake, don't go out without locking your door and taking the key. You'd better unpack and change for dinner.'

'Is the beach down there the only one in Torquay?'

'No, this isn't the centre of Torquay. We'll go to Torbay after dinner.'

'May I go down now and swim from the hotel beach?'

'No, it might not be safe on your own.'

'Couldn't you come with me?'

'I'd find the sea far too cold. You'd better keep to the hotel swimming pool.'

Kristina discovered Torquay to be a most attractive town, and from the tourist map on the Torbay Road she noted interesting cliff walks. But she wasn't allowed to leave the hotel grounds on her own. Once, when the adults were having tea on the sea front, she was given an hour to wander round the town. Instead of keeping to the shopping area she walked round the bay along the beach, as far as Corbyn Head, returning via Torbay Road. On the way she noticed a sign saying *To The Station*.

On a wet day it was decided to remain at the hotel and swim in the small heated indoor pool. Kristina disliked the smell of chlorine and being unable to swim without bumping into someone. After a few days she was thoroughly bored. Breakfast was never taken till nine-thirty, as the adults always stayed up playing bridge till after midnight. Kristina would like to have learnt something about the game, but there was no point in asking. Mrs Atkinson was a keen, competitive player with no time for beginners. Neither she nor her husband had spoken more than three dozen words to Kristina. Her father had told her how in his youth, children were only expected to be seen at certain times of day, and certainly not heard unless spoken to. The Atkinsons had something of the same attitude: Kristina was still a child who must sit still and smile and do as she was told. She detested them.

Trips were planned to local beauty spots – the River Dart, Slapton Ley, Salcombe and Brixham.

'Aren't we going to Dartmoor?' Kristina asked Tessa.

'There's nothing much to see on the moor.'

'You said we'd drive across it.'

'Well, the Atkinsons don't want to. I'm sure you'll enjoy seeing other places we're going to.'

'I particularly wanted to see Dartmoor. Dad told me there are wild ponies, and tors to climb.'

After several days of driving around, Kristina asked if she could stay behind in the garden to read, and perhaps have a swim. Denis told Tessa it was just as well. The girl was a bit of a bore on their outings.

On Tuesday morning Kristina sat in the sun lounge with *Tess of the D'Urbervilles* on her knee. But she was in no mood to persevere with a long classic. She was glad Tessa had allowed her to stay behind, but she still felt aggrieved. The holiday had turned out even worse than she'd imagined, and there were four days yet to endure. *It's a nice town,* she thought, *with lovely countryside all around, but it's been spoilt by the grownups.* An image of Jenny came into her mind. What fun they could have had in Torquay. Then she thought of Seaton, and tears of self-pity came into her eyes. Ruth was the person she longed to stay with in England.

Presently a wild scheme came into her head. Why not go to the station and catch a train to Exeter? From there she knew it was possible to go by train to Seaton, since she'd done the journey with her father. The idea of reaching Seaton Hole that very afternoon filled her with determination. There would be unpleasant repercussions, of course, but it would be worth it. She was certain her pocket money would cover the fare, as her mother had given her a generous amount for the holiday.

Having packed her few things she left a note propped on her dressing table with Ruth's address and telephone number: *I've gone to Seaton, as I'm getting so bored and lonely here, and I expect you'll enjoy the rest of your holiday better without me. If you don't want to pick me up from Seaton on Saturday, I could get an early bus to Honiton and meet you there.* She added Ruth's address and telephone number, and left the note propped up on her dressing table.

Having reached Exeter without any difficulty she bought a cup of tea and a stale rock cake and waited for a train to Seaton Junction, from where she could catch the connection to Seaton.

Emerging from the station it struck her forcibly that Ruth and her family might be away. She hurried anxiously to the cottage to find the doors locked and no one about. Perhaps they'd just gone out for the day. She sat on the garden seat in a daze for an hour, wondering what she would do if they didn't return. She was hungry, thirsty and tired, and as she began to panic she heard the phone ringing inside the cottage. She raced round the house, trying to open a window without success. Then, as the phone stopped, she noticed the two bottles of milk tucked away at the side of the back porch. The relief was so great she burst into exhausted tears.

Half an hour later Ruth and her family came up the steps to find Kristina asleep on the seat.

'Come into the kitchen', said Ruth after Kristina had followed her into the house. 'You girls go with Dad to the living room until supper's ready. I want to talk to your cousin.'

As Ruth made a pot of tea, she asked, 'Does your mother know where you are?'

'Yes.'

'Thank heaven for that. Otherwise she'd have had the police out looking for you by now. I'm sure she didn't send you to Seaton.'

'They're on holiday in Torquay with some friends. She might ring you at any moment. The phone went earlier', said Kristina, and looking at her aunt's worried face she realised the gravity of what she'd done. How could she explain what had made her come? 'I'm not running away. I just wanted to visit you until Saturday, when they can take me back to London.'

'Why didn't you ask if you could come?'

'Because my mother wouldn't have let me.'

'Well, that's understandable. It's your first holiday with her, so of course she'd want to have you to herself.'

At this point the phone rang again. Ruth went into the hall to answer it, and returned looking very grave. 'Your mother will pick you up on Saturday, about eleven. She's most annoyed, as you can imagine. They got back to the hotel, and when she found your note she rang. Getting no reply, she was frantic with worry. You must realise, Kristina, that you've caused your mother a great deal of pain.'

Kristina nodded and collapsed into a deluge of tears. Ruth put an arm round her, saying, 'Come, come, it's not the end of the world. Help me get the supper, and when you've had a night's sleep you'll feel better.'

The next three days were a mixture of shame and anxiety, combined with the sheer joy of being at Seaton. Penny and Anne created their own image of an uncaring mother and a cruel stepfather, and were full of sympathy, which Kristina lapped up. But all too soon came Saturday. Tessa arrived on her own, saying that Denis and the Atkinsons were having a drink in the town. Ruth offered to make coffee but Tessa refused. 'Are you ready, then?' she said sharply to Kristina, adding 'Thank you so much for looking after her', to Ruth.

A moment later they were walking down the hill to the car. 'I hope you realise the worry and inconvenience you've caused', said Tessa. 'You've ruined our holiday, and I shan't be able to trust you in future.'

'I'm sorry', muttered Kristina. But she felt no regret, only dislike and despair.

'Surely you're old enough to know how worried we'd be. What on earth made you go off to Seaton?'

'It was lonely with no one to talk to, and I wanted to see the twins.'

Her greatest motive had been to see her aunt, but she knew by now that to mention Ruth would antagonise Tessa.

'What a very naughty girl!' said Denis. 'We'll have to lock you up in London.'

'I'm sorry', muttered Kristina again.

Life at Harley Street resumed its tedious course. It was taken for granted that Kristina would accompany Tessa and Denis whenever they went out. Twice they met friends in a pub at lunchtime, and Kristina sat outside on the wall drinking a lemonade. Four days later Denis departed for Geneva, and Tessa took her daughter to Salisbury to visit Constance.

As they were sitting in the taxi, Kristina caught sight of an amazing spire rising high above the small town. 'That's the cathedral', said Tessa.

'Can we go and see it tomorrow?'

'Maybe.'

That evening after Kristina had retired to the small twin-bedded spare room, she could hear Constance being told about her granddaughter's behaviour. She got up and listened outside the living room door.

'You must refuse to let Kristina stay at Seaton again', Constance was saying. 'I imagine that aunt has set the girl against you, and probably influenced her for the bad in other ways.'

Kristina wanted to burst open the door and shout that it wasn't true. A year ago she would have done so, but now she'd learnt that adults could twist the truth to their advantage. Above all, they could dislike her on sight and act accordingly.

The following day she was allowed to explore the town and visit the cathedral. But there was so much to see that she returned late for lunch and was reprimanded.

'Why didn't you come with me?' she asked Tessa. 'It's no fun always going alone.'

Constance told Kristina to stop answering back, and not to sulk. It was time she smiled and joined in the conversation in a pleasant manner.

How can I be pleasant with people who don't like me? thought Kristina bitterly. She answered questions politely and said please and thank you a dozen times a day, but it was no use. She couldn't wait to leave Salisbury. Kissing Constance goodbye was like kissing a concrete statue smelling of face powder and lavender water.

A few days before the start of the autumn term, Kristina belatedly admitted she'd lost her hat. Tessa flew into a temper. Why hadn't she mentioned it the first day of the holidays? It was so irresponsible. Had she really searched for it? Miss Deacon would think it very negligent that a new hat hadn't been ordered during the eight weeks' holiday. 'I'm returning to Switzerland in five days' time, so you'll have to go back to school and face the music. It should teach you a lesson.'

Tessa said goodbye to her daughter at Paddington, almost wishing she'd never demanded to take over the rest of Kristina's upbringing. So far it had been an utter failure, and she could see no solution other than sending the girl back to her father. But this she was not prepared to do at any cost. She blamed John for the way Kristina had turned out. Perhaps five more years of boarding school would effect a radical change.

Chapter Nine

On reaching Cabot House Kristina found her hat hanging on her hook in the cloakroom. No one seemed to know who'd found it. It was a great relief, but at the same time she wondered if at the end of the summer term it hadn't been hidden deliberately by someone intent on causing trouble.

Returning to all the petty restrictions of school was made easier this term by Gita's presence. Her friend had enjoyed being at home in India, but had been obliged to praise the Dunbar lavishly. Her parents expected no less. They were paying for a very expensive education, and wanted to know it had been a good investment.

'Well, what was he like?' Miranda asked Kristina.

'Who?'

'Your wicked stepfather, of course.'

'He's not wicked', replied Kristina, 'Just frightfully boring.'

'That's even worse. Poor you.'

Gita and Kristina were in the same dormitory with Rosemary, Jackie and Fiona, and this time Mary instead of Kit Taylor, a change Kristina wasn't happy with. Mary hadn't forgiven her for becoming so friendly with Gita.

Nothing had changed for the better at Cabot House. The rooms still smelt of disinfectant and lino polish. Musty black curtains still hung at all the windows.

Kristina had written to her aunt, emphasising how sorry she was for being such a worry. She didn't mention tuck parcels, hoping Ruth would remember to keep sending them. Kristina had told her mother about the parcels, but Tessa had merely remarked, 'Surely you get enough to eat at school without cakes and biscuits as well? Your sweet ration need only be sent once a month.'

Kristina pointed out that the sweet ration was tiny, and everyone needed extra tuck. She also asked if she might have a cake sent for her fourteenth birthday. Tessa promised to order one from the local bakery in London.

Within a week a letter came from Ruth with a parcel which included a large iced birthday cake with the words *To dear Kristina, Happy Birthday* on top, and a packet of candles. *Penny and Anne iced your cake,* she wrote, *and wish you could eat it at home with us.* Even the traditional custom of being obliged to take a slice of cake to Miss Deacon didn't spoil the pleasure of sharing her cakes with everyone in the common room, and of course with Gita.

Kristina had hoped the mistakes of her first two terms might now be forgotten. But it was not to be. Miss Barrett, her new form mistress, was pleasant enough, but Kristina's reputation had gone before her, and no one in authority expected much of her. It was most disheartening to discover that Miss Deacon was still her English teacher. The class were to study Shakespeare's *Romeo and Juliet* and Jane Austen's *Mansfield Park*. The girls enjoyed the romance of *Romeo and Juliet,* and Miss Deacon was persuaded to allow them to perform it as a play reading. Kristina was desperate to read the part of Juliet's nurse, and since no one else offered, Miss Deacon allowed her to take the part.

Kristina well understood the bawdy humour in the nurse's first few speeches, and without intending it found herself slipping into the West Indian accent, which suited the lines so well. The further she read, the more marked her accent became, and the more she seemed to become the nurse. Everyone found it amusing, but Miss Deacon judged it quite unnecessary. Would she please read the lines as Shakespeare intended. Kristina's few moments of drama were spoilt. The following lesson when she was to read more of the nurse's lines, she read them monotonously in her best English. Miranda stood up and asked if Kristina could continue with the West Indian accent, but Miss Deacon replied sharply, 'No, Juliet's nurse is an Italian, not a negress.'

Shortly after Kristina had started *Mansfield Park,* she wrote to her father saying how much she was enjoying it. John replied it was his favourite too. Had she noticed that Sir Thomas owned a sugar plantation in Antigua based on slave labour. *You may not have reached the chapter where Fanny wants to ask her uncle about the West Indian slave trade. It might be good for your class to discuss this point, because it's the only time Jane Austen mentions it. People like the Bertrams would have depended on the slave trade for their riches and comfortable style of living.*

When the class reached the incident John had mentioned in chapter 21, Kristina put her hand up to ask two carefully prepared questions. 'Was Fanny not allowed to put her question because it would have been embarrassing for Sir Thomas to admit to the horrors of the slave trade in front of his family? Or was it that Jane Austen wasn't bothered about the slave trade herself, and didn't think it worth discussing?'

Miss Deacon stared at her with annoyance. 'It's quite unimportant. Jane Austen would naturally have accepted the slave trade as part of the nineteenth century way of life in our colonies.'

'What would have happened to Sir Thomas's plantation when the slaves were freed?'

'It's quite irrelevant to the novel, Kristina. This isn't a history lesson, so you'd better sit down.'

When it came to the poetry Upper 4b was to study, Miss Deacon was equally intolerant of Kristina's opinions. There were four poems, two by Rupert Brooke and two by Wilfred Owen dealing with the First World War, to be studied, and one of them to be learnt by heart. The following week Miss Deacon chose someone at random to recite her choice and say why she liked it. The first girl chosen recited *The Soldier.* Most of the class had chosen this poem. Then Miss Deacon asked if anyone had chosen one of Wilfred Owen's poems. The only one who had was Kristina, who had learnt *Greater Love.*

'Why do you like that poem?' asked Miss Deacon.

Kristina replied that it told far more about the details of war. In *The Soldier,* a man dies and is buried, but we aren't told how he and the soldiers with him suffered. He could just as well have been a civilian who happened to die abroad. 'In *Greater Love*', she continued, 'I like the way the poet tells his girl friend that the love he feels for her can't equal the love he now feels for his comrades who died so horribly.'

Then before Miss Deacon had time to comment, Kristina said 'I found a war poem by Wilfred Owen called *Dulce et Decorum Est* in another anthology. It was horrifying. I'd like to recite it to you.'

'Certainly not, Kristina, you've had your say.'

Miranda leapt to her feet, saying, 'Oh, do let her, Miss Deacon.'

'Yes, please do', choroused the class.

Kristina announced the title loudly, and plunged into the poem, trying to communicate the horrors of poison gas warfare, and reading phrases such as *the blood come gargling from the froth-corrupted lungs* with great feeling. The girls clapped, and Kristina, elated by her small success, said 'Wilfred Owen is such a super poet. It's ever so sad to think he was killed at the end of the war. And', she added, 'He was so handsome.'

Miranda burst into loud laughter at Kristina's last remark, and Miss Deacon declared angrily, 'That's quite enough showing off, Kristina. You weren't asked to read poems from other books.'

'What's wrong with reading more Wilfred Owen poems?'

'Will you sit down and be quiet.' Then Miss Deacon chalked *Dulce et Decorum est* on the blackboard, and asked the class, 'Can anyone tell me what it means?'

Rosemary translated the Latin as *It is sweet and right to die for one's country.* 'Honourable might be a better word', said Miss Deacon. 'A poet called Horace wrote that line. And of course it's still true today.'

'It never was true. Wilfred Owen says it was a lie', muttered Kristina as the bell rang for break. But she missed her bun and milk that morning, for Miss Deacon kept her in as a punishment for being insolent.

At the beginning of term Gita had told Kristina her aunt and uncle would be pleased to invite her again for the half-term weekend. But a few days before the break Gita said she was so sorry they couldn't have her after all.

Her grandparents from India had suddenly decided to visit London, and they would naturally want to see their granddaughter over the weekend. Gita had in fact been granted permission not to return to school until Monday lunchtime. Kristina dreaded the thought of remaining at Cabot House on her own with Miss Deacon and Matron. Miranda said she would have invited her, but for Kate, who always joined her family for half term.

Then to Kristina's surprise Cynthia, a girl she hardly knew in Upper 4c, asked if she'd like to come to her home, a few miles away at Weston-super-Mare. 'I'm sure Mummy would say yes. We're going to have a fireworks party for Guy Fawkes.'

It would be better than nothing, and Kristina replied that she'd love to come. Miranda told her Cynthia's parents owned a luxurious house with a large garden and a tennis court. Her two brothers were at Eton.

'Is that a good school?' asked Kristina.

'Of course it is. The very best.'

Cynthia's parents saw to her every need and asked questions about her own parents and background. In some subtle way Kristina could feel them becoming slightly patronising. Her mufti clothes had become very worn, and out of doors she had only her school coat and shoes to wear. The moment Cynthia reached home she changed into an attractive skirt and jumper. She then took out a blue velvet coat from her well-stocked wardrobe. 'As you've only got your school coat', said Cynthia, 'You could borrow one of my mother's coats for the weekend. She's almost as tall as you. As a treat we're getting taken to the poshest hotel in Weston for dinner tonight. Have you got a frock to wear?'

Kristina went hot with shame, as Cynthia debated which of two frocks to wear. Having decided on one, she offered the other to Kristina.

They drove to the hotel in an Armstrong Siddeley, Kristina feeling a sham in her borrowed finery. The dark green frock in soft wool with a wide lace collar and cuffs suited her very well, apart from being rather too short, but she felt so mortified she hardly enjoyed the excellent four-course dinner.

At bedtime Cynthia came to Kristina's room to chat, bringing mugs of hot chocolate. 'What heaven to be home!' she said, sitting on the luxurious pink satin eiderdown.

'Don't you hate being at the Dunbar when you could live at home and go to day school?' Kristina asked.

'It's a bit of a bore at times, but the local grammar school's an awful dump. Daddy was determined to send me to the Dunbar. I had to have private coaching in Latin and Maths to get in.'

The fireworks party took place on the Saturday evening. A bonfire was lit in which potatoes were baked. Cynthia's mother and her maid provided mulled wine, cider, grilled sausages and ham sandwiches. Several well-to-do families in the vicinity had been invited and there were two Lower Sixth boys from a Bristol public school, hoping to get into Oxbridge. Cynthia knew them quite well, and introduced Kristina. However, it was impossible to join in the conversation, since they were talking of the ski trip they were going on straight after Christmas. Then one of the boys said his father had just bought a yacht. They were hoping to take it down to Salcombe in Devon for a month in the summer.

Kristina had never spoken to a public school boy before, though she'd seen a few from Clifton College on the Downs. Cynthia's friends in spotless white shirts, ties and smart blazers with gilt buttons, looked so formal. They were polite but distant, with sardonic expressions. Miranda had told her that English schoolboys were painfully awkward, and hadn't a clue how to treat a girl. 'My dear, I wouldn't be seen dead with a pimply schoolboy. Give me a mature male any day.'

'Where do you live?' Kristina was asked by one of the boys, who smelled unpleasantly of hair oil.

'Nowhere in particular.'

The boys laughed. 'Nowhere sounds like a good place.'

'Sometimes I live at Seaton in Devon with my aunt.'

'Do you get good sailing down there?'

'Yes, very good', Kristina replied, thinking, I don't have a home any more. I wish people wouldn't ask. I wish my parents weren't divorced. It's horrible staying with families I don't know.

Back at school, Kristina fervently hoped Cynthia wouldn't tell everyone about the borrowed coat and frock. Tessa was to blame for this situation; she should have foreseen that one needed suitable clothes for visiting.

During the weekend some girls had been to see *Gone with the Wind,* a very popular film starring Leslie Howard, Clark Gable and Vivien Leigh. They'd said how wonderful it was, and Kristina suggested to Gita that they go on their afternoon off.

'How can we, Miss Deacon often goes round the house to check on us.'

'Oh, do let's go. I've been dying to see it. It's on at the Embassy, just round the corner at the top of Park Street. It won't take long to get there.'

'Someone might report us.'

'Well, let them. I don't care.'

The prospect proved too tempting, and after lunch they managed to reach the cinema without mishap. They hadn't reckoned, however, on the length of the film. Tea was over and prep had begun by the time they returned to Cabot House. The Toad was awaiting them in the hall. Kristina was given a conduct mark, and Gita a severe warning. But the romantic atmosphere stayed with them for several days, and Kristina thought it well worth the punishment.

One Sunday afternoon, having run out of fiction, Kristina took her Virgil up to bed to tackle the homework passage for translation. The Aeneid was so dull she opened her sewing box and took out the book entitled *Growing Up*. She'd glanced through it hastily the year before, and then forgotten all about it. Now it seemed to be more interesting. The first half dealt with how the body worked in relation to sex and reproduction. The second half described the concept of real and faithful love in all its manifestations. The last two chapters discussed the dangers of sexual promiscuity, and even touched on homosexuality

Kristina lent it to Gita, who read it by torchlight under the bedclothes. Soon everyone in the dormitory had read it, except Mary, who having glanced at the illustrations, pronounced it a disgusting book. 'You'd better see that Matron doesn't find it', advised Rosemary, and Kristina returned the book to the bottom compartment of her sewing box. But Fiona, who'd gathered a great deal of hitherto unknown information from the book, couldn't resist giggling about it to the girl sitting next to her in the dining room. Miss Deacon demanded to know the cause of all the giggling, and Fiona tactlessly replied, 'I was just laughing at a book Kristina lent me.'

Kristina had to produce her book, which Miss Deacon confiscated, saying that such books were not permitted at school. She should know the rules. Any books from home must be checked by Matron.

'My father gave it to me, so why can't I keep it?' said Kristina.

'Because it's not a suitable book to be passed round at school. Your father should have realised that, and I shall be writing to him.'

Kristina was wretched on her father's account, and furious on her own. Gita said it was bad luck. Fiona had been tactless, but after all, the book would be given back at the end of term, so why not forget it?

But Kristina saw it differently. Miss Deacon already disliked and mistrusted her, and now had further reason to make life unpleasant. And as it happened, the very next week Kristina was in contention again with the house mother in class, this time over an essay set for homework. It was to be a portrait of a family, using dialogue as much as possible. Kristina decided to write about a Trinidadian family she knew. She had no long term experience of an English family other than her aunt's, and she suspected that English families weren't so loud, uninhibited and amusing as the West Indian ones she knew. Kristina's essay included an ambitious mother in despair over two difficult teenagers, a gambling husband and an interfering grandmother. The dialogue came easily, and the description was colourful. She was pleased with her effort.

When the essays were handed in Miss Deacon told the girls to continue with the next exercise in their grammar book while she started to mark their homework. After twenty minutes she said, 'Kristina, I wonder that you dare send in work like this.' She picked three sentences from the essay and read them out in her stiff, monotonous voice: *"You go bawl when I tell you what happen to she"* and *"You should see all them sexy magazines she does be reading"* and *"He's jus' crazy like hell, man!"* Hardly the kind of grammar we use in England.' The class tittered, and Kristina said indignantly, 'It's how the West Indians talk. Lots of people here speak in dialect.'

'You're here to write and speak good English.'

Kristina got a D for her essay, and felt most aggrieved. She lost all interest in creative writing, and for the rest of term did the minimum amount of work.

The dancing sessions continued on Saturdays, but as Kristina told Gita, they hardly made up for the utter frustration of life. 'If only we could put on a play or a concert. We ought to be taken regularly to the Theatre Royal or the Colston Hall.'

'Next year fifth formers can go to two concerts a term, and one play. And in the sixth they go to Stratford as well', said Gita.

'I want to go now. I've only seen one play, and never been to a symphony concert, and my Dad keeps asking if the school has arranged a trip. He says the Bristol Old Vic performs wonderful plays.'

'Even the day girls aren't allowed to go during term time.'

'This posh school is crazy like hell, man!' said Kristina in her best West Indian accent. Gita giggled. 'What you is gigglin' for?' She pointed out that in Trinidad there were no theatres or concert halls, only cinemas. But at the High School they put on a school play each year, a Gilbert and Sullivan opera, and one-act house plays. Whenever a professional music group or pianist did manage to visit Port of Spain they always went to hear them play.'

'It was the same in India', said Gita. 'I played Mustard Seed in *A Midsummer Night's Dream*..'

Kristina couldn't understand why there were no classes in music, craft or drama. Even the drawing and painting class was considered inferior to the academic lessons. The one and only art mistress, a harassed-looking woman, had to teach an overloaded class comprising both the Lower and Upper Fourth. The one-hour lesson barely allowed her time to hand out paper and paints, much less give tuition. Most girls used the time merely to chat.

In the dormitory Kristina asked her friends why they didn't find the lack of arts infuriating. Rosemary pointed out there wasn't time in the curriculum when such a high standard was demanded and reached in academic subjects. She herself only just managed to fit in one private violin lesson a week after school. There was of course the élite madrigal group and the small choir which led assembly.

'We're expected to go to plays and concerts during the long holidays', added Jacky.

'Anyway, who'd want to go on a school trip?' said Fiona. 'Marching down to the Theatre Royal in uniform, with a sergeant major shouting at us in the foyer, and not being allowed to buy drinks! I'd much rather go in the hols. And imagine a coach trip to Stratford! My mother thinks coach trips are awfully vulgar,'

Yet during the half term break, Kristina and Gita did have a chance to see a play. Gita's aunt and uncle took them to Stratford to see *Much Ado about Nothing*. They were entranced with the production, and on their return to school could talk of little else. Kristina decided that she was going to be a theatre director.

Lengthy conversation with her friend could only take place in the dormitory, but as their beds were far apart it wasn't easy to keep up a whispering dialogue. Mary was constantly requesting them to be quiet. Gita tried sitting on Kristina's bed, but it was far too cold, so she got under the blankets. In this way they were able to talk eagerly for an hour or so, until Gita returned to her own bed.

For the next few days they repeated this convenient way of having private talks. One night, however, the door opened abruptly at half past ten and the light was switched on. With a grim look, Matron ordered Gita to get out of Kristina's bed and follow her out of the dormitory. The light went off and the door closed. There was a stunned silence for a minute, then Rosemary said, 'You are an idiot, Kristina. You must have known they'd go berserk here if you share a bed.'

'I wonder how Matron knew', said Fiona, and Mary added smugly, 'I did warn you about being close friends with a girl in a different year.'

In the morning Kristina was told by a stern Miss Deacon to report to Miss Craig's study after assembly. Gita was nowhere to be seen, and Kristina had to walk to school close behind two other girls. She couldn't understand what she was to be accused of, other than talking after lights out. On entering her classroom there was a sudden silence, and she guessed everyone had been discussing her. Miranda came up saying, 'We're all on your side. I should have warned you the Toad's a demented hysteric when it comes to close friendships.'

But even as she knocked on Miss Craig's door, she still couldn't see what the fuss was about. The headmistress asked Kristina to sit down before saying, 'Miss Deacon is very perturbed about your behaviour. You already have a conduct mark, and you're insolent and argumentative. But two recent incidents are more serious. First, you brought a book to school without permission, which you then circulated among your friends. The book contains chapters and pictures quite unsuitable for children of your age.'

'My father gave me that book. I put it in my sewing box and forgot about it until this term. He wouldn't have given me a book which wasn't suitable. What's wrong with it?'

'It's not for you to question me, Kristina. Just make sure you get all books checked at the beginning of term. Apart from that, I gather you've made friends with Gita Rau, in the year below you.'

'She'll be fourteen in April', broke in Kristina indignantly.

'Don't interrupt. Miss Deacon tells me that you and Gita were found sharing the same bed.'

'Only so we could talk quietly and not disturb the others. We don't get much chance during the day.'

'Surely you know it's most unhealthy to be sharing a bed?'

'Why should it be? In the olden days whole families had to share a bed.'

'Don't be insolent. Close physical friendship with another girl is not encouraged at this school. Gita's parents might well think you're a bad influence on their daughter.'

Kristina was going to protest again, but Miss Craig wouldn't let her speak. 'Not another word! I have decided that Gita shall be moved to another house.'

At this, Kristina burst into hysterical tears. 'It's not fair! She's my best friend. We haven't done anything wrong except talk after lights out.'

'Kristina, will you please control yourself. Miss Deacon and I think you need some time to calm down and get over this unhealthy relationship. So we're sending you to the sanatorium for a week.'

'Why should I be punished? I've done nothing bad.'

'Going to the sanatorium isn't a punishment.'

'It is a punishment. Miss Deacon knows how I hated it when I was ill.'

'You're not ill now. You can take some homework, and there are books at the sanatorium you can read. A week isn't long.'

'I won't go, I won't!'

'Stop being so childish. I've asked a prefect to walk back to Cabot House with you now.'

Miss Craig rose and opened the door. A sixth former was waiting outside. For a wild moment Kristina considered running away, but something told her she was up against an invincible force. She had no option but to follow the prefect to the classroom to collect her satchel as the bell rang at the end of the first lesson.

As everyone was hurrying along the corridor to the next lesson, a girl in Upper 4A approached Kristina, thrust a note into her hand, and dashed away. This was Laura Parker, from Penn House, a tall, rather solemn-looking person in horn-rimmed spectacles, whom Kristina had been aware of in the art class, but had never spoken to. Miranda had mentioned once that Laura was so brainy she even confounded the teachers, but she was also very shy and hadn't made any close friends in all the years she'd been at the Dunbar.

'She's too skinny', said Miranda. 'Her clothes hang onto her body as though she's a scarecrow. And have you noticed her elongated face? It's rather like the face of a sad basset hound. I can't imagine her ever having been a child.'

In the taxi conveying her to the sanatorium, Kristina read Laura's note. *Miranda was saying in the cloakroom you might end up in the San, where anyone who has what they call 'improper relationships', gets sent. I spent two weeks there with that Gestapo matron. I thought I'd warn you it's better to do what you're told, be very polite, pretend to be grateful, and offer to help with the chores. If she thinks you're being sulky or openly defiant, she'll keep you there longer. You can't beat the system at the Dunbar. – Tear this up when you've read it.*

Chapter Ten

Kristina was in a state of confused anger and despair, but the note changed the perspective on her fate. She would follow Laura's advice as though she was acting in a play. The challenge might enable her to get through the week.

To begin with, her role playing did help. She endured Matron's caustic remarks, the tasteless food, the dusting, sweeping, washing up and peeling potatoes. There were five girls with chickenpox from year two in one of the dormitories to be catered for. But the worst aspect was the overwhelming boredom, especially in the evening. She sat in the large, chilly day room, with its tepid radiator, hard chairs, dirty grey paint, black curtains, threadbare carpet and row of dog-eared books, all of which she'd read or didn't wish to. She could hear Matron's wireless, and once or twice, when the hateful woman emerged from her private apartment, caught sight of a comfortably furnished room and cheerful coal fire. The days took on a relentless air of unreality, like a bad unexplained dream. She would remember it in adulthood as one of the worst experiences of her life.

When the day came for release she hung about for hours until she wondered if she was to leave after all. At four o'clock, however, the maid told her to pack quickly, and she left the sanatorium without seeing Matron. At Cabot House she slipped back into the routine. Sitting next to Miss Deacon three days later she made no attempt at conversation.

Gita's bed was empty. Fiona thought she'd been transferred to Colston House. At school Kristina looked out, but never saw her. There were three more weeks of term, and everyone in the common room was talking of Christmas. It seemed to Kristina that there was no one else in her position; each girl had a settled home life, usually with siblings and certainly with friends. There would be parties, carol concerts and family gatherings. Kristina dreaded Christmas at Harley Street with Tessa and Denis.

She'd been waiting for weeks to hear from her mother, but when the letter came she was stunned by the news, and had to read it twice before taking it in. *I'm afraid Denis is very ill. He's to go into hospital for an operation on December 18th. This means we won't be able to come to London for the Christmas holidays. This will be a shock for you, and I'm very sorry. However, I wrote to Miss Craig, asking if she could possibly find a family to take you for the holidays. She said there's a clergy family called Wilson in Bristol who would be glad to have you. They have two daughters, who are younger than you. Last year they had two girls from the D.A. whose parents are abroad, so they're quite used to having paying guests. It sounds a very suitable family, and you'll enjoy having companions at Christmas. Mrs Wilson will be getting in touch with you…*

Kristina wrote back immediately to her mother, begging to be allowed to go to Seaton. The idea of going to strangers was unbearable, but she knew Tessa wouldn't relent.

Kristina received a note from Mrs Wilson, inviting her to tea on Sunday, to meet the family. *I'll come and fetch you at 3. pm, she wrote. Then you could get a bus back to school on your own. Our vicarage is on the south side of the river, in Coronation Road, not far from St Mary Redcliffe Church, which you must have seen. Miss Craig tells me your father is a Rector in Trinidad, so you'll be used to vicarage life.*

Kristina doubted that life at the Rectory in Sangre Grande could possibly resemble life at a Bristol vicarage. Miranda said, 'Mrs Wilson sounds quite pleasant, but it must be awful not having your own home. If I were you I'd ask to be moved to another house next term. The Toad's really got it in for you.'

'She'd only tell the next house mother I'm a trouble maker, and anyway, I'd still have her for English. So I may as well stay here.'

Mrs Wilson arrived on Sunday, a soft-spoken, lively-looking young woman, who smiled at Kristina, saying, 'Goodness, aren't you lucky to be so tall. Look at me, five foot two! People often talk to me as though I'm still a schoolgirl. I have to wear high heels to make any impression.'

Kristina, who'd been expecting someone middle-aged in a shapeless felt hat and lisle stockings like the vicar's wife at church, smiled back, feeling encouraged and thinking she did look rather young to have two school-aged daughters.

On the bus, Pam Wilson told Kristina that her husband, Patrick, was officially the Vicar of St Matthias. However, the church had been bombed during the war, and was going to be rebuilt. In the meantime, services were conducted nearby at a rather dismal mission chapel. 'Unfortunately the vicarage isn't inspiring either. It's a monstrously ugly Victorian house with four bedrooms and two large attic rooms for the servants, in the days when vicars had them! At least we're within walking distance of the centre of town, and in the other direction we can get into the country quickly. Are you a town person?'

'No, I like the country better.'

'Well, that's good. You may borrow my bike.'

They got off the bus along Coronation Road beside the site of the bombed church. 'Isn't it sad', said Pam, 'That's the River Avon across the road. We call it The Cut, because this section of the river is a man-made canal. When the tide's low it's a nasty muddy mess, full of rubbish.'

Kristina looked across The Cut to a widespread flattened area covered with bits of rusting metal and rubble. The shells of a few bombed-out houses were still standing.

'Not a pretty view, as you can see. But then most of the centre of Bristol was bombed or neglected during the war. It's lucky your school's up on the downs, one of the few pleasant places left.'

Before entering the vicarage, Pam took Kristina round to the large wilderness of a garden at the back, including what had once been a grass tennis court. 'Some of our very elderly parishioners, who live in the big houses further up Coronation Road, remember the days before the first war, when tennis parties were held in the vicarage garden, and a maid in a smart uniform brought round trays of home-made lemonade!'

Kristina looked at the lawn, covered with greyish-green coarse grass, and found it hard to imagine tennis parties.

'We struggle with the ancient hand-mower, and try to keep down the weeds, but that's all. We can't afford to buy plants. Still, it's nice to have those few trees and shrubs, with space for the children to play. Come inside and meet the girls.'

The Wilson children, Hilary and Jane, were aged eight and nine. They sat silently to begin with, at the kitchen table, watching Kristina eating bread and jam and a rock cake, and giggling when she spilt her tea on the check tablecloth.

'My best friend's mum says the Dunbar's a snobby school for swots', announced Jane.

'Don't be rude, Jane. The Dunbar's said to be one of the best schools in England.'

'Will we go there?'

'Goodness, no! It's horribly expensive.'

'Can you climb trees?' asked Hilary. 'The girl we had to stay last year could get right to the top of our highest tree.'

Kristina laughed, thinking of the trees in Trinidad. 'I expect I'll get to the top of it too.'

'Come out and see if you can', said Jane.

'Not today', said their mother. 'Kristina's only here for tea.'

Patrick Wilson appeared for a few moments and shook hands with Kristina. He looked a lot older than his wife. Then he took away a mug of tea, saying he had a sermon to finish. Kristina was glad to note he didn't resemble the Reverend Kenneth Speare.

Pam showed Kristina over the house, saying, 'This place is quite a challenge. We've been here for nearly three years, and it still looks awful. The church authorities repaired the roof and bought us some paint to re-decorate a couple of rooms. They find it very expensive to keep up these old vicarages.'

Kristina felt quite hopeful about living with the Wilson family, but when she went out to catch the bus up to the Downs, it was most discouraging to look at the surroundings. Where would she go for walks in such a dismal place? And would she be able to go out on her own? Probably not, since the Wilsons might feel doubly responsible for her safety.

The next day came a surprising letter from Gita. She was now living with her relatives in London. *I told my uncle how we'd been treated,* she wrote, *He rang my father, who agreed to take me away from the Dunbar. Miss Craig tried so hard to make out that I was the innocent one who'd been led astray by you. I told my uncle it was all lies, and the school was awful in every way. Just think, I'm now going to a brilliant day school for girls in London, where they do music and drama and domestic science and art appreciation. At lunch time we don't have to sit next to a Toad and make conversation.*

If you're in London with your mother for Christmas do let's meet and have some fun.

Kristina was relieved to hear from her friend, and envious of her luck. Her first impulse was to write and say how glad she was that Gita was happy. But then she felt let down by the tone of the letter. Gita had no concern for what had happened to her. In the end she didn't reply.

At the first opportunity, Laura had asked about Kristina's experience at the sanatorium. 'The main thing is not to let them get us down.'

'Why were you sent there?' asked Kristina

'It was all a fuss about nothing. When I was eleven, I was rather miserable because I hadn't made any real friends. A very pretty sixth former came a few times to supervise us when a teacher was off sick. She noticed what I was reading, and actually deigned to speak to me. She asked if I liked poetry, and offered to lend me a book. She smiled at me so kindly that of course I fell for her. I saved my sweet coupons to buy her a box of chocolates and wrote an admiring note. I left it in her pigeon hole, and someone pinched it and took it to our house mother.' Laura laughed. 'Actually the most annoying thing was that whoever took it kept the chocolates.'

Kristina had heard of girls who had crushes on sixth-formers. It seemed to her that having a crush on someone implied being subservient; there was something cringing about it which didn't appeal. The notion of giving away her sweet ration to a prefect was ludicrous. Keeping such a relationship secret was another aspect she didn't care for, but life was so boring at school that anything involving secrecy might enliven the deadly routine. But not for Kristina. Her relationships had always been open, uninhibited and full of shared laughter.

Laura Parker seemed to be an unlikely best friend, being solemn, bookish and very much of a loner. But by the end of term Kristina had changed her mind. They shared the same rebellious nature, passion about injustice, sense of humour and lack of vanity. But whereas Laura, in the face of being found out, deceived authority by retreating humbly behind her spectacles with quiet acquiescence, Kristina stood up vociferously for herself and for others, and invariably provoked authority. In addition to the characteristics they shared, Kristina realised for the first time that an interesting personality could exist behind a nondescript appearance. Laura would come out with surprisingly witty remarks about the teachers and girls, and she seemed remarkably mature in her judgment of people and awkward situations.

Mr Parker worked for the British Council in Cairo. His daughter spent the Christmas and Easter holidays with her maternal grandparents in Torquay, and joined her parents each summer.

'Do you tell them how awful it is here?' asked Kristina.

'No, there's no point in upsetting them. I've got to go to a boarding school, and I expect they're all much the same.'

'My father wanted me to go to Dartington Hall. It would have been better than the Dunbar. But my mother refused to let me.'

'What a coincidence!' said Laura. 'We might have met at Dartington, because my grandparents tried to persuade my father to send me there.'

'Why wouldn't he?'

'He maintained it would be wasting my brains going to a progressive school. "Strict routine and discipline are needed to fulfil academic potential", was how he put it. He compared the Dunbar's Oxbridge successes with Dartington's. That was the deciding factor. Having been to Oxford himself, he wants me to go too.'

'D'you want to?'

'I don't think so. Oxford is full of wealthy public school types. I'd rather mix with students from different backgrounds. My grandparents sent my mother to Torquay Grammar School, and I think she had a much better education than my father's at public school. She was lucky, because my grandfather has very modern ideas on the upbringing of children. He even thinks schools should have beautiful pictures and sculptures and colour schemes – and that pupils should be allowed to ask questions and be given honest answers, and be treated as friends by the teachers.'

'He'd get on well with my father. He thinks childhood is the only time when you can have moments of pure happiness. Adults should enable children to have as many of these moments as possible.'

'That's just the kind of thing my grandfather would say. And children should be allowed to take a few risks on their own. My father has a book called *The Child is Right.*'

'He ought to send it to Miss Craig.'

At the end of term carol service, Kristina was seated in one of the galleries overlooking the stage where Miss Craig was emphasising how God had deliberately caused his Son to be born in a humble stable with the ox and ass and hens. Listening to her perfect upper class accent Kristina had a sudden image of a two-roomed shack in Trinidad, one for the family and the other for the animals. Scruffy hens pecked the ground while a small naked boy sat smiling happily in the dust playing with coconut shells. *Once the angels and the kings had gone,* she thought, *and the tinsel star put away, would Jesus have had a similar childhood? What if he were to appear on the school stage at this minute? Or better still, what if he arrived as a young man straight from a long, hot preaching trek, in a faded robe and dusty sandals, with long matted hair and a sweaty face? What if he were to start gesturing with his brown arms and addressing Miss Craig in a harsh, unrecognisable language? What would she do? Call the police? Or ask for a chair to be brought to welcome Jesus to the school's celebration of his humble birth?*

She became so wrapped up in her speculations that she was surprised when the girls began filing out in the usual orderly lines.

Kristina had written to her mother, asking for money to buy Christmas presents for the Wilson family and for her cousins. She added that she needed some new clothes. Until recently Kristina hadn't worried much over her own clothes or anyone else's. In the dormitory everyone was used to Fiona making fun of other girls. Remarks such as 'Did you notice Kate's wearing one of her mother's hand-me-downs?', or 'Have you seen Gillian? – my dear, such appalling taste! Her mother must shop exclusively at C & A's', had always seemed ridiculous. But recently she herself had been embarrassed when invited out. She'd also been angry at cocoa time when she heard someone in the Lower Fifth saying her clothes looked as though they'd been bought at a jumble sale. Kristina had marched up to the culprit, declaring in a challenging West Indian accent, 'You not lookin' so good yourself, man! Where you get that blouse? It not matchin' your skirt.' A fracas ensued, causing much amusement in the dining room. But as always, it was Kristina who was punished.

The girls were constantly discussing the fashionable things they wanted their parents to buy when clothing coupons were abolished. Kristina noticed that one or two girls from the wealthiest families were already wearing nylon stockings with suede court shoes, beautifully cut calf-length skirts, twin-sets in softest lambs' wool and Fair Isle jumpers, all bought abroad. Some even dared wear tiny gold earrings in pierced ears, hoping Miss Deacon wouldn't notice.

Tessa wrote that she'd suggested to Mrs Wilson it might be sensible not to exchange Christmas presents, so Kristina needn't worry about buying anything. As for her aunt's family, there was no need whatsoever to send presents. Kristina was bitterly disappointed. She'd been looking forward to buying small gifts to wrap up, for which she'd already been painting name tags. She would have liked to send her father a present, but the post wasn't reliable, and it was too expensive. Her mother promised to send clothes for Christmas, and had contacted the school, asking Miss Deacon to accompany Kristina to Merchants to buy items of uniform that needed replacing. Kristina shuddered to think of shopping with The Toad. She wished she could have had a say in the choice of her own clothes.

Tessa had enclosed a cheque to put in her Post Office savings account. She was to spend her money carefully, as it would have to last over the four weeks' holiday and cover the cost of the taxi to take her to and from school.

When Kristina arrived at the Wilsons' vicarage on a cold December day Pam apologised for the inadequate heating. It was a difficult place to keep warm. There was an ancient Rayburn in the kitchen, and a small Victorian fireplace in the living room and study; otherwise only two electric fires, conveyed from room to room as needed. 'In winter we do tend to live in the kitchen', said Pam.

'I'm used to being cold. Sometimes at school I wear my coat to do prep in the common room', said Kristina.

Pam laughed. 'Well, you might have to go to bed in it here! We try to keep the living room fire going over Christmas. It has a silly little grate, and is a devil to light.'

Kristina followed Pam up the uncarpeted stairs to the guest bedroom, high-ceilinged and papered in a gloomy pattern of indeterminate colour. An enormous clumsy brass bedstead and an equally large wardrobe filled half the room. A threadbare rug beside the bed was the only carpet on the expanse of pitted beige linoleum. Two faded floral curtains had been stitched together to form a bedspread matching the curtains at the single sash window framed in peeling dirty white paint.

Pam switched on a curly brass lamp beside the bed. 'I'm afraid it's a depressingly dark room. The furniture came from my grandmother's home, and we haven't yet been able to afford to strip off that ghastly wallpaper and redecorate. In fact the whole house needs redecorating. Most of the windows don't open properly, the frames are so rotten.'

Kristina walked over to examine a reproduction of Vermeer's *Girl with a Pearl Earring* over the mantelpiece, and then another Vermeer, *The Cook,* on the adjacent wall.

'I bought those reproductions for my room at university, but here they look quite ludicrous. It's an insult to the painter, Vermeer, to hang them on these walls.'

Next, Pam showed Kristina the bathroom. 'This is the room we're most proud of', she announced solemnly, opening the door with a flourish, and then bursting into laughter as she watched Kristina's expression. 'Isn't it quite the worst bathroom you've ever seen?'

'No', replied Kristina, laughing. 'The one in Trinidad was worse.'

The bathroom was painted in a harsh green with cracked white tiles surrounding the monstrously large brown and yellow stained bath tub and hand basin. One gained an overall impression of numerous rusting, mostly redundant pipes, running up and down the walls, along the skirting board and round the heavy black cistern and toilet bowl, covered with a cracked black seat. Two bath mats lay on the uneven dusty floorboards.

'Our next project is to put some good lino on the floor, but we can't do it until a plumber comes to remove some of the pipes and replace that ancient gas-fired geyser over the bath. When you take a bath, don't forget to bring up a kettle of boiling water. The geyser only runs a trickle of warm water. After a few weeks here you'll be dying to get back to school!'

In Trinidad Kristina had always been aware of the primitive bathroom, but all she'd needed was cold water. If the tap ran sluggishly, then a bucket of water in the garden from the outside tap had sufficed. But in this cold vicarage courage would be required to take a bath.

By and large it seemed that St Matthias's Vicarage had nothing to recommend it. Kristina felt sorry for Pam, who put up with it so cheerfully.

'Next year', replied Pam, 'I intend to start teaching again. Then we'll be able to make the house more habitable. The parishioners will disapprove, of course, since they expect the vicar's wife to be available at all times.'

'What do the parishioners expect you to do?'

'Make jam and cakes, etc., for the bring and buy sales, help run coffee mornings, organise the Mothers' Union and the Young Wives, help with the youth club, read the lesson in church, take my turn to arrange the church flowers, prepare for the summer garden party and the Christmas bazaar, help to clean the church, and answer the phone and the door bell all day to take messages. And so it goes on.'

'My father didn't have a wife to do all those things.'

'I expect his parishioners did them perfectly well on their own.'

The only pleasant place was the living room, Pam's creation. The furniture was simple and the carpeting and curtains cheap. But the walls in pale yellow were hung with pictures, and there were flowers in pleasing pottery, books on the shelves and a piano.

Patrick Wilson was an approachable man who was good with young people when he had time. He was in and out of the vicarage, but most days rarely spent more than half an hour with his family. At home, he would be in his study preparing services and sermons, writing articles, editing the parish magazine, answering piles of letters, planning confirmation and bible classes, making lists and choosing hymns, among a host of other things. Unfortunately he wasn't practical about the house. Since he couldn't always afford to call in the experts for minor repairs, Pam had either to cope herself or put up with it. When her husband was out she showed Kristina the study, where the walls were almost completely lined with books of all kinds.

'I'm afraid we neither of us can resist books. Most of them are second-hand. You're welcome to browse and see if there's anything you'd like to read.'

During the next few days Kristina began to feel part of the family. She enjoyed helping Hilary and Jane make Christmas cards and paper chains to decorate their bedrooms, and walking three miles with Pam to cut holly in Leigh Woods. On Christmas Eve, because Patrick had always insisted it shouldn't be done before, they decorated the small fir tree.

Kristina was overjoyed to find that Pam took it for granted she would go out alone. 'There are good second-hand book shops in town, besides our excellent main bookshop, George's, in Park Street. If it's dry you can ride my bike to Ashton Court park and Leigh Woods, or even up to Clifton village and then onto the Downs.'

Now at last she could explore Bristol. In one second-hand bookshop she found a large children's section. She'd noted that Hilary and Jane owned a sizeable selection of books. There were a number of titles in the shop she knew they didn't have, and thought they might like. There were also books Anne and Penny would appreciate. In defiance of her mother's instructions she bought four books, and derived immense pleasure from wrapping them up and posting two off to Seaton. Just before Christmas three parcels arrived for Kristina – a dress, skirt and jumper from her mother, six books ordered from a London store from her father, and a soft leather handbag from her aunt.

On Christmas morning Kristina woke late, for the family had been to Midnight Mass, and no one went to bed before one-thirty. She was childishly delighted to find a bulging brown stocking beside her bed. So Pam too had ignored Tessa's request. How glad she was to have bought something for Hilary and Jane.

Christmas dinner was very special compared to the everyday meals the Wilsons could afford. But halfway through the first course Kristina noticed that Pam had scarcely had any turkey or sausage. She'd already suspected that Pam consumed minute portions of meat or fish at a meal. Perhaps it was Pam's way of saving money. She wondered how much her mother was paying the Wilsons to have her for the holidays, and hoped they weren't making a loss because of the extra Christmas treats.

On new year's eve Patrick and Pam had been invited to a dance. Normally two elderly parishioners were happy to baby-sit as a favour, but for a dance ending after midnight, they couldn't be expected to stay up so late. The were glad to have Kristina to baby-sit. Hilary and Jane crept downstairs when their parents had gone, and the three girls played Monopoly until midnight. Then they listened to Big Ben on the wireless while eating the last of the mince pies with mugs of cocoa.

'It's 1949', said Hilary. 'What do you wish for in the new year, Kristina?'

'To go home to Trinidad', she replied.

'When will you go?'

'The summer of 1950.' It seemed so far ahead, Kristina couldn't believe it would ever happen.

These Wilson girls were lucky, for their father had often stated that he and Pam would never consider boarding school, even had they been wealthy. 'Children need their own space', said Pam, 'Besides, a child needs to get away from the school atmosphere at weekends.'

'It's just like being in prison', said Kristina gloomily.

'I'm sure it is', agreed Patrick. 'Probably no experience in your adult life will be anything like as bad. At least you'll appreciate freedom so much more when it comes.'

The day before leaving, Kristina decided she could just about afford to buy some flowers for Pam. At the local florists she saw some exquisite rosebuds. Having no idea of the cost of roses, particularly out of season, Kristina asked for half a dozen with some foliage. She was surprised and confused to find out she would have to pay all her remaining pocket money. But the flowers were already gift-wrapped and she couldn't retreat. Now she wouldn't have enough to pay for the taxi to school or for shampoo, toothpaste and soap.

The pleasure she gained on presenting the flowers, and Pam's obvious appreciation, staved off thoughts of money for a while. But she became very quiet during supper, and at bedtime Pam knocked on her door and asked if she could come in and talk for a few minutes. Her sympathy immediately reduced Kristina to tears, and feeling like a small child, she told Pam about her lack of a taxi fare.

'Don't worry', said Pam, 'We can sort out your problem. I won't give you the money for the taxi, because that would make your lovely gift less precious. Our verger has a van, and I'm sure he'd take your trunk to the school.'

Before they left to catch the bus, Pam gave Kristina a parcel to put in her holdall. 'Not to open till you get to school', she said. An hour later in the dormitory, Kristina unwrapped a jam sponge cake, soap, toothpaste and shampoo.

Kristina was relieved to find Mary no longer in her dormitory. She was sure it was Mary who'd suggested to Matron her relationship with Gita wasn't a healthy one. And since their friendship had ended, it seemed Mary continued to triumph every time Kristina got into trouble.

Miranda and Kate livened life up at bedtime, but she wished Laura was in Cabot House. The snatched conversations they managed to have were not enough, so they took to writing letters, which they gave each other on arrival at school.

Laura had been told about the difficult situation in Kristina's family. She herself felt fortunate in having doting grandparents. Nevertheless, it wasn't entirely easy living with an over-protective elderly couple out of touch with post-war attitudes.

'I wish you could come and stay in the holidays, but my grandparents would be much too nervous about being responsible for you. They're bad enough about me.'

'Do your parents know you're unhappy at school?' Kristina had asked.

'Not really. My father was so proud when I passed the entrance. Like your mother, he's convinced the Dunbar's the best school in England, if not in the world, and I should be grateful to be here. He thinks young people should be brought up with definite rules, no luxury and a strong Christian background.'

Since Penn House was only a few minutes' walk away from Cabot House, Kristina knocked on Miss Deacon's door and asked permission to go round to see Laura for half an hour at the weekend.

'Good heavens, girl, of course not! The rule is, only upper fifth and sixth formers are allowed to visit other houses.'

Kristina should have known better than to pursue the matter, but she couldn't resist it. 'Well, how can I talk to my friend if I can't visit?'

'Don't argue, Kristina. We can't have girls running to and fro between houses. You must be content with the girls here.'

The Reverend Kenneth Speare announced on the first Sunday of term that confirmation classes would commence the following Tuesday. A muffled groan greeted this information. The Vicar had a reputation for being the most tedious of the clerics in spiritual charge of the Dunbar pupils.

'Do we have to be confirmed?' Kristina asked Miranda.

'Yes, unless you're a Jew, or belong to some other Christian sect.'

'I don't see how they can make me.'

'Go and ask The Toad, and see what happens!'

'D'you want to be confirmed?'

'Not much. It's just one of those things one does, like being christened. The worst thing will be having to go to Communion at eight as well as Matins at eleven.'

Miss Deacon had informed Tessa it would be impossible for Kristina to miss any lessons in order to be taken to Merchants. Matron could purchase the odd item, such as a tie, but otherwise Tessa would have to make arrangements for uniform to be bought in the holidays. Fortunately Kristina hadn't grown any taller, but her blouses, skirts and cardigan were looking distinctly shabby, making her look unkempt from the moment she dressed in the morning. Inevitably week after week Mirabel complained, saying what a bad example she was to the younger girls in her deportment group.

In her next letter, which Kristina received one Friday lunchtime, Tessa wrote that regrettably she couldn't come to London at Easter. *So I'm afraid you'll have to stay with the Wilsons again. As you like the family, you won't mind. Unfortunately Mrs Wilson is starting a new job after Easter, and has decided not to take any more paying guests. So, if Denis isn't well enough to come to London for the summer I'll have to find you another family to stay with. Mrs Wilson has very kindly agreed to take you to Merchants during the holidays.*

Full of anger and resentment, Kristina walked back to school with Kate in silence, thinking, She made me leave Trinidad, and now she can't see me in the holidays. And she's determined not to let me go to Seaton, where she knows I'll be happy. I may be dumped in another family in the summer. 'Sorry, I don't want to talk', she said to Kate. 'I've just had a horrible letter from my mother. I hate her, I really do hate her!'

She decided she couldn't face lessons, so she went up to the art room, which was always empty on Friday afternoons. She read the letter again and felt like crying.

She felt in desperate need of a reliable mother-figure. She had loved Ruth in this role, and when that was thwarted she had turned to Pam as a substitute. Now even this relationship was to be snatched away. She found a piece of drawing paper, and spent the afternoon devising a letter, not just asking but begging, as though life depended on it, to be allowed to go to Seaton in the summer.

Kristina was given a detention for missing lessons, and Tessa didn't reply to her letter.

Confirmation instruction took place in a classroom at 4.30 pm. One of the fifth-formers warned that Mr Speare droned on so tediously that the best thing to do was to take some prep. He'd never notice. Kristina recalled her father saying he always enjoyed taking confirmation sessions, and encouraging the teenagers to ask difficult or even awkward questions. That was what confirmation classes were for, to have a debate on some of the problems of Christianity. The beliefs Kristina had taken for granted during her childhood, had begun to turn into questions in her mind. She wondered if Mr Speare might be prepared to discuss, or even give her an answer to some of them. Perhaps he would be less tedious in a discussion group than when he was preaching.

She'd been puzzled from an early age as to whether the divine nature of Jesus would affect his human nature. It had been a comforting thought when she was confronted for the first time with the horror of the crucifixion, that fortunately Jesus, being a supernatural being, couldn't feel pain. She put it to Mr Speare that as Jesus was God, then he couldn't be sinful. At the same time he'd become Man, and therefore must have sinned.

Mr Speare conceded the dual personality of Christ was a problem many leaders of the church had pondered over the centuries. 'But with God, all things are possible', he said, 'And we have to accept the mystery.'

But as the classes continued he became more and more irritated by Kristina's persistent questions. Suicide was another subject he absolutely refused to pursue, though the girls were all very curious about it.

'Why is it a sin to kill oneself?' Kristina asked. His answer, that God gave us life, and only God can decide when to take it away, didn't satisfy her, or Rosemary, who began to argue with Mary. In no time the whole class was having a vehement debate and taking no notice of the Vicar.

'So', Jacky said to Mary, 'If someone's being tortured to death, you think it's God's decision?'

'Just as it was God's decision Jesus must be crucified', put in Rosemary.

'God doesn't decide anyone must be tortured to death. But he gives a person strength to bear it, if they ask', said Mary.

'Bearing it doesn't mean it becomes painless', Jacky pointed out. 'And what about children?'

In subsequent classes Kristina posed further questions: 'Why do we have to worship God, and if we don't, will it make any difference to our salvation? Will God damn everyone who isn't a Christian, and if He doesn't, then why should it matter if we aren't believers? And what is the point of praying for oneself or for others? What about the many people who lived before Christ?'

Mr Speare explained the Christian view, but didn't satisfy the girls.

'Why do we have to believe in Christianity?' asked Rosemary.

'Yes, why do we?' asked Kristina.

'Because it's true, Kristina White – far and away more good and clever people than you have, and do', snapped the Vicar.

Rather than welcoming challenging questions, Mr Speare went on the defensive, becoming angry, and even confused. He preferred his candidates to sit quietly and accept everything he told them. He particularly abhorred Kristina for making trouble. Though aware of his hostility she couldn't resist trying to stir him out of his complacency and determination to make the girls accept everything he said without question.

Laura decided she wouldn't be confirmed. She told her house mother that her parents were Quakers.

'What are Quakers?'

'I'm not quite sure what they believe. I know they're pacifists, and helped to abolish slavery, so they must be OK.'

'I wish I could refuse too, but my father would be disappointed. And my Aunty Ruth is coming to take me out to supper after the service.'

The girls were to wear stiff ugly squares of white gauze over their hair. Kristina worried hers would slip off in church. And it did, just as she was kneeling at the chancel step. Someone retrieved it, but not before Mirabel had noticed. Nothing, however, could spoil Kristina's delight at seeing Ruth afterwards and going to the Royal Hotel for dinner.

'Are you staying the night here?'

'Yes', replied Ruth.

'It's so decent of you to come. How did you know about my confirmation?'

'Your father wrote to your mother, saying it would be very sad if you had no relation present, so she agreed to let me come.'

Ruth was smiling as she spoke. But Kristina said angrily, 'She ought to be grateful. I hate the way she wants to stop me from seeing you. It's so mean of her.'

'Well, we mustn't worry about it tonight. Anyway, she's paying the hotel bill, so let's have a good dinner!'

'I'm going to stay with the Wilsons at Easter. But in the summer they can't have me. I'm to go to a different family.'

'Don't worry, I'll tell you a secret – you won't be going to a new family in the summer, and your mother won't be coming to England.'

'So can I come to Seaton?'

'Better than that. You'll be going to Trinidad a year earlier than planned.'

Kristina couldn't speak for a moment, caught between unbelievable happiness and the thought that it was too good to be true. 'Why didn't my parents tell me?' she demanded.

Ruth looked at her bewildered niece sadly, saying, 'The situation between your parents is very difficult. Try to imagine how your mother feels. It's most unfortunate that her husband doesn't care for children and is now ill, so she can't be with you during the holidays. She must be feeling unhappy and guilty...'

Kristina opened her mouth to interrupt, but Ruth said, 'Let me finish. I know the sensible answer would be to let you stay with us, but she's frightened we might prejudice you against her. Your father was annoyed when he heard you were to go to yet another family in the summer. He phoned your mother, saying it was quite wrong to keep you in England living with strangers for two months when you could go to Trinidad. I don't know exactly what persuaded your mother. Maybe he threatened to take the matter to court in the hope of gaining custody.'

'I wish he would!' burst out Kristina. 'I just wish he would. I don't care what you say, I hate my mother. She's selfish and mean, and whatever she does, I'll never love her, so she might as well give me up.'

'It's understandable you should be resentful. But you'll feel happier if you stopped feeling sorry for yourself. Your parents' marriage was a mistake which thousands of people make, and of course the children suffer. But it doesn't mean your whole life is blighted. There are still things to look forward to and enjoy. There's Trinidad this summer, there's your friendship with Laura, there's Pam Wilson, who seems to have taken to you, and I'm sure there are other good things.'

'There are, but I've got four more years at school. That's my youth gone, just obeying stupid rules with bossy prefects waiting for me at every corner, living in prison conditions and putting up with boring lessons. You can't imagine it, because you've never been to a school like mine. We used to grumble about the High School in Port of Spain, but actually we had lots of good times, and the teachers were human beings, not sadistic warders.'

'Aren't you exaggerating just a little? There must be some teachers who are human beings. It was most unfortunate they put you in Cabot House with Miss Deacon.'

'I'm not exaggerating! They won't even let me see Laura at weekends, so there's hardly any point in our being friends.'

'I'm afraid, my dear, it's time I returned you to your prison. You'll have a pleasant Easter with the Wilsons, and after that, just think of Trinidad.'

The following morning the newly confirmed girls had to attend the service at 8 a.m. They all grumbled at having to rise early and march forth in a cold drizzle to the church. Kristina wasn't sure what she'd expected as she knelt at the end of the row – some earth-shaking conversion, or a vision of light. As it was, she got half of the melting wafer stuck to her tooth, and when the chalice was tipped towards her there was so little wine left at the bottom that she failed to get a sip at all. This upset her so much that she stumbled as she rose to her feet.

Miss Deacon wasn't in the congregation. But as Kristina reached the door, with a rush of pleasure, she saw Pam Wilson trying to reach her from behind the queue of girls. 'I couldn't come to your confirmation, so I decided to come to your first communion', she said.

'How did you get here?' asked Kristina, astonished that Pam had taken the trouble to come.

'A friend gave me a lift in her car.'

There was no time to chat, but Pam gave Kristina's hand a squeeze, saying, 'The kids are so looking forward to seeing you at Easter.'

At breakfast Mary stated solemnly that her first communion had been the most inspiring experience of her life. Rosemary remarked that at least it had been more interesting than Mr Speare's sermons.

'One of the servers was rather dishy', was Fiona's only comment.

Chapter Eleven

When Kristina arrived at the vicarage, Pam said 'I'm afraid you're going to be very bored this holiday. I've got to do some preparation for my history lectures.'

Kristina pretended not to mind. She'd come to know the centre of Bristol quite well during the Christmas holiday, but the idea of a month without anyone to go out with seemed bleak. After a week of reading, and a few rides on Pam's rickety old bike, she became increasingly frustrated. Yet she was glad Pam would soon be earning money. The vicarage seemed shabbier than ever, and needed so many improvements that it would be hard to know where to start.

'The stair and hall carpet will be the first thing we'll buy. It's been awful clumping up and down for three years.'

A letter arrived from Kristina's father. I'm sending you some money as an Easter gift. You could spend it on a special day's outing to London, if Mrs Wilson is willing to take you. There should be enough money to cover both your train fares plus meals and any other incidentals. You mentioned that Mrs Wilson liked art, so she might be glad to take you to an art gallery or a museum, or both.

Pam was delighted at the idea, and they set out on the day after Hilary and Jane started school. Pam suggested going to the National Gallery, saying that visiting one gallery would be enough for a day's outing. Kristina agreed, remembering her visit the year before, when she and Tessa had hurried from room to room, taking in very little.

'It would be better to concentrate on just a few famous artists, Michelangelo and Titian to start with. The trouble is that the works of the great masters are scattered among various art collections in other countries. So we can only see the ones the National gallery has managed to acquire.'

'Which d'you like best out of Michelangelo and Titian?' asked Kristina.

'I'm not sure. Perhaps when I see them again I'll be able to decide. Apart from the Italian paintings I'll show you a picture I like by Jan van Eyck from the Netherlands.'

By mid-morning they were staring at the two unfinished paintings by Michelangelo – *The Entombment* and *Madonna and Child*. Kristina had heard of the great sculptor and painter and had seen a photograph of the Sistine Chapel ceiling. Now that she was looking at two of his original paintings she felt she ought to be gasping with admiration.

'When I first came here as a teenager', said Pam, 'And saw the fifteenth and sixteenth century Italian paintings, I did marvel, of course, at the wonderful way they were painted, but I wasn't sure I liked them. I was more in awe of them. So, how do you feel?'

'I do agree they're wonderful. But when you see the Italian paintings all at once as I did last year, somehow it seemed too much. So many people in each picture, and all on religious themes or classical myths. My father said the Italians were paid to paint Madonnas and saints and angels to decorate the churches. They had to earn a living, but it's a shame they couldn't choose their own subjects.'

'Well, what d'you think of these two Michelangelo pictures?'

'I don't like *The Entombment.* Palestinians couldn't have looked like these people. St John looks like a woman, and the two women aren't even looking at the body of Christ. I'm sure they would have been. It must have looked gruesome. In this picture he hasn't any wounds, and can't possibly have been crucified. No, I don't like it.'

'How about the *Madonna and Child*?'

'Mary's face might have looked like that, but she would never have been dressed in rich silky robes. The little boys are just ridiculous, looking so plump, with golden curls. I'm beginning to get tired of angels. Last time I came it seemed nearly every Italian picture had angels hovering above or standing around.'

Pam laughed. 'You've got a point, but we have to realise that in the fifteenth and sixteenth centuries the religious works of art weren't meant to be realistic. They were mostly symbolic. For instance, the angels in this picture are studying a symbolic scroll. And Mary's book must be symbolic too.'

'Mary wouldn't have owned a book like that', said Kristina emphatically.

'If you think about it', said Pam, 'An artist must paint whatever he or she is inspired to paint. You don't have to like it, but it's worth trying to understand why a picture is painted in a particular way using a particular subject. Let's see what you think of Titian, who died in his nineties and was almost as famous as Michelangelo. 'You probably won't like this one', she continued, as they stopped in front of *Bacchus and Ariadne.*'

'Well, of course it's beautifully painted, but I hate it. Ariadne must have been scared stiff of all those horrible gods.'

When confronted with Titian's depiction of Christ revealing himself to Mary Magdalen in the garden, Kristina was still unimpressed. 'How could Mary Magdalen have mistaken Christ for a gardener? No one could garden properly draped in a sheet. And like in Michelangelo's *Entombment,* Christ doesn't look as though he's been crucified.'

But Kristina did like *Portrait of a Man.* It was a relief to look at a painting of a single person after pictures filled with people. The fourth picture they saw of Titian's was another one Kristina didn't like as a whole. *The Vendramin Family* included all the male members venerating a cross-shaped reliquary of crystal and gold on an open-air altar.

'I only like the boy with the dog', she said, 'And why hasn't he painted the six daughters? They had such peculiar ideas at that time. I'd have hated to live in such a family.'

'Well, let me show you a famous picture I particularly like', said Pam. In another room they approached *The Arnolfini Marriage,* a double portrait by Jan van Eyck. 'Before you look at the date, d'you think that picture was painted before or after the ones we've just seen?'

'I'd guess after', said Kristina.

'It's not surprising you should think so. But actually it's early fifteenth century – 1434, whereas the

Michelangelos were late fifteenth century and the Titians early sixteenth. 'It may not be strictly accurate, but it was said at the time that van Eyck was the first to work in oils. Whether he was or not, he certainly devised a new method of painting in oils, by putting on layers of paint to produce more depth. His subtle colours have been described as glowing with an amazing lustre from inside.'

'Who are the man and woman in this picture?' asked Kristina.

'We don't know much about them. They're a couple in a merchant's house who might have been through a marriage ceremony, or who might be in the process of being betrothed.'

'The woman looks pregnant', said Kristina. 'I wish we could see the man's hair. With those hooded eyes he looks ugly and rather stern – a bit of a dried-up old stick.'

Pam laughed. 'Yes, I suppose he does. But I don't think the woman is meant to be pregnant. It's just her skirt bunched up.'

'She was probably forced to marry, poor girl.'

'Well, whatever the story behind it, would you agree it's a marvellous painting? Before you answer, have a look at all the objects in the room, apart from the couple.'

Kristina stared at the clogs, the little dog, the mirror, the rosary on the wall, the lit candle and the fruit on the window-sill and table. Suddenly the picture came alive. 'That dog is so cleverly painted!' she exclaimed. 'But would he have stood still in that position long enough. He ought to be sitting or lying at the woman's feet.'

'I agree', said Pam, 'When you're older, go to Bruges in Belgium, and see other van Eyck works. There's an exquisite painting of the Madonna which you couldn't help but like, even though you've had enough of Madonnas! The way van Eyck painted has enabled his works to look as new as though they were done yesterday.'

They were having lunch in the National Gallery café when Kristina caught sight of Gita sitting at a nearby table with two friends. Wearing Indian dress and make-up, she could have been taken for eighteen. Gita noticed Kristina at the same time, and hurried over to her table, saying, 'How wonderful to see you! Are you in London for the holidays?'

'No, only for the day. This is my friend, Pam Wilson.'

'So glad to meet you. May I join you for a moment?' The gold bangles on Gita's arm jangled as she pulled out a chair. 'Do tell me how things are going at The Dunbar.'

'Bad as ever. Are you still happy at your school?'

'How can one be happy at any school? But at least I'm in London, which is so exciting.'

'Are you still hoping to be an actress?'

'Good heavens, no! I hope to study at the London School of Economics.'

'How clever', said Kristina.

'Anything to stay in London. It's the only town with the best Indian restaurants, and the only place to buy good clothes. You'll have to come and stay with us. I'm not going to India this summer.' She chatted on for a few more minutes before rejoining her friends.

Kristina felt envious of Gita's advantages, but also wondered what they'd ever had in common, other than hating the Dunbar.

'What an attractive girl', commented Pam. 'She looks much older than fourteen, but I suppose Indian girls do avoid the English schoolgirl look.'

'Like me', said Kristina glumly.

'Like you now, but of course, dressed up like Gita with make-up, you'd look older too.'

'She'll probably get a first at university and marry a rich man.'

'You could get a good degree too. And perhaps marry a rich man', said Pam, smiling.

'I won't get into university, because I'm not learning anything at school.'

'It might not seem like it, but you must be taking in a lot of necessary basics.'

'Like what?'

'Well, grammar and vocab. And maths, and facts in history and geography and so on. In the fifth and sixth year your lessons might become more interesting. It depends so much on whether you get a good teacher.'

'The teachers think I'm a trouble-maker. All they do is tell me to sit down and be quiet whenever I say anything. Once you get a bad name you haven't a hope. My house-mother teaches me English literature, and probably tells everyone in the staff room that I'm no use.'

'That should give you all the more incentive to prove you're worth taking notice of. D'you know what you want to do after university?'

'To be a theatre director.'

'What inspired you to make that decision?'

'Seeing two plays, acting at school in Trinidad, and reading a bit of Shakespeare. It sounds silly, but I'm sure I could direct if I was trained.'

'Which plays did you see?'

'Pygmalion, and Much Ado About Nothing.'

'It's a good start. If I can get a baby-sitter, we could go to see *Hamlet* the day after tomorrow if you like. There's some of your father's money left.'

Kristina was ecstatic, but then she said, 'Won't Patrick mind?'

'No, he works most evenings, and when he's at home he's happiest reading in his study, and listening to the Third Programme. He's not bothered about going to plays.'

They sat in the circle at the Theatre Royal to give Kristina the best view. As they walked back to the vicarage after the performance, Kristina was very quiet.

'I saw my first *Hamlet*', said Pam, 'When I was about thirteen, and it's fascinated me ever since. On that occasion it just seemed a good, but very sad, story. What do you think?'

'It was so, so sad, especially Ophelia's madness and death. Why did Hamlet treat her so cruelly?'

'Because he's suffering so much himself over his mother's betrayal that he's turned against all women. He says there should be no more marriages. It's not an easy play to understand. Every time I see it there's some new aspect I hadn't noticed before.'

'I'd like to see it again.'

'Well, go alone tomorrow to the matinee. In the morning you could have a quick look at the text.'

Kristina did so, and after lunch, sitting in the gods on a narrow bench, she gathered a great deal more about the intricacies of the play. To be in a Bristol theatre on her own made her feel guilty and thrilled at the same time.

This time next week, she thought, *I'd be expelled if they caught me here.*

'Did you enjoy *Hamlet* more this time?' asked Pam as the family were eating spam and lettuce sandwiches and hard-boiled eggs in the kitchen.

'Yes, I took in some of the witty bits – Hamlet teasing Polonius, and later when he's talking to Rosencrantz and Guildenstern. But I didn't understand why the chap named Fortinbras became King of Denmark at the end.'

'No, it is rather muddling. Briefly, Hamlet's father killed the King of Norway in single combat, and gained some of his land. The King of Norway's son, Fortinbras, gathers an army, hoping to regain those lands. He also decides to plunder a part of Poland, and is given permission by Claudius to take his soldiers across Danish land. That's when Hamlet meets Fortinbras on the shore. It's all to do with Scandinavian politics, and personally I don't find it very important.'

'I didn't like the costumes. All that black and white was a bit dull.'

'It does fit in with a sombre castle where many deaths take place and the main characters are all suspicious of each other.'

Kristina was to return to school the following day. It was gratifying to be told that the Wilson family had enjoyed having her, and hoped she'd have a happy reunion with her father in the summer. 'But we'll see you again before you go. You could spend the Saturday of half term with us if you like. And you can have your trunk sent here at the end of term, and just take what you want on holiday.'

'You won't need three pairs of thick green knickers in Trinidad!' said Jane.

Everyone laughed, and Kristina said she was going to burn her uniform the day she left school.

'Won't you get into trouble?' asked Hilary anxiously.

'They'll be very angry', replied Kristina, grinning, 'But it won't matter if I'm leaving.'

'Mum always uses our old knickers as dusters.'

'You could donate yours to us', said Pam, and Kristina burst into the loud laugh Miss Deacon so abhorred. Hilary and Jane giggled all through lunch.

When they'd recovered, Kristina said, 'It's all right for you, for the next three months I won't be able to laugh at all.'

As the summer term began, conversation in the common room centred on the opposite sex. Nearly three months of segregation lay before the girls, when the only male they could speak to was the Vicar. Those who weren't having a love affair made one up. Miranda was, as she put it, just wild with passion for her brother's best friend in his first year at Oxford. He'd invited her to the May Ball, but when Miranda's parents braved Miss Deacon for special permission to let her go, they were repulsed in no uncertain terms. 'Certainly not!' Miranda mimicked. 'Miranda must wait until she's at university, though I must add that if she doesn't make more effort, she won't gain her School Certificate, never mind get to university.'

On one of their free afternoons, Kristina and Laura arranged to meet in a secluded grassy basin behind some bushes on Clifton Down. Being indoors during the perfect summer weather was most depressing, and it was worth sneaking out and risking the consequences. They reached their destination without mishap, and stretched out on the grass, luxuriating in the sunshine.

'Everyone in our common room seems to be in love', said Kristina. 'Have you got a boy-friend?'

'No, of course not, but I rather like a fisherman I often see on the harbour in Torquay. He's good-looking in a rugged kind of way, and very pleasant. But he only talks about fishing. If he knew I was at this school he'd run a mile.'

'Perhaps I'll meet some boys in Trinidad.'

At four o'clock, as they crept out from behind the bushes, they almost collided with three Clifton College pupils, older boys who had to shave and whose voices had broken. But Kristina thought they looked too baby-faced to be taken seriously.

'Hi!' she said. 'Have you been eavesdropping?'

'You're out of bounds', said one boy sternly.

'So, if we are, why should you care?'

'We could report you.'

'That'd be a sneaky, goody-goody thing to do. You ought to be honoured we're talking to you. I bet you've never spoken to a Dunbar girl.'

'We thought the Dunbar Academy was a nunnery', said a second boy.

'You'd be surprised at what goes on under a nun's habit', said Laura, in a deadpan voice. Kristina burst into a loud cackle, and the boys fled.

At half-term, Kristina began to tick off the days until the end of term. The girls in her year became mildly curious about her life in Trinidad.

'I expect you had lots of black servants?' said Fiona.

'No, we didn't, only my nanny.'

'Did you play with nigger children?'

Kristina felt uneasy at her tone of voice. 'Of course, all the kids at my primary school were black. And at the high school there were very few white girls. They were mostly Negro, East Indian, Chinese or of mixed blood.'

'Surely the whites didn't marry coloured people?' said Kit.

'Why shouldn't they? The mixed blood kids were by far the best looking.'

'They were still half-castes.'

'I had an ayah in India', put in Jacky, 'And I played with Indian kids before I went to an all-white junior school.'

'What's the point of an all-white school' asked Kristina.

'It's OK mixing races at primary school level, but surely not later', said Rosemary. 'Can you imagine Indian girls learning Greek and Latin, or playing hockey?'

'Of course I can. Gita learned Latin and played hockey.'

'There's always the odd exception.'

'All the girls at the high school in Port of Spain learned Latin and played hockey.'

'Would you have a negro as a boy friend?' asked Miranda.

'Yes, if I met one I liked. Trinidad is full of good-looking black boys.'

'Think of kissing a nigger!' said Fiona. 'It makes me shudder.'

'I've read they're more sexy and passionate than English boys', said Kate.

'I expect they are', said Kristina angrily. 'If you really want to know, I wouldn't fancy kissing any of the English boys I've seen, especially the ones at public school.'

Miss Deacon was to take Kristina into Redland to have inoculations prior to flying to Trinidad. Miranda had already described her one experience of visiting the school doctor – a sweet old thing, she said. 'The Toad insisted on coming in with me, instead of staying in the waiting room. My dear, it was most embarrassing. I had a boil on my bottom. Afterwards, when I was getting dressed behind a screen, the doctor said, "What good-looking girls the Dunbar is producing these days, Miss Deacon. It must be all that wartime milk and cod liver oil." You can imagine the look on Toad's face.'

Miss Deacon sat so grim-faced while Kristina was having her injections, that the doctor made no attempt at genial remarks. Kristina too was put off by Miss Deacon's expression, and they walked back to Cabot House in silence.

In history, geography, English Literature and Scripture, Kristina was gaining a reputation among her teachers for side-tracking the syllabus and asking irrelevant questions. They considered it time-wasting when revision for the end-of-year exams had to be covered quickly.

In one geography lesson Miss Barton said, 'We've been studying the Nile and Ganges deltas with all the problems of irrigation and water control. Can anyone name another important river delta?'

Someone named the Mississippi, and Kristina added, 'The Orinoco'.

'And where is that?', asked Miss Barton.

Does she know?, wondered Kristina, *If not, I can tell her all about it.* And she launched into a detailed description, remembered from a geography lesson at the High School. 'It's in Venezuela, opposite Trinidad, where I live. It's the third longest river in South America, after the Amazon and the Plata. The river water, which looks a milky white colour, flows into the Gulf of Paria, which is almost a land-locked sea. Boats can go from the port, La Guaira, all the way to a place called Cuidad Bolivar. It's named after, Simon Bolivar, the hero who liberated Venezuela and other South American countries. A tributary of the Orinoco links up with a tributary of the Amazon, which is in…'

'Kristina, I did not ask for a lesson on South America. Please sit down.'

But Kristina's enthusiasm for describing South America was not to be dampened. The next opportunity came when Miss Barton mentioned waterfalls. Cynthia had recently visited Niagara, which she said were the greatest falls in the world.

'They aren't the highest falls', said Kristina. 'The Kaieteur Falls in British Guiana are five times as high as Niagara.'

'Have you seen them?' asked Cynthia.

'No, but my father has. He went on a hiking trip along the Potaro river to find them, and took some wonderful photos.'

'I still think Niagara are the greatest falls in the world.'

'Stop arguing, girls', said Miss Barton. 'The Niagara Falls are known as the greatest in the world in terms of the volume of water.'

But Kristina hurried on to say she was sure the Kaieteur Falls were more impressive. Very few white people had seen them, and it was much more of an adventure reaching them after a trek through the jungle.

'That's quite enough from you, Kristina.'

At half term, when Kristina arrived at the vicarage, the Wilson children grabbed her hands, saying, 'Come and see what we've got!'

In the garage was a second-hand Morris Eight. 'It's such a luxury for Patrick, not having to cycle up hills in the rain', said Pam. 'We can get out into the country at weekends. And we've ordered a stair-carpet! So life has really changed for the better.

Before putting Kristina on the bus, Pam said, 'Your father's asked me to take you to the air terminal in London at the end of term. I'm sure you could manage on your own, but understandably, he's worried you might miss the plane.'

'It's very decent of you.'

'I've arranged to stay overnight with a friend, so it'll be quite convenient.'

In bed that night Kristina wondered why it was that Pam, who wasn't even a relative, talked to her as a sensible person, while all the teachers talked to her as though she was a bad, rather stupid servant.

At the end of the week of exams, Kristina developed a sore throat and sinus pain. This time she was determined to avoid the sanatorium. She forced herself to try and appear normal, wishing she could get hold of some pain-killers. 'No, I'm fine, just a bit tired after the exams', she assured a teacher who'd noticed she was looking very pale. Fortunately nothing more was said, and Kristina struggled to keep going with the thought of Trinidad in two weeks' time.

Then came surprising news from her father. *By the time you come to Trinidad,* he wrote, *I'm afraid I shall have left Sangre Grande. It will be a great disappointment to you, but after nearly fifteen years in the same place I felt it was probably time for a move. When a parish just outside Port of Spain was offered to me, I decided to take it. You might prefer to be within easy reach of town, so you can meet up with your old school friends, particularly with Jenny, who's looking forward to seeing you. Dodo hasn't come with me. She didn't want to live so far from her family and friends. But we'll go and see her and your friend Yvonne. My maid, Leonie, lives in the village and comes every day except Sunday. I've got a wide area to cover, but it's very interesting having a great mixture of races in my parishes. Unfortunately the Rectory is new, which might not please you. We were lucky at Sangre Grande, having that old plantation house...*

Initially Kristina was upset at the thought of not returning to Sangre Grande. But then she began to think it might be pleasant to live in a modern rectory. She pictured a white house with a proper bathroom, a pretty garden and a verandah, like the Morrisons'.

Chapter Twelve

S tanding on the sizzling runway at the airport, Kristina experienced the midday heat slapping against her like a hot, damp blanket. Her fellow passengers, mostly American tourists, were dressed in keeping with the humid climate. In contrast she felt clammy and constricted in a cotton frock with sleeves, collar and belt. Kristina had scarcely noticed the Trinidad heat as a child, but now she wondered how she was going to tolerate it.

Waiting in the queue to go through customs, Kristina picked out her father waving beyond the barrier. She'd been feeling somewhat shy at the thought of meeting him after nearly two years – two years which had seemed a lifetime. But when she saw the kind bright eyes in his deeply tanned and lined face, her fears were allayed. His figure, clad in the familiar khaki shorts, aertex shirt and white stock with clerical collar, seemed even thinner, and there were grey streaks in his auburn hair.

She put down her bag and rushed towards him, filled with pity and a love she'd almost forgotten she could feel. At an English airport she would have restrained herself, but in Trinidad public emotion was natural.

'Take care, man, you letting she squeeze you to death!' exclaimed a grinning West Indian lady.

When they reached the Eastern Main Road, Kristina asked, 'Is it far to Morvant?'

'No, we're in my parish of Barataria now, and we turn off here for Morvant. It's just a hilly village with a rum shop, where a steel pan group practises day and night.'

'I'm dying to see the modern rectory.'

'Don't expect too much. Both the church and the rectory aren't quite finished. In fact the church hasn't any side walls as yet. But except in the rainy season it's quite pleasant to have the breeze blowing through.'

'Is the garden like the one at Sangre Grande?'

'Nothing like it. The rectory's built on a small rocky hill standing by itself in the centre of the village. There's very little soil. A few shrubs struggle to grow, and there are three coconut palms on a patch of weedy grass at the back.'

The little her father had told her of Morvant didn't quite prepare Kristina for the disappointment she felt on seeing the concrete, cream-rendered building stuck on the side of the hill, with a garage and two rudimentary servants' rooms beneath the house. The front door opened into a large living/dining room. A poky study, three bedrooms, a shower room and toilet, and a long dark narrow kitchen completed the accommodation. The palm trees at the bottom of the steps to the rear were growing too far down to provide any shade. Thus the rooms lay exposed to harsh sunlight till early evening. John himself had been dismayed by the lack of a verandah to relax on at dusk with his rum and pipe after a tiring, sticky day.

As at Sangre Grande, the rectory was sparsely furnished. Scratched and pitted bare boards in the living room lay unadorned by rugs, and there were no curtains. Two Morris chairs and a small settee, all with limp, dusty brown cushions clustered at one end, and a dining table and four chairs at the other. The room was so large and bare that Kristina's voice echoed round the walls.

Predictably, an ancient stove, a juddering refrigerator and three roach-infested cupboards comprised the kitchen furnishings. The shower room was a replica of the concrete horror at Sangre Grande. The only light came from a small ventilator.

'There isn't a proper bathroom!' complained Kristina. 'You told me it was a modern house.'

'Only modern in the sense it's been built recently. There wasn't enough money to finish it properly. The parishioners are trying to raise money to complete the church. They're remarkably generous, but also very poor. So the rectory probably won't be finished.'

'I hate this horrible shower room! The concrete should at least be tiled over, and it's so dark.' 'Why isn't there a window?'

'It all costs money, my dear. I don't suppose our parishioners' shower rooms are any better. We can't expect to live more comfortably than they do. You didn't mind the shower room at Sangre Grande.'

'I did wish we'd had a bathroom like the Morrisons'.'

'The water pressure here is very low, due to our being on a hill. Some days water doesn't come through to the house till late at night. Leonie collects water in a bucket from a tap in the garden.

'So I can't have a shower till midnight?'

'It might happen sometimes.'

'How awful!' Kristina could feel the sweat running down her back.

'I've given Leonie the day off, so we can have the house to ourselves', went on John. 'Don't compare her to Dodo. She's just a young woman of nineteen or twenty who dislikes housework and, unusually for a West Indian, she's taciturn and rarely smiles.'

Leonie had left a pot of calaloo in the oven. The steaming mix of fresh crab, split peas, onions, coconut, dasheen and okras tasted wonderful, but it wasn't as good as Dodo's. Sitting in the large room, where a single naked bulb hung over the cheap veneered table, Kristina's eyes suddenly filled with tears at the thought of Dodo and the pewter bowl of dark red impatiens standing on the gleaming cedar table. This Morvant rectory wasn't home, and even the presence of her father couldn't quell the feeling that her Trinidad paradise had gone for ever.

After lunch the house became unbearable as the glaring white walls reflected the heat. Sweat trickled down Kristina's arms as she sought a cool place to sit and read. John usually snatched a short siesta after lunch, but this had never appealed to Kristina. Eventually she went outside and sat on the steps running down the side of the house. The surroundings were rock-hard, with no green softness or colour to be seen. She watched an army of red ants marching over the baked earth, and a yellow lizard basking in the sun.

For supper they ate fried bananas and hops bread. Several jack spaniards zoomed into the living room, and giant moths flitted round the bare bulbs. Kristina retired soon after dark to her room and unpacked. She took the towel hanging on a rail beside the small stained hand basin in her bedroom and ventured into the dark shower room. As she switched on the light several insects scurried into cracks in the concrete. Yellowish-brown water dripped slowly from the shower head, and twenty minutes passed before Kristina could rinse off all the soap on her body. The Cabot House bathroom seemed the height of luxury in comparison. It struck her more forcibly that John wasn't much concerned with modern domestic comfort, or with clothing and food for himself. The only indulgence he allowed himself out of his meagre stipend was books. The many touches of colour and comfort at Sangre Grande must have been Dodo's doing. She did recall Dodo bullying her father into buying a beautiful locally made rug for the living room. It was typical of him to have left it behind.

Her school pyjamas being too warm to wear, Kristina changed into clean pants and then stood at the window. A thin streak of grey cloud lay across a huge bright moon. The familiar scraping of crickets had started, and the louvred leaves of the palms creaked in a welcome breeze. Lights were twinkling all over the village below, and there was a faint smell of curry. Presently she was startled by the noise of a steel pan group striking up. It wasn't an accomplished sound, it wasn't always in tune, but all her exciting memories of Trinidad carnival came flooding back. She lay on her bed, listening in delight till she fell asleep.

The following morning as the sun rose higher, Kristina's dislike of the rectory increased. From her window could be seen the many little houses and shacks in the village –and beyond, the hills of the Northern mountain range outlined against the relentless metal-blue sky. She longed for the tall trees of Sangre Grande, for luxuriant green growth in the garden, for jasmine, morning glory and trumpet vine clambering in at the windows. There was nothing to gladden the eye on this hard Morvant rock, where every blade of yellowing grass had to struggle for existence.

'Yes, I know, it's not like home', agreed John. 'I miss Sangre Grande too, and I wish this house wasn't so stark and unfriendly. But, as I said in my letter, you do need to be near Port of Spain. My working life is particularly demanding at the moment with three parishes, but I can probably drop you in town most days, and you can get a taxi home. Mrs Morrison has kindly suggested you might like to spend a few weekends with her family.'

'At Ballandra?' said Kristina, her hopes rising.

'No. They've sold their villa, and started taking holidays to other islands: Barbados last summer, and possibly Tobago at Christmas.'

It was a relief that Mrs Morrison, as usual, had come to the rescue, for Kristina had already realised there was absolutely nothing to do at Morvant except read. She wondered if her high school friends would be pleased to meet her again – the English girl whose mother thought Trinidad education wasn't good enough. But at least Jenny wanted to see her.

Leonie arrived, and greeted Kristina pleasantly enough, but wasn't inclined to chat. She attacked her chores in a grim-faced way, sweeping clouds of dust into the air with a broom.

John had to go out at ten, and he offered to show Kristina his other two parishes. The crowded area of Barataria spread south of the Eastern Main Road, where the houses looked somewhat better off than the shacks of nearby Laventille to the west. Kristina found it quite a culture shock to be on the Eastern Main Road again. In post-war Bristol, cars in sombre colours moved sedately along clean, odourless streets, and quiet drably dressed people walked past shops with closed doors. In contrast, the Eastern Main Road was a riot of noise, colour and smell with merchandise displayed outside the shops. Every door was open, every person seemed to be shouting, laughing or screaming. There was a sense of dramatic life being lived on the streets. John became stuck, first behind a truck and then behind a cart, and Kristina felt close to fainting in the heat.

Her father deposited her in his large wooden church at Barataria to keep her out of the sun while he made a couple of calls. Two elderly ladies entered the church full of friendly greeting, and when Kristina informed them she was the rector's daughter, they asked many questions, starting with, 'How old you is?'

This well-remembered West Indian patois made Kristina feel at home. For a while it was like being back in the church at Sangre Grande, where, ever since she could walk, the parishioners had always clustered round her, full of solicitude over her motherless condition. Better still, they had often slipped cakes or sweets into her hand. Kristina enjoyed talking to these ladies at Barataria, and now felt eager to meet West Indians of her own age. It was depressing to return to the emptiness of Morvant rectory.

'Are there teenagers in the village?' she asked her father.

'Of course there are, but as you probably remember from Sangre Grande, young people start work at an early age unless they're going all through secondary school. I doubt there'd be more than one or two in Morvant taking School Certificate. Even at Sangre Grande you'd have found it impossible to resume your old life. Young children can be great friends, whatever their background, but sadly, it often changes when they become teenagers. You wouldn't have much in common with your old friends, with the exception of Yvonne Thomas.'

At lunch time Leonie produced thin slices of aubergine fried crisp, with plantains, sweet potatoes and home-made mango pickle. She recalled her first lunch at Cabot House –gristly liver, a splodge of greyish potato and some kind of vegetable, boiled until it had lost colour, texture and taste. It was delightful to eat West Indian food again.

John had received a letter that morning from Tessa. The most disturbing aspect of her having taken over their daughter was the way she hadn't provided a consistent home for Kristina. Now she wrote that she and Denis hoped to come to London in December, and stay for six months.

'I wish she wasn't', said Kristina. 'I'd rather go on staying with the Wilsons. And what about next summer? Can I come out here again?'

'It's up to your mother to decide.'

After their meal John sat in his study writing his Sunday sermons. Every now and then he pulled out one of his many books, ranged as at Sangre Grande on lengths of wood, balanced on red house-bricks. Kristina sat beside him, waiting impatiently, but also nervously, for Mrs Morrison to ring. She'd never spoken on a phone, and when it rang she hesitated before picking up the receiver. It was disconcerting to hear Jenny's bright, self-confident Trinidad accent. Her own Trinidad accent had disappeared, and she felt self-conscious in trying to resume it.

'Hi there, Kristina, it's Jenny. Did you have a good trip?'

'It was OK – a bit long.'

'We went to Barbados last summer by plane. I loved it. Mum wants you to come over at four if your Dad can bring you. She'll drive you home. Bring your swimming things. Carla and Di will be here. D'you remember them?'

The girls Jenny mentioned, both white Trinidadians, had been in the same class. All the while she'd endured boarding school, these girls had continued their pleasant life in Port of Spain, living with their families in the same houses and consorting with the same familiar friends. How would she fit in with them now?

When John dropped her at the Morrisons' gate her worst fears were confirmed. All three girls wore sundresses, sunglasses and sophisticated sandals. The twelve-year-old Jenny she remembered with pigtails, socks and short skirts, had metamorphosed into a sleek beauty with wavy perm, pink lipstick, nail varnish, and dangly earrings in her pierced ears.

'Hello, Kristina', said Jenny. 'Did you have a good time in the UK?'

'It was all right, but I'm glad to be back.'

'You don't speak like you used to', said Di. 'You've got a posh accent, like some of the expats.'

'Everyone speaks like this at my school.'

Carla giggled, saying, 'You don't look the same. Your skin's so white.'

The other girls asked questions, and Kristina became more and more embarrassed. She felt the scrutiny of three pairs of inquisitive, critical eyes, and wished Carla and Di hadn't been there. Once it was she who'd been the more confident, bossy one with Jenny. Her friend had moved on into new relationships, and she felt at a loss.

But when Mrs Morrison came out and kissed her fondly it was more like old times. 'The girls are about to have a dip. Have you brought your swimming things?'

'Oh, gosh, I forgot', lied Kristina, who'd no intention of appearing in her regulation school costume. 'I'll just watch this time.'

The girls changed into colourful bikinis, a fashion that hadn't yet caught on in England. Kristina regarded them with envy, plunging into the blue pool. How lucky they were to have mothers who provided holiday clothes – clothes they could look attractive in. Her own mother only bothered when she was actually with her daughter.

However, Mrs Morrison sized up the situation, and on the way back to Morvant with Kristina, she said, 'Don't be offended if I mention your clothes. As we both know, your father was never any good at fitting you out. So, would you like my dressmaker to run you up half a dozen sundresses? Material is so cheap here. We could go and buy some early tomorrow.'

'Yes, I'd love to.'

'We needn't let Jenny know. I'll ring your father and discuss it. We'll go down to Frederick Street, and at the same time we'll get you a swimsuit, some cheap sandals and some shorts. Then you won't feel so awkward. It's hard for you, having a mother in Switzerland and a father in Trinidad.'

Kristina was speechless with gratitude.

At eight the following morning Mrs Morrison drove from Morvant along the bumpy country road and down the hill to the Savannah on Queen's Park East. They turned into Frederick Street and then into Keate Street, where Mrs Morrison left the car in the British Council park.

'It's fortunate', she said, 'That Malcolm still does part-time work for the British Council, so I can park here. Otherwise it's a nightmare trying to find a space.'

Kristina wasn't surprised. The centre of Port of Spain looked far more crowded with traffic, people and animals than she remembered. There even seemed to be more policemen, looking incredibly smart in spite of the heat, in their white cork helmets and well-pressed navy shorts.

As they walked back to Frederick Street, a vendor beside a donkey cart laden with coconuts tried to sell them one. Kristina would love to have stopped to watch the man slice off the top of a coconut with three strokes of his machete. She and Jenny had often bought coconut milk after school, though Mrs Morrison would never countenance buying refreshment from a street stall, particularly roti. Yet all the girls at school had done so, with no ill effects. Heavily spiced goat roti with pepper sauce, which set fire to your mouth, was wonderful, and Kristina longed to try one again.

It was a relief to leave the baking hot pavements and to enter the cool department store where bales of colourful crisp cotton were ranged from floor to ceiling. Half an hour later they emerged from the shop and made for the dressmaker's house. By the time they returned to the rectory the sun was beating down and the living room was like an oven. John was out, and after a hasty lime juice Mrs Morrison got up, remarking how hard it must be without air conditioning or fans.

'It's a horrid house. I hate it!' burst out Kristina.

'I'm sure you do. I expect most rectories are rather primitive. But at least you're near Port of Spain. I'll be up on Monday, about five, to take you back to my dressmaker. We shall look forward to having you to stay next weekend.'

On Saturday John agreed to drive to Sangre Grande to seek out Dodo, and possibly Yvonne. Ugly blocks of flats were being built behind the Eastern Main Road, but otherwise the route looked the same. There was the usual overwhelming smell of dust, dung and rotting mangoes. When the Rectory at Sangre Grande came in sight Kristina was horrified to see the trees along the drive had disappeared.

'It's our house! How dared they cut down the trees?'

John smiled, but he felt for her. It had been her childhood home, the memory of which would remain very strong throughout her life.

They drew up outside Dodo's son's house, where she was now living. Dodo herself answered their knock, greeting them with her usual broad smile, and asking why they hadn't warned her they were coming.

'We didn't want you to go to any trouble, Dodo. All we need is a soft drink. We'll sit out here on this seat, and if you've time we can have a chat.'

Kristina hadn't quite imagined how it would be on meeting Dodo again. In the past Dodo had fondly addressed her with rude phrases, such as *Who the hell you think you looking like? Hush your mouth before I vex,* or *You is the most uselessest girl I ever meet.* And Kristina would reply in a similar vein. It had been their way of showing affection once Kristina had grown out of a babyhood in which her nanny had smacked or smothered her with kisses in equal measure. It would be impossible ever again to speak in such a familiar way. Kristina sat unhappily drinking pineapple juice and eating banana bread, while her father talked about his work, saying how much he missed Sangre Grande. She was fast discovering that she couldn't slip back into the old life. People grew apart, and now she even felt shy with Dodo. She felt apprehensive too about meeting Yvonne, but her father said they must try, as news of their visit would be all round Sangre Grande.

Yvonne was at home alone, so John dropped his daughter and went to visit old acquaintances. Kristina wasn't surprised to find Yvonne with her bird books spread out on the kitchen table. Her friend was taller and had filled out a little. She'd lost her Trinidad dialect, though not her accent. Otherwise she had the same serious, bright-eyed face, sudden wide smile and enthusiastic manner. Her delight at seeing Kristina again was genuine, and there were no awkward moments before they were chatting away. And yet – yet the relationship wasn't quite the same. Yvonne had another, more urgent intellectual life to absorb her. She was just about to go on holiday to British Guiana, with the family of her best friend at school. She reeled off a long list of the new birds she wanted to see – bell-birds, puff-birds, trogons, trumpeters... Kristina could hardly take them all in.

'Next year they might take me to Brazil, where the birds hardly sing at all, but have even more brilliant plumage than the ones here. The most beautiful bird in the Brazilian forest is the suruqua. I'll show you my painting of it, which I copied from a book in the library.'

Yvonne fetched a sketch book full of water colours of birds. Kristina marvelled at her painting of the suruqua, in purple, gold, red, grey and white. 'You're so clever', she said. 'I wish I could paint like this.'

'Going to the High School was such a wonderful opportunity for me. Mrs Henry taught me how to paint, and Mr Raymond, the new biology teacher, has been so encouraging. He lent me a book on Australian birds, the best songsters in the world. Look at this honey-eater, so small, but so colourful. At the moment I'm writing an essay on the development of birds. A fossil they discovered in Bavaria is the oldest bird we know about. It's called archaeopteryx. It even had teeth, which birds no longer have.'

It had never occurred to Kristina whether birds had teeth or not. Suddenly she felt very bitter. No teacher at the Dunbar had shown the slightest interest in her. Since she hadn't any great academic talent no one was going to single her out for special encouragement.

'Last term', continued Yvonne, 'We had a school trip at night to the Aripo Caves to listen to those amazing oil birds who live in the dark most of the time. I discovered that the proper name is Guacharo. They're as big as crows, and make a kind of high-pitched screaming noise. It was quite scary. Have you ever been there?'

'My father promised to take me, but never got around to it.'

If only Yvonne lived in Port of Spain. Of all her old friends this was the one Kristina valued most. And now, just when Yvonne had blossomed at the High School and widened her experience, there was to be no possibility of continuing the friendship. She suspected Jenny and her group were not so interesting. 'What do you do in the holidays?' she asked

'Mostly read and paint, and help my mother with her stall.'

When the time came to go, Yvonne said, 'We should write to each other.'

'Yes, I really will', promised Kristina. She and Jenny had promised to write, but hadn't. Perhaps it would be easier to write to Yvonne about the horrors of boarding school life. She couldn't imagine Yvonne, a black girl from a very poor home, going to the Dunbar.

Equipped with her new clothes Kristina felt equal to spending the following weekend with the Morrisons.

On Friday after dinner she and Jenny spent the rest of the evening catching up on their long separation. Kristina made much of the Spartan life at the Dunbar in general terms, omitting to talk of her personal miseries. She didn't want to be pitied even more by the Morrisons. Jenny had always found Kristina amusing, and her description of the teachers, the daily routine and the food kept her laughing till bedtime.

Jenny said their old circle of school friends had now joined up with some of the Queen's College boys together with several students studying in the US or Canada. They all met frequently to play tennis and swim, to see films, to dance at parties and to picnic at weekends when parents were available to drive them to Maracas or other beaches. Some of the girls, including Jenny, had 'boy friends', which often caused rivalry and adolescent heartache. Kristina gathered that to be popular it was necessary to be attractive, to dress well, and to have parents living in a smart residential area with enough space to throw a good party and hire a steel pan group for dancing. Saturday evenings were usually taken up with going to the Country Club weekly buffet and dance. It was a lovely place, said Jenny, just north of the town, with gardens, pools, tennis and squash courts as well as the restaurant and dance floor. One had to be a member, but guests could be taken.

Kristina realised that without the Morrisons she'd have had no social life. Her father's vocation was regarded as a respectable profession among those white people who attended the various Christian churches. But clergy families on low stipends couldn't expect to keep up socially with the white Trinidadians and expatriates who inhabited the wealthy suburbs and a few rural beauty spots. At the age of nine Kristina had been 'adopted' out of kindness by the Morrisons, and now it became painfully obvious how much she owed to Jenny's parents. Jenny too was now fully aware that Kristina was a 'dependant', and could sometimes be slightly patronising.

At school in Bristol Kristina had never considered what would happen on her return to Trinidad. If the Morrisons hadn't been so forthcoming she wondered if her father could have coped with her for the eight-week holiday. She began to see him in a new light, realising that he was spurned by certain sections of society. The fact that he never bothered about social divisions, taking people of every colour and background on their own merits, made him seem an oddity, even among the clergy. He was a man whose company was tolerated but not actively sought. For the first time Kristina understood why her mother had left her father.

Going into his study when he was out, she looked at the surprising titles of the books on his table. She picked up an open book entitled *The Leviathan,* by Thomas Hobbes, published in 1651. Her father had jotted down a quote and some notes on a piece of paper. '*Christianity is like a pill, swallow it at one gulp and it may work; chew and you will retch*' …*Leviathan – sovereign power. Average man's life: solitary, poor, brutish and short. State of nature, general war and self-seeking. Laws of nature…* Reading on, Kristina was astonished at how modern and sensible Hobbes' ideas seemed.. This was not the kind of book The Reverend Kenneth Speare would like to have discussed, and neither would her mother. On looking up the name, *Leviathan,* in a dictionary, she discovered it was the name of a sea-monster in the Bible.

Kristina was glad enough to join the teenage holiday life, but there were two drawbacks. The first was being invited to lavish parties in private houses, but being unable to have one of her own. The thought of Jenny's friends coming to the rectory, even had her father been able to afford a party, made her shudder. None of them had even heard of Morvant. Secondly, she was too tall. The boys preferred to dance with small, slender girls. So she often had to sit and watch the dancing she excelled at herself. Not that she was attracted to any of the boys;

they all seemed to be rather inarticulate and painfully shy with her.

'What do you see in Lawrence?' she asked Jenny.

'Not much', she replied, 'But he's crazy about me, and he dances well. At the moment he's only interested in cricket.'

One Sunday a picnic had been planned to Maracas beach. In the grey dawn four cars set out up the Saddle Road. The sun hadn't yet risen above the mountains as they joined the North Coast Road, which had been carved out of the mountain side. Below lay a valley of fruit trees, a mangrove swamp and small lagoons. At the coast the road rose high above the sea, and they could look down at the waves pounding the rocks at La Vache Bay.

By the time they'd parked the cars the sun had appeared. Kristina had expected to find the beach deserted so early in the morning, and was surprised to find the sea already full of bathers, most of them just standing in the water. There were Indians wearing shifts and a number of plump middle-aged black ladies clad in bright bloomers and bras, shouting happily to each other across the green water.

'No jellyfish today', shouted one lady cheerfully as Jenny and Kristina swam past. All the teenagers were strong swimmers, and many of them made for some rocks, putting the pelicans to flight. Unlike Toco, the beach had been developed as a tourist attraction, with carefully laid out strips of palms, grass, seats and Coca-Cola kiosks well behind the shoreline. Kristina was warned to look out for serrated bottle-tops half buried in the sand.

The morning was spent in and out of the water until brunch, which they ate under the trees – bacon and egg rolls, cold sausage, mango pickle and fruit. After the meal everyone flopped out on towels and dozed. As a child in Sangre Grande Kristina had never taken a siesta, and now, after living in England, it seemed a waste of time.

Instead, she wandered off by herself along the blinding white sand and then inland among the deep shadows of the trees. Suddenly she came across a middle-aged and a young man, each leaning against a palm trunk with a chess board between them. Both had fallen asleep with their chins resting on their chests, and their straw hats slipped down over their eyes. Observing them closely, Kristina couldn't help laughing loudly. The young man woke, pushed his hat up and grinned. His smooth black facial features were flawless, and he had the most benign expression in his eyes. She admired his tight orange trousers and white shirt patterned with green palms.

'Sorry, I woke you up.'

'I forgive you.'

The young man rose in one graceful movement. It was a relief to find he was taller than she. The older man continued sleeping, so he moved away, saying, 'Let my old man have his siesta. I'm Edmund Vesey.'

'I'm Kristina White.'

'I've seen you before, coming out of the High School.'

'I'm at school in England now.'

'I'm going to England in October, to study law at university.'

'Were you at Queen's College?'

'Yes. I noticed you because you're so tall, and also because of your hair.'

'What's wrong with my hair?'

'Nothing – you've got lovely hair.'

'At school they say it looks a mess. They want me to cut it short.'

'No, it's lovely as it is. Where d'you live?'

'At Morvant.'

'Morvant!' he said in surprise. 'Do English people live there?'

'Only us. My father's the Rector.'

'My family live at Diego Martin, on the other side of Port of Spain. My dad's a lawyer.'

At that point Edmund's father woke up and Kristina said hastily, 'You'll want to finish your game. I'd better get back to my friends. Good luck in England.'

She walked away thinking what a dream boy he was, far better looking than all the white boys she'd seen, and not only that – he seemed a really nice guy. She'd like to see Edmund again. However, she said nothing to Jenny about meeting him.

She'd arranged to meet Jenny two days later on the seat outside the back entrance of the High School. They intended going to see a film starring Margaret Lockwood at the Embassy cinema. Kristina arrived on time, but three quarters of an hour later Jenny still hadn't turned up. Her father was to pick her up from the school at six. She'd just decided to stroll up to the Savannah, when Edmund Vesey passed by.

'Fate has arranged a second meeting, and since you've a couple of hours to spare, shall we take a walk?' said Edmund when Kristina had explained the situation.

'But weren't you going somewhere?'

'Only the library. It can wait till tomorrow.'

Not for an instant did Kristina question whether she should go walking with a boy she didn't know. 'Yes, I'll come.'

They walked up Chancery Lane to the Savannah. The subsequent two hours proved to be the most pleasant Kristina had ever spent in Port of Spain. They bought bottles of Coke and strolled slowly round the old walled cemetery. Then they watched some small boys playing cricket, shouting 'Him's out!' all too frequently. Eventually they sat down under a cannonball tree. Round them hung the rope-like strands of sticky blossoms with pinkish-brown petals which gave out a sickly-sweet smell.

Kristina told Eddy, as he was known, about her life at Sangre Grande and Bristol. In return he described his family and home, saying that if he managed to qualify in law, he'd return to Trinidad to practise.

'Will you come back?' he asked her.

'Not if I still want to work in theatre. There's no professional drama going on here.'

'You could start a company.'

'Oh yes, if I was rich.'

Eddy laughed. 'Borrow the money, and then get rich.'

He didn't ask her age, but Kristina suspected he thought her older than fourteen.

'When will you go back to school?' he asked.

'The second week in September'.

'I have to study two hours each day, but otherwise I'm free. Perhaps we could meet sometime. Would your father object?'

Perhaps he would, thought Kristina. The Morrisons certainly wouldn't have allowed Jenny to walk around Port of Spain alone with her boyfriend. 'You could come to the Rectory tomorrow if you like.' She realised she'd asked him to Morvant without worrying what he'd think of the house. He'd described his own home at Diego Martin as having a pretty garden and a large veranda, but she felt instinctively he wouldn't be snobbish or critical.

They walked back to the school, where John was already waiting in his car. Going back to Morvant, Kristina explained what had happened, and he showed no outward surprise. He was perfectly willing for Eddy to visit the Rectory.

Jenny was full of apologies on the phone for having got the wrong date, but Kristina said it had all turned out well, since she'd met a good-looking guy called Eddy, who'd just left Queen's College. Her friend was agog with curiosity. 'Do bring him round on Saturday. He could come to the Country Club with us.'

Kristina hesitated before saying, 'I'd better not bring him to Cascade. Your parents might object. In any case, he's not allowed in the Country Club.'

'Don't tell me he's coloured?'

Yes, he's black – very black, and very handsome.'

'You can't go round with a black boy.'

'Why not? He's really nice.'

'That's not the point. The girls in our group don't have black boyfriends.'

'I don't care. Anyway, he's coming to our house on Friday.'

As she thought about it, Kristina became angry, and fiercely protective of Eddy's rights as a human being.

He'd told her he was good at tennis, and she wished they could play at the Country Club. It was time people stopped this stupid colour bar. She'd had enough of the Morrisons' social life. She didn't really care if she never saw any of Jenny's friends again. But of course she was still so grateful to Mrs Morrison. She'd have to keep up a façade.

Eddy came to Morvant the next day at five. Kristina heard him chugging up the hill on his motorbike, and went out to meet him. He was dressed more soberly this time, in a sparkling white shirt, pressed grey trousers and polished black shoes, as though he was going to church. John was amused. It was obvious Eddy had dressed to please an English Rector, little realising that this particular Rector didn't judge people by their clothes. It reminded John of his first few weeks at Sangre Grande, when the men at his first Church Council meeting turned up in dark suits, starched collars and ties, while he himself wore shorts.

'You do look smart', said Kristina. 'I should have mentioned that Dad never dresses up, except for church.'

They sat in the creaking Morris chairs drinking lime juice and eating biscuits. Eddy conversed easily with John about politics, the future of Trinidad and his own ambition to be a lawyer. Kristina guessed her father was impressed. In a while he retired to his study, and Kristina showed Eddy the house and the church.

'And this is our beautiful garden!' she said, as they stood on the scrubby patch of yellow grass under the coconut palms.

'Yes, I see what you mean, but you do have a good view of the hills.'

Kristina laughed. 'My father doesn't mind living in a dreadful house. He'd be content living in a hut in the jungle.'

'An unusual person.'

'My friends think he's very peculiar.'

'I like peculiar people.'

'D'you think I'm peculiar?'

'Very peculiar indeed!'

When Eddy had gone, promising to ring her, Kristina said to her father, 'Isn't he wonderful? What a coincidence he's going to Bristol University.'

'He does appear to be a very pleasant, clever young man, but it might be wise at this point not to start a serious relationship.'

'D'you mean because he's black?' exclaimed Kristina, on the defensive.

'You probably won't heed my advice, but let me give it nevertheless. First, you're very young, and still have four years at school. Secondly, you've only two and a half weeks left before you return to Bristol, and much of that time will have to be spent with the Morrisons, as I'm sure you'll admit. And thirdly, Eddy studying in Bristol is going to be very frustrating for you both. You won't be able to meet, as you know, and at Christmas you'll be in London with your mother.'

'Eddy could come to London. He's got an uncle living there.'

'He may do. But your mother won't want you going out alone with a boy, and certainly not a West Indian.'

'Why not?'

'Most people in England, and some in Trinidad, don't approve of mixed relationships. Your mother would be criticised. I would be too, but I don't mind what people say. It's high time colour prejudice came to an end. But if you tell your relatives and friends in England you have a black boy friend, you'll be ostracised. When you become an adult is the time to decide on the kind of people you want to mix with.'

Kristina had always listened carefully when her father was explaining how one ought to think or behave, but this time she'd no intention of following his advice. She'd fallen in love with Eddy, and was determined that if he cared for her they'd contrive to meet somehow, whatever people said.

'Eddy wants to show me some places in Trinidad I've never seen. Will you let me ride on the back of his motorbike?'

When John hesitated, she went on, 'Please, please let me, he doesn't drive fast. We won't do anything silly.'

John knew he was courting enormous disapproval in allowing his daughter to go around alone with Eddy, especially on a motorbike. And yet he couldn't face her disappointment. She'd only have a few days with him before returning to Bristol, and then no doubt the affair would die out. Eddy would meet more mature girls at university, and Kristina would suffer the rejection of a first love affair. So why not let her enjoy her holiday before returning to the austerities of boarding school? Possibly some busybody would complain to the bishop, but it would blow over once Kristina left.

The following evening Kristina went reluctantly to the Country Club with the Morrisons.

'Did Eddy come to your house?' asked Jenny.

'Yes, and on Monday he's taking me out on his motorbike.'

'Does your father know?'

'Of course.'

Jenny expressed amazement, and Kristina sensed her envy.

For the next three days Eddy called early each morning, wearing brightly coloured tight pants, a pastel shirt with deep cuffs and two-tone shoes. With his wide shoulders, narrow waist and long legs, Kristina thought he looked the ultimate in elegance.

Equipped with sandwiches, fruit and water, they explored the centre and southern parts of the island. They would set off down the Southern Main Road, above which a row of vultures perched on the telegraph wires; then past flooded rice fields towards the town of San Fernando, thirty-seven miles south. Here they branched off along tracks and deserted roads built by the Americans during the war. Much of the terrain they covered looked familiar enough to Kristina – rolling hills, swamps and forests – but many of the mud and thatch Hindu villages spreading inland from Fyzabad, in the district known as Bengal, had a different atmosphere. On their third trip, after looking at a Hindu temple, they stopped to drink and rest under a group of trees in the heavy torpor of midday.

Kristina felt the sweat running down her back and trickling between her breasts. 'How do people put up with this heat?' she asked.

'They're used to it.'

'It never seemed to be this hot at Sangre Grande.'

'You'd get more of a sea breeze there.'

After a pause Eddy said, 'I'd like to hold your hand, but I think it's melting away.'

He took off his shirt and hung it on a branch, suggesting that Kristina did the same. 'Don't look so worried, I'm not going to seduce you.'

Without her shirt, Kristina felt as sticky as ever. 'Does black skin make it cooler for you than for me?'

'Of course not.' He put his arm, glistening with drops of moisture, next to hers.

'I wish I had velvety black skin like yours.'

'I like you as you are.'

'I wish I didn't have to spend the weekend staying with the Morrisons. We've got so few days left together.'

'Never mind, I'll see you in England.'

How could she explain the situation to Eddy? Meeting Laura had been hard enough. Even in London they'd have to meet secretly, owing to her mother's prejudice. It was all so horrible, and so unnecessary.

Their remaining time together was spent wandering around Port of Spain. They visited the Anglican Cathedral, where Eddy pointed out the elaborate roof made from Trinidad hard woods. They bought peeled oranges and roasted corn cobs in Picton Street, and ate them in Jackson Square. They went into a Chinese shop which sold everything from cooking pots to ladies' underwear, and an Indian shop where Eddy bought Kristina a filigree necklace. They watched huge stems of bananas being loaded onto a boat. They rode to the Caroni Swamp to look out for Scarlet Ibis. In Marine Square they strolled past tourist shops selling gifts – stuffed alligators, beads, carved coconuts and miniature steel drums. For lunch they ate curried shrimps under an awning outside a shabby little café. In the early evening they listened outside the neon-lit Queens Park Hotel to a jazz group playing Duke Ellington and Count Basie. Everything looked, sounded and smelled magical. Being in love was better than anything Kristina had imagined.

Just before dusk on their final evening together, they drove up Lady Chancellor Road to the Belvedere Hotel. Here they parked and stood looking over a parapet at the city spread below, with the silhouette of palms poking up from between the white houses.

'You're going to hate Bristol', said Kristina. 'It's cold and windy and grey, even in October, and it's covered with bomb-sites.'

'I'll like it with you being there. You can show me round.'

'Eddy, I have to tell you, English boarding schools don't let you go out to meet friends. It's not like the High School. Even relatives can only see you for a few hours twice a term.'

He couldn't conceive of such nonsense, so he only laughed, saying, 'Well, we'll have to do a Romeo and Juliet, without the balcony. I seem to remember Juliet was only fourteen, just like you.'

'How did you know I was fourteen?'

'It wasn't difficult to work out.'

'I'll be fifteen on September the eighteenth.'

'And I'll be eighteen on September the fifteenth. It must be significant!'

After a pause, Eddy said, 'This is a romantic place to say goodbye, better than a film set.'

'You're always laughing at me.'

As the bats began to fly, and fireflies glimmered in the bushes, Eddy kissed Kristina for the first time. She clung to him desperately, but he eased her away, whispering, 'Not now. We'll meet in Bristol. Look how bright the fireflies are.'

'What are fireflies?'

'Luminous male beetles. They're showing off to the females.'

'They're lovely. My nanny, Dodo, told me people in the jungle used fireflies as lanterns, and girls would stick them in their hair as ornaments.'

A few tears trickled down her cheeks. 'I can't bear the thought of four more years at school.'

'Never mind, I'll write you passionate love letters.'

'It's not funny, Eddy. You can't begin to imagine how awful my boarding school is. The teachers and the prefects all hate me, and I'm not learning anything. I'll fail my School Certificate. Dad will be disappointed, and my mother will kill me! Then what will I do as a career?'

'If your mother kills you, you won't be needing a career.'

'If you can't take me seriously we'd better not see each other again.'

Eddy put his arms around her and smoothed her hair. 'Of course I take you seriously. You're the most interesting, intelligent, lovely girl I've ever met, and I'm sure you can do anything you set your mind to. So don't let a few insensitive, ignorant teachers wreck your life. You must stand up to them. Remember, I love you, and it'll all come right in the end.'

How useless it was trying to make him understand the public school system.

The last two days Kristina stayed at home with her father. A whole morning was spent writing letters – to Mr and Mrs Morrison, to Jenny, to Yvonne, and finally to Eddy. She'd been so indebted to the Morrisons over the years that it was difficult to convey adequate thanks. John said he would write, and send a large bouquet of lilies. He also suggested that now she was older she should correspond with Mrs Morrison. But what could she write about? She'd already told the family that boarding school was awful, but they thought she was exaggerating. Jenny, who'd read boarding school stories by Enid Blyton, sometimes wished she could go too.

To Yvonne she wrote, *I've fallen in love with a boy who was at Queen's. He's going to Bristol to read law. Just think, one day, we might get married, and come back to Trinidad for good…* But as she wrote these words a small doubt arose in her mind. She was no longer a proper Trinidadian. She didn't belong, as Yvonne did. Would she ever be fully accepted, even as Eddy's wife?

At the start of her holiday, Kristina's greatest desire had been to return to the High School. Now she'd met Eddy she wanted to go back to Bristol. But she'd be subject to the strict vigilance of the Dunbar. Suddenly the idea of planning secret meetings seemed impossible. The school year stretched ahead in all its grey dreariness. The holidays promised nothing better. She felt imprisoned in a hostile world where adults made unpleasant decisions from which there was no escape. She loved her father. He was kind, good-tempered, and always tried to be reasonable. Yet subconsciously she blamed him for being unable to save her, and fell into a half-sullen mood.

John himself had continued to worry about Kristina. Her school reports painted her as a lazy, uncooperative pupil who might do better if she were to apply herself. Tessa grumbled to him about these reports, but still wouldn't consider an alternative school. Then on the last day of Kristina's holiday further news came from her, destined to make life even more uncertain for his daughter. Sadly, Denis was entering the final stage of terminal cancer, and would be dead within weeks. Tessa still intended being in London by Christmas, but would be preoccupied with buying a house and settling in England. The holiday with Kristina was not likely to be a success.

'Why didn't she tell me Denis had cancer?' asked Kristina.

'Because cancer's a taboo subject for many people. It's such a dreadful illness, and usually ends in death. Anyway, the main thing is that she'll be in a state of bereavement, and you'll have to make an effort to be supportive. However bored or misunderstood you feel, try and think of her rather than yourself at the moment. Disaster should bring people together, so this may be your opportunity. You're old enough to understand something of how devastating it must be to lose someone you love.'

Saying goodbye to Kristina was going to be even more painful than the first time, when he'd hoped she might be happy in England. As it was, there seemed to be no possibility of her settling down at school or with her mother.

Chapter Thirteen

On her arrival at the air terminal in Buckingham Palace Road, Kristina took a taxi to Paddington and caught a train to Bristol, where Pam met her. She was to spend a night with the Wilsons before returning to school.

It was a pleasant September afternoon, but sitting in the drab, smoky railway carriage, looking out of the grimy window, Kristina was struck once more by the contrast between the colour and warmth of Trinidad and the muted English scenery.

It was a relief to see Pam's friendly face and to be welcomed at the vicarage. But nothing could alter her tired, depressed mood, not even the thought of seeing Laura.

'It won't be so bad once you get there', said Pam hopefully. 'And you must come to us at half-term.'

But how could anyone who hadn't been there know the deadening effect of the Dunbar Academy. As soon as she entered Cabot House the unfriendly, dismal atmosphere overwhelmed her. She wanted to run down the steps and flee. Instead she dragged her case up the stairs, noting that Miranda and Kate weren't in her dormitory. After unpacking she made her way to the Senior Common Room, to be greeted by an indignant Miranda.

'Kristina, she's left you in the Middle Common Room list? It's so unfair. Do go and complain. Maybe it's a mistake.'

But it was no mistake. When Kristina marched furiously into Miss Deacon's study, she was told she'd have to stay in the Middle Common Room until her deportment marks improved. No one in Cabot House had ever had such consistently bad marks. Until she behaved like a senior she would continue to be regarded as a junior. Should she show a marked improvement she would be moved up next term. To add to her humiliation, she would have to obey the monitor of the Middle Common Room.

'I refuse to be in the Middle Common Room', she burst out. 'All my friends are in the Senior Common Room.'

'You'll do as you're told, or be sent to Miss Craig. And I might point out that girls like you who constantly refuse to cooperate often end up in a girls' reformatory.'

Kristina had never heard of a reformatory, but guessed it was some kind of children's prison. The idea shocked her profoundly. Could it be that Tessa in her soon-to-be-bereaved state might be persuaded by the school to place her in a reformatory? It was a chilling thought. If she was ever to see Eddy again she must conform as Laura had advised.

On the eighteenth of September Kristina received a birthday card from Tessa, saying a present would follow at Christmas. At the moment she was too occupied with looking after Denis. That she'd forgotten to order a birthday cake didn't worry Kristina. She'd already written to Ruth requesting her please not to send a cake, and promising to explain why in a future letter. She'd no intention of sharing a cake with the Middle Common Room girls, and certainly not with Miss Deacon. Her fifteenth birthday would have been a miserable occasion had not Eddy sent her a pair of delicate gold earrings with a letter, saying he'd arrived in London. But how soon would her mother allow her to have pierced ears?

If Kristina had been in the Senior Common Room she could have invited Laura to tea on two Sundays during the term. Fortunately Laura herself was able to invite Kristina to Penn House, but this necessitated Laura walking to Cabot House with another girl to fetch Kristina. After tea she would have to walk back with the same companion, in spite of only being a few minutes away. Uniform, including hats, had to be worn. The inconvenience and utter absurdity of these rules meant that invitations were rarely given. It was awkward appearing in the dining room in uniform, and inevitably the conversation became stilted. After tea Laura and Kristina only had fifteen minutes together in a corner of the drawing room.

Laura had returned from Cairo in much the same mood as Kristina. She too had enjoyed her holiday, though as yet she hadn't embarked on a romance. 'Public school boys seem so immature, and there was no opportunity to meet local boys, as my parents and their friends don't socialise with the Egyptians.'

Kristina confided all her longings and fears about Eddy, and they discussed ways in which they could meet.

'I don't see how you can meet', said Laura.

'I know it's hopeless. What makes it worse is if too many letters arrive with the same handwriting and a

Bristol postmark, Matron will get suspicious and open one.'

'Would she really dare to read your mail?'

'It happened to someone else.'

'Couldn't you get that Vicar's wife you stay with to help? Eddy could send letters via her. And if she could take you out one weekend or at half-term, perhaps she would invite Eddy as well.'

This attractive idea had occurred to Kristina, but it seemed too much to ask of Pam.

Kristina decided to brave Pam, saying that Eddy would naturally pay the post. Pam was quite willing to enclose letters in an envelope with her own name on the back. She even promised to try and contact Eddy when she was lecturing at the university, and she would consider asking him to the Vicarage.

Throughout the term Kristina set to with grim determination to keep out of trouble. Every free moment at Cabot House was spent checking her clothes, hair and nails. She tidied her drawers and polished her shoes. Her deportment marks went up, except for conversation with Miss Deacon. She was quiet in class, never challenging a teacher or putting herself forward in any way. The only time she relaxed was at break with Laura, or walking to school with her friends in the Senior Common Room. Miranda was particularly concerned about Kristina, and considered getting up a petition to request her removal from the Middle Common Room. Rosemary said it would only make things worse.

Kristina wrote to Eddy in London, telling him how Pam would help them to meet, and giving him the dates of half-term and the vicarage address. In October she received his reply enclosed in an envelope addressed by Pam. It was like writing to a nun locked up in a convent, he said. How could a House Mistress stop a girl having her boyfriend visit at the school, especially as he'd been approved by her father? He'd already been to the Downs and located the school and Cabot House. So if he was to see her before half-term, he'd actually have to wait on the road to see her pass by. He wouldn't be able to say hello, or wave. It was crazy like hell!

Kristina had asked him to make no sign if they met in the road, for besides the friend she would be with, there were always other girls, especially prefects, walking in front or behind, who might investigate. And how could she tell Eddy that because he was black everyone would be more suspicious.

The University had recommended Eddy to digs in nearby Redland, so it was easy for him to watch out for her. Each day she would walk to and fro from school, hoping against hope to catch sight of him. Eventually she saw him, not at a distance, but directly in front of her, standing on the pavement, chatting to another student. They stepped aside as the girls passed, and Eddy smiled at Kristina. It was the most frustrating moment of her life, and required all her self-control to walk on without speaking. She felt most unattractive in her school coat and hat, and the clumpy lace-ups which made her large feet look even larger. It was a wonder Eddy had recognised her. Seeing him left her in a state of confusion for the rest of the day, making it difficult to concentrate on her studies.

In his next letter Eddy wrote that he was inundated with work, which kept him up till after midnight. It was perhaps as well they couldn't meet at the moment, for he'd no time to socialise. It was difficult settling down to English life, and he loathed the food. Pam Wilson had spoken to him very kindly, and invited him to lunch on the Saturday of half-term. Kristina could hardly believe her luck. Pam had been so kind and understanding from the moment they met. Meeting Eddy at the vicarage wouldn't be breaking any school rules, yet Miss Craig would have judged it quite unacceptable, especially in a clergyman's wife.

Laura was intrigued. 'Eddy must have bags of charm', she said. 'For Pam to collude in your scheme, especially as you said she's hard up. What does the Vicar think?'

'He doesn't mind as long as his meals are on the table at the right time. He often doesn't notice what's going on in the family. Anyway, he's very tolerant.'

'Are they happy together?'

'It's hard to tell. I haven't heard them quarrel. But she hates being a vicar's wife and living in that ghastly house. Now she's got a lecturing job I expect she's happier.'

Kristina warned Laura never to mention Eddy or Pam in the notes they wrote frequently to each other. 'I feel I'm being watched all the time, particularly by Mary.

'Of course I won't mention Eddy.'

Kristina poured out all her troubles to Laura, and her friend replied with sympathy – exchanges which would have horrified Miss Deacon. Laura had long since come to terms with her own problems. Being plain and often painfully reserved, she took it for granted she'd always be on the outside of life looking in. Retreating into the world of adult literature from an early age had given her a precocious understanding of human nature. The one emotional gesture she'd made towards an attractive older girl who'd smiled at her, had rebounded most unpleasantly and had taught her to be wary of relationships. She rarely gave way to strong feelings. Her unlikely friendship with Kristina was partly based on the fact that her friend voiced enough strong emotion for them both.

'You're so lucky', said Kristina. 'No one pounces on you two or three times a day for misbehaving, and yet you're not a goody-goody like Mary.'

'It's true', agreed Laura. 'It's because no one notices me, whereas you're always making a noise and protesting about everything. You expected boarding school to be like the outside world, when really it's a kind of prison. It's better to do one's time quietly according to the rules. I despise and hate everything about the way this place is run, but I'd never let on. Miss Deacon knows you hate her, so she's determined to bring you into line.'

Kristina was wildly excited and also apprehensive, when Pam came to collect her at half-term. 'It's so nice of you to ask Eddy. I do hope you'll like him.'

'If he can eat sausages and mash and sprouts, followed by chocolate blancmange, then I like him', said Pam, laughing. 'It won't be a spicy West Indian meal.'

'He must be used to English food by now, and at least your sprouts won't be reduced to a yellow mush.'

At the vicarage Kristina hurried to take off her uniform before Eddy arrived. She was glad to see he was wearing a bright red tie with his white shirt, which helped offset his camel toggle-coat and dark brown cord trousers. He looked very different from the flamboyant figure he'd cut in Port of Spain. But of course it was the same Eddy who hugged her tightly and looked her over with bright, kind eyes.

Kristina enjoyed the most civilised meal she'd ever had. The children were out for lunch, and though the many meals she'd shared with the Wilsons had always been pleasant, this occasion was special. Having Eddy there charged the atmosphere with added interest. He seemed very much at home, and endeared himself immediately to Patrick by showing an intelligent interest in his books. He was even able to converse quite knowledgeably about some of them. With a tinge of envy Kristina realised that Eddy at eighteen was being regarded as an adult. He used words she understood, but would never have used at school. Rosemary and Jacky were the only teenagers she knew who used erudite words in their conversations to each other, and because of it were regarded as rather tedious. Kristina and her friends had become so immersed in schoolgirl jargon and superficial gossip, with no opportunity to talk to older girls, teachers or even parents on an equal basis, that they couldn't easily join in a cultured conversation.

Pam had laid the table in the dining room, with a lacy white cloth and the flowers Eddy had presented her with, in a blue bowl. There were starched white napkins and wine glasses with delicate blue stems. Sausage and mash it may have been, but Pam had disguised them with plenty of wild mushrooms she'd collected, and home made pickle. Patrick didn't treat Kristina as a child; she was given a full glass of wine.

Surprisingly Eddy loved the food, and kept them amused describing the horrors of the evening meal at his digs. Pam was wearing an attractive dress instead of her usual trousers and shabby jumper. Kristina saw for the first time that she could look rather beautiful. Patrick for once didn't dash away after lunch. The October sunshine lit up the little gold-rimed coffee cups the Wilsons had received as a wedding present and the tiny glasses of Cointreau.

Eddy said he'd been reading an interesting book about Sidney Smith, but couldn't remember its author.

Patrick smiled. 'Probably Hesketh Pearson', and went on to say that Sidney Smith was the wittiest man of his time, besides being a most compassionate and courageous person. His comments on marriage, female education, religion and almost every other subject were most entertaining and often true. 'You might care, Eddy, to read Hesketh Pearson's biographies of two other witty characters – Bernard Shaw and Oscar Wilde.'

'You'll be able to see some of their plays at the Theatre Royal', said Pam.

'It's all right for you', said Kristina bitterly. 'You can go whenever you like. I can't go till I'm in the Senior Common Room, and even then only once a term, to a play the school chooses.'

After Eddy had left, Pam said, 'He's a very personable young man. I imagine he'll make a good lawyer. We'll invite him again, Kristina, so you'll have something to look forward to,'

On the Sunday afternoon, Eddy returned, and they walked to the Ashton Park Estate and sat on a massive fallen tree trunk.

'How shall we meet in the Christmas holidays, when you're in London?' asked Kristina.

'I'm not keen on the idea of secret assignations. It's rather childish', admitted Eddy. 'I'd rather come round to your flat and ask your mother if I can take you out.'

'She'd never let you', said Kristina.

'Well, ask her to invite me to tea. I'll be very polite, and maybe she'll relent and let us go out alone.'

But Kristina knew her mother wouldn't invite Eddy to tea.

'It's because I'm black, isn't it?'

Kristina nodded miserably.

'Well, don't tell her. I'll just arrive, and if she dislikes the colour of my skin, she can throw me out.'

'It would be awful. I couldn't bear it.'

'Tell her I'm a black Trinidadian who knows your father, and you want to invite me round. It's worth a try.'

Kristina burst into tears, saying, 'I hate her, I hate her!'

Eddy kissed her wet face. 'Don't get so worked up, my sweet Kristina. She won't be in charge of you for ever. She's not worth all this hate.'

'She's in charge of me for another four years, and she'll put me in a reformatory if I don't do what she says', said Kristina, and she started running down the grassy slope.

'Whatever gave you that idea?' shouted Eddy, dashing after her.

Kristina had calmed down by the time they reached the vicarage, but the pleasant weekend had been spoilt.

Chapter Fourteen

On the train to Paddington at the end of the autumn term, Kristina was dreading the thought of meeting Tessa again after so long. This time she made her own way to Harley Street by taxi, and lugged her heavy case up the stairs.

She wasn't sure how a recently bereaved widow would behave, but outwardly Tessa looked and acted the same. She was slightly thinner, but still attractive and as always, beautifully dressed. Kristina, who in the company of the Wilsons had begun to learn how to relax when talking to adults, found it impossible to talk naturally to her mother.

It was hardly going to be a happy time with Tessa grieving for Denis. Worst of all, her grandmother was coming to stay over Christmas and new year. Tessa had said in her last letter that it would be less dismal if Constance was there. She also intended asking a friend to lunch on Christmas day, an American she'd known for years, who was on his own.

'You've not lost your hat this term', said Tessa as Kristina pulled it off and threw her coat onto a chair.

'Someone deliberately hid it that time.'

'Oh, surely not. Why would anyone want to hide it?'

'A prank, I suppose.'

'Your uniform looks grubby. I must send it to the cleaners. You haven't grown any taller, thank heaven, but I suppose you'll need some new mufti clothes.'

'Can I choose them myself?'

'We'll see.'

Tessa did compromise a little. However, when it came to buying an expensive dress for special occasions, she refused the long-skirted wine-red frock with a plunging neckline, which Kristina had set her heart on. 'It's much too sophisticated for you.'

She had to settle for a more youthful style with the usual Peter Pan collar, belt and shorter skirt.

'As you're not growing any taller, this frock should last quite a while – no, you're definitely not old enough for high heels.'

Kristina returned to the flat in disappointed fury. She'd planned to look sophisticated for Eddy. All the girls at school were into the long, full New Look skirts or dresses, and yet she was still condemned to continue looking like a schoolgirl. But at least she was allowed to go out alone for short periods, enabling her to escape from her grandmother's constant nagging.

Constance conceded that Kristina's behaviour had improved a little. She would sit quietly with a book after supper, and answer questions about school politely. Tessa intended selling the flat and buying a house with three bedrooms and a garden. She and Constance spent hours discussing where she might go. Kristina hoped it would be somewhere in central London, so she could see Eddy in the Easter holidays. She received a card from him, with his uncle's address, saying he was coming to London on Christmas eve, and would be in touch.

Christmas lunch was enlivened somewhat by Leslie, Tessa's rich American friend, who arrived laden with gifts wrapped in glossy paper tied with red ribbon. He'd been to Fortnum and Mason's to buy smoked salmon, Stilton, caviar, chocolates and liqueurs among other things. Tessa had known him in Switzerland, and now he was based in London for a year, and as yet hardly knew anyone. Constance and Tessa preened themselves and tittered at his jokes. Kristina squirmed at his attempts to flatter her. Though the meal was excellent, she was relieved when it was over.

The adults sat round the electric fire drinking coffee and liqueurs while listening to the King's speech. The sky darkened, and a persistent drizzle trickled down the window pane. The room grew steamy and claustrophobic.

'May I borrow your umbrella?' Kristina asked Tessa.

'Goodness, you can't go out in the dark', said Constance.

'It's only four o'clock.'

'We should all get some exercise', said Leslie, but none of them moved.

Kristina hurried downstairs with Eddy's card. She took the London map out of her handbag, and studied it under a lamppost. Lancaster Gate looked quite near, just along Wigmore Street and then keep going along Bayswater Road. She could walk to the house where Eddy was staying with his uncle and aunt. She wouldn't call on him this time, merely note where he lived. Now the rain had eased a little she began to measure out the lampposts along the endless wet, shiny road. At one point she was almost for turning back, but the thought of Eddy kept her going. Perhaps she'd ring at the door, just to see him for a moment.

Behind curtains in lit-up rooms people could be heard celebrating Christmas, which gave Kristina a sense of isolation. At length she reached the house. The curtains in the ground floor bay window were open. A brilliantly lit Christmas tree partially hid a room full of people. She made out the scratchy recording of a well-known calypso, and tears came to her eyes. She felt sure she could hear Eddy's voice, and went weak with longing. As she debated whether to ring the doorbell it began to rain so heavily that Tessa's skimpy umbrella offered little protection. Her shoes and coat became soaked.

If she made herself known, she guessed she'd be welcomed in with the usual warm West Indian hospitality. Once she'd explained herself, she'd have to join the festivities, eat and drink and wait for her clothes to dry before being able to leave. And Eddy would obviously feel obliged to escort her to Harley Street. Her hand was on the doorbell when she decided it was impossible. She must go home without seeing him.

There being no entry hall to the Harley Street flat, Kristina stood dripping onto the carpet in the living room. Tessa and Constance vied with each other in loud condemnation. Leslie had gone, and the washing up had started. They'd been worried sick about her, there was nowhere to hang her wet clothes, and she'd ruined Christmas day. She was not to be forgiven.

Kristina woke late the following morning to hear Constance's voice raised in irritation. 'You must put a stop to her going out in the dark.'

'It's dark so early', said Tessa. 'You have to admit, when she left yesterday we were glad to be rid of her. She's so gloomy, mooching about the flat, hardly speaking. You said, when you went to Trinidad, that Kristina was always shrieking with laughter. Well, I've never heard her laugh. I suppose if this is what all teenagers are like, I'll have to put up with it.'

'You certainly didn't behave like Kristina.'

Tessa had hung her daughter's coat over a chair in front of the fire, and the room smelt of steaming material. 'You should have worn your mac yesterday', said Tessa when Kristina appeared.

'I hate my mac, even more than my coat. It's so ugly, and much too short.'

'You shall have a new one next winter.'

'It'll still be ugly.'

She couldn't explain how awkward and childish, even ridiculous, she felt in uniform. In her grubby, ink-stained skirt, thick shapeless blouse, green and yellow tie and horrible lisle stockings she dreaded being seen by anyone outside school. At least she now had some nylons, though one stocking had already laddered.

Kristina sent a note to Eddy, asking him not to come to Harley Street. Even you, she wrote, won't charm my mother and my abominable grandmother, who's staying with us. They'd never let me out of the flat with you. She suggested meeting in Regents Park, near the zoo, and if he couldn't make it, she'd come the following day at the same time.

But as Eddy had told her, he'd no intention of making secret assignations. If he was to continue his relationship, her mother would have to accept him. The fact that her father had taken to him and trusted him so readily made him sure her mother would feel the same, once she'd met him.

Thus at eleven a.m. on Boxing Day before he received her letter he presented himself at Harley Street. Tessa answered the doorbell, and he could see how taken aback she was. He explained he was a friend of Kristina's from Trinidad, and in slight confusion she asked him to come up and sit down. Constance and Kristina both appeared from their bedrooms, having heard his deep voice. For entirely different reasons both were horrified, and when Eddy asked if he could take Kristina for a walk, Constance said firmly 'Kristina's not old enough to go out alone with boys.' And her cold tone implied, *And certainly not with black boys!*

'I don't know how it is in Trinidad', said Tessa, 'But in England we don't allow under-age girls to make dates with their boyfriends. Of course you may come here to see her.'

Kristina had been thinking all the while, You fool, Eddy. Now they probably won't let me out of the flat at all on my own, in case I meet you. The only way was to keep it secret.

Eddy was offered a cup of coffee. As he drank it, seemingly with no embarrassment, he attempted to make conversation with Constance and Tessa, asking them what they'd thought of Trinidad, and telling them he was studying law. Kristina prayed they wouldn't ask where he was studying. If Tessa were to find out she'd ask Miss Deacon to make sure there was no communication between them. Tessa had nothing against coloured people in general, but not for her daughter, and certainly not while at school. It was a pity Kristina had returned to Trinidad. She must write to John and find out if he'd encouraged the affair.

When Eddy got up to go, he shook hands very politely with Constance and Tessa. Kristina said she'd go downstairs to see him out, but on reaching the front door, she said, 'I don't care what they think. I'm coming with you.'

Fortunately she was wearing a thick jumper, and the weather wasn't unduly cold. They walked towards Regents Park, and Eddy said, 'You were right, I haven't won round your mother. But at least now we can see each other in her flat.'

'Oh, wonderful, with mother and grandmother sitting there!'

'Wouldn't they leave us alone together?'

'Not for two seconds.'

The sun came out in the park, and they sat on a seat. Kristina told him what a miserable Christmas she'd spent, and how she'd walked to his uncle's house.

'You're crazy like hell, Kristina, why didn't you come in?'

'Your uncle and aunt might not have liked me barging in. I was soaking wet.'

'They would have welcomed you like a daughter. They're very hospitable.'

'And I'd probably have got home about midnight. It's no good, Eddy, we can't see each other in London. I'll be made to promise not to arrange a meeting.'

'Pam told me she'd invite you out twice next term.'

'She's such a kind person. How lucky she likes you so much.'

They talked and kissed while an hour flew past. Kristina leapt up suddenly, crying, 'It's long past lunchtime – they'll kill me!'

'I'll write every day', said Eddy.

'So will I', and she hurried away.

Kristina crept up the stairs and hesitated outside the flat door. Inside, she could hear a quarrel going on.

'All this is entirely your own fault', Constance was saying. 'You insisted on marrying someone you'd nothing in common with, an eccentric with no money and no prospects, who took you to live in a jungle. I told you at the time it was stupid and irresponsible.'

'If you and Daddy hadn't been so liable to condemn, we needn't have married. We neither of us thought it was going to work – but I was pregnant.'

'Pregnant! – Before your marriage? How could you, Tessa, after all we sacrificed to give you the best possible upbringing?'

'You see, that's what I mean. You wouldn't have helped me as a single mother. You'd have kicked me out to fend for myself. Anyway, John and I didn't want our child to be illegitimate.'

'So you married, and then divorced and ran off to Switzerland, leaving your daughter to that hopeless clergyman.'

'I couldn't take Kristina. Denis refused to have a small child in his life.'

'You didn't have to marry Denis. If you couldn't keep your marriage vows, at least you should have brought Kristina to England.'

'And where would we have lived? How would we have lived? I couldn't have worked. I barely had the fare to come home.'

'We would have looked after you.'

'Don't lie, Mummy. You'd have been far too ashamed to have a divorced single mother in your house. What would the people at church have thought? And at the bridge club? And you never did like children, any more than I do.'

'If you were going to remarry, you should have found a man with money who did like children.'

'We can't always choose. As it happens, Denis provided me with a good home, and we were very happy together.'

'If you were so happy, why did you bother to take over the care of Kristina? Why did you beg me to go to Trinidad and face her father in that primitive rectory?'

'Because Denis didn't want me to go and stay at Sangre Grande with John. It was unreasonable, but I suppose he was jealous. As for claiming Kristina, I imagined it would be lovely to have a teenage daughter. We'd have so much in common, and we'd be good friends. Even Denis thought a teenage daughter might be pleasant. We were stupid, utterly stupid, to think she wouldn't be resentful. As it is, she hates me, and I'm beginning to hate her.'

'Well, as I said, you've brought it all on yourself. You're too lenient with the girl. You should give her a good talking to, instead of keeping silent.'

'What good would it do at this stage? She'll rebel against everything I ask of her.'

'As she's doing now, out with that black fellow.'

Kristina opened the door and burst in, shouting, 'He's not that "black fellow", he's the person I love best in the world!'

Tessa, aware that Kristina might have heard the last few exchanges, fled to her bedroom. Constance went to the kitchen and brought out a plate of food she'd been keeping warm in the oven.

'I don't want any lunch' muttered Kristina, though she was actually very hungry, having run all the way from Regents Park.

'Take it or leave it', said Constance.

Kristina picked up plate, knife and fork, and retired to her bedroom. Fifteen minutes later, hearing the flat door click, she guessed with relief that Constance had gone out, and took her plate very quietly towards the kitchen. It was then that she heard her mother crying. She stood listening for a few moments, while a succession of painful and contradictory thoughts ran through her mind – *It was hard to believe Tessa could cry – she deserved to be utterly miserable after the things she'd said – this was the first opportunity when it might be possible to offer sympathy to her mother in the hope of establishing some kind of intimacy, perhaps even forgiveness on both sides – but what would be the point? Tessa wouldn't change her opinions, especially with Constance in the background – did she or didn't she feel sorry for Tessa, who had had to marry John – but it was Tessa who insisted on keeping her at the Dunbar – and now it was these two hateful women together who were preventing her from seeing Eddy.*

And so the moment passed, and Kristina returned to her room. Half an hour later she emerged to find Constance and Tessa drinking tea. She'd decided to follow Laura's advice yet again, and act the role of dutiful dependant. It was useless fighting women like Constance and Miss Deacon. They would always win. So Kristina ostentatiously never went out alone. Instead, she tagged along with Tessa whenever possible, and rarely spoke unless spoken to.

One interesting excursion, however, to see Oklahoma, kept her mind occupied day and night for the rest of the holiday. It was her first experience of an American musical, and she was bowled over by the idea of combining music and dialogue with jazzy dancing. In bed that night she devised a satirical, comic musical for the Senior Common Room to perform, sending up the horrors of school life. Rita, a girl in the Upper 5th, an accomplished improviser of popular tunes on the piano, could provide the music. There was a fair amount of potential acting talent among the girls, and of course there was Miranda, who would make a perfect Miss Deacon. Soon the whole musical had taken shape. Some of the lyrics and the spoken dialogue had been written, and the dancing outlined. Her creation would have to be performed in Cabot House, but she had grand visions of it being transferred to the school stage.

On New Year's Eve, after working all day at her musical she'd gone to bed straight after supper, waking just before midnight. She got up and found Constance knitting in the living room.

'Is my mother in bed?'

'She's gone to a party', said Constance. No more was said, and as Kristina settled back in bed, 1949 became 1950.

Chapter Fifteen

When the idea of a musical was broached to the Senior Common Room, to which Kristina had now been admitted with loud cheers, there was little initial enthusiasm. But Kristina persisted. 'It's a fairly short musical with piano accompaniment, and parts for those of you who want to act, sing and dance. I've already sketched out a story line, with dialogue and lyrics to fit popular tunes we all know. We'll need to add more dialogue and lyrics, and choreograph some dances. Rita's already agreed to play the piano. Costume could be a problem, but two of you live near Bristol, so perhaps your mothers might help out. It'll be enormous fun.'

'Yes, it will', agreed Rita, and opening an ancient, untuned piano kept in an alcove, she started bashing out a couple of tunes.

'Try singing this, Miranda', said Kristina, handing her a sheet of paper. 'You'll be impersonating a lovelorn Toad, who dreams of running off with a woman-hating organist. There's a chorus of teachers all vying with her for his attention.'

'Whose attention?' asked Fiona.

'The organist's, of course.'

'D'you mean grumpy old Cyril? How could the Toad want to run away with him?'

'Oh, Fiona, it's meant to be a satire. Of course, we won't use real names.'

Miranda, who'd been looking through the song, was giggling. 'The Toad will certainly recognise herself in this.'

'Of course she will. All the teachers and prefects will recognise themselves, but there's nothing malicious in it.'

Miranda struck a pose, and began to sing with as much zest as any cabaret star. There was a two-line chorus, which everyone picked up, and by the end the Senior Common Room was completely won over. Jacky and Rosemary were keen to write a comic lyric in Latin. And Cynthia was sure Mummy would help with the costumes. Roles and back-stage jobs were allocated.

'Who shall we ask to beard the Toad for permission?' said Kristina.

'A prefect would be best. Try Judith Prescott', suggested Kate. And Judith did gain permission for the girls to rehearse in the common room, with one rehearsal a week in the drawing room.

The musical progressed with amazing speed. For three weeks the girls worked hard in every spare moment, writing witty songs and dialogue and learning lines, after lights out.

Cynthia's mother, who belonged to the local operatic society, drove to the school, laden with borrowed costumes and props. The cooperation was excellent, and much enjoyment was gained in working on a difficult project together. Kit Taylor and her two friends imitated the sports staff to the last detail, and all being good gymnasts, performed a clever dance incorporating handstands and cartwheels.

Finally all was ready, and Miss Deacon was invited to the dress rehearsal along with Matron and the prefects. It didn't take her long to grasp that the cast were lampooning the teachers and prefects. Whenever Miranda in a grey wig delivered lines in Miss Deacon's voice and made faces and gestures which everyone recognised, the prefects tittered. But it was Kristina's imitation of Miss Craig which quite literally stopped the show. With hair scraped back into a hairnet, and pince-nez perched on her nose, Kristina had barely uttered half a dozen lines in her strong voice before the prefects collapsed with laughter and from outside the door came more laughter from a group of eavesdropping 3rd and 4th formers.

The hilarity came to an abrupt halt as Miss Deacon ordered the show to stop immediately. It was a disgracefully discourteous performance, and certainly couldn't be shown to the rest of the house. The girls were to clear up and get to bed as soon as possible. Before leaving the room she added, 'Will whoever thought up and produced this musical please report to my study after you've cleared up.'

The drawing room was put to rights by a silent, furiously disappointed Senior Common Room. Then one of the Upper 5th said, 'We're in this together, and we'll all go to the study. So, when someone knocked and Miss Deacon opened her door, she found the Senior Common Room girls lined up, almost standing to attention.

'It was a joint effort', stated Miranda.

'I can hardly believe that', said Miss Deacon, 'Since you insist on taking corporate responsibility, you will all suffer the same punishment. None of you will attend the theatre outing this term.'

'I was the producer', admitted Kristina loudly.

'I might have known', said Miss Deacon.

'We've all worked very hard, and consider your stopping the show to be most unfair', said Rosemary, who was particularly annoyed at not being able to try out her very clever Latin duet with Jacky. But the house mother was not to be moved.

Kristina had begun to study ten subjects for the Ordinary level exams to be held in June 1951. These included art, but tuition hadn't improved. Those who'd persisted with art all had some talent, and Miss Cook counted on this to scrape them through the exam. She had long since run out of impetus as well as inspiration. The only advantage to the girls was the relaxed atmosphere in which they were allowed to talk quietly.

It was during an art class that Kristina was able to tell Laura about her disastrous Christmas holiday.

'And has Pam arranged to take you out this term, so you can see Eddy?'

'Yes, next Saturday. I can hardly wait.'

'The trouble is, Kristina, you spend all your time dying to see him. But when you do it's so short and unsatisfactory you get plunged into gloom. How on earth are you going to get any work done?'

'I don't know.'

'Being in love is so time-wasting. You ought to be reading more. My father says referring to books other than the set books in the English exam, will help to get better marks. One must avoid just regurgitating the notes we're given in class.'

Kristina knew this was true. But her inward response was, *Just wait till you fall in love.* In contrast to Laura,

Miranda was wholly in sympathy, being constantly in love herself. 'My dears', she'd announced at the beginning of term to the Senior Common Room, 'Je suis désolée. I'm wildly in love with two chaps, and simply can't decide which one to cultivate.'

'The question is, are they both wildly in love with you?' asked Jacky.

'Of course they are. Jonathan's looks are just too, too divine, but Jean-Paul, who's half French, is more poetic. You should hear him reading Baudelaire. It almost makes me swoon with desire.'

'Oh, do keep your voice down, Miranda. I've got two Latin unseens to finish tonight', said Rosemary.

When Kristina told the girls in her dormitory that her boy-friend was black, they were fascinated. She showed them her photograph of Eddy, and everyone agreed he was rather stunning. 'How romantic!' said Miranda. 'You are brave, Kristina. If I fell for a black chap, Daddy would cut me off with a farthing. I'd be out on the streets in my petticoat, like Queen Elizabeth.'

'You've got it wrong', said Jacky. 'Queen Elizabeth was never on the streets in her petticoat. She only said that, were she to find herself on the streets, she'd be quite capable of earning her living.'

Kristina's current form mistress was a Miss Winter, who also happened to be her Latin teacher. One afternoon she told the class to get on with homework, since she wanted to talk individually to each girl in alphabetical order about university entrance to Oxford or Cambridge. When Kristina's turn came, Miss Winter said crisply, 'We won't be entering you, Kristina. You may sit down.'

'But I might want to go to Oxford.'

'In the sixth form you may apply to some provincial university. You certainly won't be able to sit the Oxford or Cambridge examination.'

Laura had been put down as a potential candidate. Miranda and Fiona hadn't even bothered to queue up. They were quite indifferent, but Kristina felt indignant and humiliated. She would show them she could pass the Oxbridge entrance. She would work particularly hard at Latin, which was mainly a question of memorising grammar, vocabulary and chunks of Virgil – very tedious, but it could be done. The notion that nearly three and a half years before sitting before her A-levels she'd been written off as too stupid to sit the university entrance exam, seemed most unfair.

Miranda too was indignant on Kristina's account. 'Poor, poor you!' she exclaimed, in her usual generous fashion. 'How dare they stop you taking the entrance, when you're so brainy? I'm rather dim, I know, and wouldn't want to spend years swotting away at university. And of course, poor Fiona's an absolute dumbo. But thank God for that. We both want to leave at the end of next year, and go to a finishing school in Switzerland.'

Don't take Miss Winter's decision as final, Laura wrote in a note to Kristina, Of course you'll be able to sit Oxbridge if you really think it's worth staying on an extra term to do it.

Saturday came at last, and Kristina stood watching at the window for Pam to arrive. They walked down Park Street to look at the shops, and then caught a bus to the Vicarage. 'The kids are dying to see you, and wish you could stay the night. It's such a pity there's no half-term break.'

The comfort of the Vicarage had improved immensely since Pam had started working. Even the bathroom was tolerable, with an efficient hot water system. The ancient, rusting pipes had been removed, the walls had been painted a sunny yellow, and the floor tiled in pale green. It was good to be able to walk upstairs on carpet instead of clattering up on the bare boards. Kristina wished her Easter holiday could be spent with the Wilsons, where she felt happy and secure, and able to be herself without censure. She'd begun to trust Pam as much as Ruth.

Hilary and Jane liked Eddy, who teased them and didn't mind personal questions. After lunch, Pam drove everyone to Ashton Park, where they ran races with the children to keep warm in the freezing February wind. It was very pleasant to return to an open fire in the living room, to enjoy buttered crumpets and gingerbread. Eddy began to talk to Pam about his studies in the law, remarking how glad he was that Latin had been compulsory in the sixth form. It was so useful now. Kristina let her mind wander onto other things for a while, and then found Pam and Eddy were discussing law in seventeenth century England, and the writings of the philosopher and lawyer, Francis Bacon. Kristina was studying the Tudors for O-level, and knew little as yet about the Stuart period.

As Pam and Eddy continued their discussion, she felt neglected. 'Do we have to talk about history?' she said. 'I have enough of that at school.'

'Quite right', agreed Pam. 'Let's talk about the present. What did you think of the election?'

'I heard Attlee had won, but I don't know anything about him', said Kristina.

'Don't you get a newspaper at school?'

'There are some in the library, but the prefects always bag those.'

'We used to have current affairs at school', said Eddy. 'And a debating society. I enjoyed debating politics, and learnt a lot about public speaking.'

'I'll save some newspaper articles to send you, Kristina', said Pam. 'You really ought to know what's going on. I wonder they don't provide a paper in your common room.'

When the time came for Kristina to go, Patrick said he'd drive her to Cabot House to save her sitting in a draughty bus. Hilary and Jane clamoured to come too, and Eddy offered to tackle the washing-up with Pam. Kristina was disappointed she and Eddy weren't going by bus together, but she could understand that Pam must have help with so much washing-up.

She and Eddy kissed goodbye in the drive, while Patrick was getting the car out. 'You're so lucky, being able to stay for the evening, while I have to go back and do my rotten Latin homework.'

Tessa wrote to say the flat was sold, and she was in the process of buying a small house in Hampstead. She'd been invited to visit some friends who lived in Kenya, and was planning to go in the middle of February. She'd be back in April. Her Kenya address was enclosed. So now there would be no question of her coming down to the school, for which Kristina was thankful.

This term for the first time, those girls in the Senior Common Room wishing to attend concerts were to be allowed to go unaccompanied by a member of staff. A few of the girls who chose to go had never been to a symphony concert before, and were most excited at the prospect of hearing a live orchestra. Kristina walked down to the Colston Hall with Kate, and discovered that the Cabot and Penn House girls were sitting on the bench seats just behind the orchestra. These were brilliantly lit, as they were often used to accommodate a choir. By a lucky chance Laura was sitting directly behind her.

Kristina glanced through the programme notes. Schubert's 5th symphony in B flat was to be played first. She discovered it was one of Schubert's youthful six symphonies, written before he composed his two great symphonies. She read about its original melodies, high drama, deep feeling – about its being so completely Schubertian. Each movement was described in language she didn't entirely understand. She did remember the meaning of the words, *minuetto, allegro, andante* and *vivace* from the music lessons at the High School.

Kristina knew Beethoven's 5th was considered, unlike Schubert's 5th, as one of the greatest ever written. She read about the phrase, *Fate knocking at the Door,* but again she didn't quite understand what it meant. Phrases such as *thematic resemblances* and *germinal themes¸* made no sense to her at all.

Laura, who'd heard the Beethoven 5th before, said, 'The programme notes don't help much. Just listen to the music, and I'm sure you'll love it.'

'At school in Trinidad they used to tell us about a composer's life, then play one of his pieces, and finally explain it, letting us ask questions.'

'I can't think why the Dunbar hasn't got time for music. It's so essential to education.'

Just before the concert started Kristina suddenly noticed Eddy, sitting in the second row of the stalls amongst half a dozen other students. She tried but couldn't attract his attention. In her excitement she found it hard to concentrate on the Schubert symphony. At the interval she left her hat on the seat and hurried down into the stalls with Laura. They struggled through the crowd to reach Eddy and his friends. He greeted her warmly enough, and introductions took place. Yet for the first time there was a certain awkwardness in his manner. When she and Laura resumed their seats for the Beethoven, she suspected Eddy had been embarrassed at having a girl-friend dressed in school uniform. At the end she saw him hurriedly leaving the auditorium with his friends.

'Wasn't the Beethoven absolutely wonderful?' said Laura.

'Yes, it was', replied Kristina. 'What did you think of Eddy?'

'Very handsome', pronounced Laura, 'He looks older than eighteen.'

Kristina felt great pride in being his girl-friend, but the question remained in her mind: was he as proud of her as she of him?

The next time Kristina was invited to the vicarage, Eddy was late. On his way he'd dropped into the second-hand department of George's bookshop and picked up some bargain copies of Shaw's best-known plays and prefaces. Patrick and Pam were very fond of Shaw's works. They regarded him highly as a theatre and music critic, and spent lunchtime talking about him. Kristina knew almost nothing about Bernard Shaw. She knew that Jacky had been captivated by *Saint Joan,* and she remembered enjoying the play, *Pygmalion,* she'd seen with her mother. But she felt so ignorant as Patrick held forth on the social and political themes in Shaw. Eddy asked questions about the socialist Fabian Society to which Shaw had belonged, and they began a long discussion about the future of socialism in the post-war world.

Eddy had progressed into the adult intellectual world, leaving her far behind. He was currently interested in the poet T.S. Eliot, but when she glanced through his copy of *The Waste Land* she was utterly baffled. The four-year age gap was constantly widening. Eddy was coming to regard her as she regarded Hilary and Jane – intelligent, interesting kids, but only kids as yet. If her father had been able to keep her in Trinidad, she might already have absorbed some ideas on literature and other subjects. So far at the Dunbar she'd had no access to intellectual discussion. The library was full of literary and erudite books. But she'd been so intimidated by the chief librarian in her first term that she never ventured to find out how the library functioned. Besides, she needed guidance as to what to read.

After lunch Hilary and Jane urged Kristina to come to their bedroom, as they wanted to show her a secret. 'Only Kristina', said Jane, 'Not you, Eddy. You can stay and wash up with Mum.'

Kristina had sensed the children were in a state of excitement, and she let herself be led upstairs. Hilary took out a small box from under her mattress. Inside it lay a delicate coral necklace.

'How lovely', said Kristina,'

'It's for Mum's birthday', whispered Jane.

'When is it?

'Tomorrow. She's going to be thirty-five.'

Jane made thirty-five sound very old, and even Kristina felt that Pam was definitely leaving youth behind. 'I wish you'd told me before, so I could have bought her a present. There isn't time now even to send her a card.'

'We should have told you', said Hilary, 'But you could give her something next time you come.'

'Yes, I will', *But it wouldn't be the same*, she thought.

'I'll tell you another secret', went on Jane.

Hilary gasped. 'Mum told us not to.'

'You'll have to tell me now', said Kristina, smiling. 'And I promise not to tell your mother.'

'Mum's having a birthday party tomorrow evening, but she said not to let you know. She asked your horrible house mother to let you come, but she refused, and Mum didn't want to disappoint you. You'd have got to know on Monday anyway, because she's going to save you a quarter of her birthday cake and bring it up to the school.'

'How very kind of her.'

'She's really sorry you can't be at the party, especially as Eddy's coming.'

'Eddy?'

'Yes, she's invited some friends and a few people from the university. It's a wine and cheese party, and we're going to make sausages on sticks and other things.'

'Sounds like it's going to be a good party', said Kristina brightly, but inside she felt sick. She followed the children downstairs and agreed to go for a walk with Eddy, since it was a bright March day.

He told her as usual about his work, his friends and his social life at the University. He'd been to see an Ibsen play at the Theatre Royal, and heard Moiseiwitsch play at the Colston Hall. A season of chamber concerts had started in the Great Hall of the University.

Once Kristina would have described incidents at school – talked about Laura and Miranda, and the constant difficulties of trying to get work done amidst the petty rules which occupied so much time. Lights Out was at ten, and often she had to finish essays or learn her notes by torchlight under the bedclothes in the cold dormitory. Books had to be secreted upstairs under the watchful eye of Matron. Life continued in a nightmare of strategic planning to meet deadlines.

Initially Eddy had laughed at or commiserated with the repetitive routine of school life, but it had ceased to interest him. Now she did most of the listening, recounting very little of her own life. But on this particular afternoon she did say, 'My mother's bought a house in Hampstead. Here's the address. But I don't suppose we'll be able to meet.'

'Not this Easter vacation, as I've agreed to go on a walking tour of Cornwall with a couple of chaps.'

'If only I could come!'

'It's a pity you can't. If we were able to meet in London, to go to theatres and art galleries and so on, I wouldn't have joined this walking trip. But you really have become a prisoner of your school and your mother.'

'So, will I ever see you again?' Kristina said miserably.

'Yes, of course. Pam will invite you out next term.'

'It's not so easy as you think. My parents share the cost of my holidays, and of course have been paying Pam to have me to stay. But I'm sure it hasn't included having me at weekends. If I tell my mother she ought to pay Pam for all the extras, she'll probably come to Bristol next term and take me out herself.'

'Let's not think beyond this term.'

'If only we could both go to Port of Spain this summer.'

'I can't go home till I've got my degree. It's costing my father a lot to send me to university, and there will be years more studying after my degree.'

They walked on, and then Kristina said, almost accusingly, 'Jane told me about Pam's party.'

'Yes it's a shame Miss Deacon wouldn't let you come. Pam was most annoyed.'

'She's always so good to me.' She paused, and then added, 'I was surprised you were invited without me.'

'Pam's been like a mother to us both, I suppose. She knows it's been hard for me to settle in England. She encouraged me from the beginning to drop in if I needed any advice, or just moral support.'

'And do you drop in?'

'Not now, I'm too busy. I used to, and like you I almost feel like one of the family. I shan't stay long at the party.'

'It doesn't matter to me how long you stay.'

'We must keep in contact', said Pam as she drove Kristina back to Cabot House. 'And if your mother can't manage to come and take you out next term, we can have you again. It's only a year and a term until you're in the sixth form, and then you'll be able to see us – and Eddy too, of course – more often.'

'It's a long time to wait. Eddy will have fallen for someone else by then.'

Outside Cabot House, Pam kissed Kristina goodbye, saying, 'Don't despair, my dear. You've got a whole lifetime ahead of you.'

Kristina smiled and thanked Pam for all her kindness. But at that moment she decided she was going to the party on Sunday night, come what may. She'd had enough of the Dunbar Academy.

At cocoa time that Saturday evening, word passed round that Miss Deacon, who was away for the weekend, might not be back till Monday. Matron, with the help of the prefects, was left in charge. She liked to retire early to her two attic rooms, and Kristina's hopes rose.

At rest time on Sunday afternoon Kristina took from the wardrobe a green dress she'd acquired in Port of Spain. Unlike her sun dresses, this one had sleeves, a scooped neckline and a tight-fitting skirt. Mrs Morrison had encouraged her to have a dress she could wear on special occasions in England. It went well with the filigree silver necklace Eddy had bought her in Marine Square.

Miranda was full of admiration when Kristina told her she was going to a party at the vicarage with Eddy. The Toad being away, it would be safe to slip out of the cloakroom door in the basement and take the key.

'But what a risk, Kristina! You'll be expelled if they find out.'

'I don't care. I'm going to go.'

'I'll put some clothes in your bed to look like a body, just in case.'

The other girls in the dormitory were all eager to support Kristina. 'Make sure you catch the ten-ten bus from the Downs', said Cynthia, 'Otherwise you'll have to walk all that way, and arrive very late.'

The kitchen staff went home on Sunday after lunch, but for one maid, who left after cocoa time. Thus by nine o'clock the basement was empty. Matron had gone to her room, leaving a prefect to lock the front door and turn off the lights, except for two dim bulbs in the upstairs hall and the bathroom.

The buses would have ceased running by the time the party ended, but Kristina knew Eddy would walk back to Cabot House with her. The sky was overcast, but it was dry and unusually warm for March. Kristina dressed by torchlight, and was ready to leave before ten.

'Coast's clear', whispered Miranda, and Kristina, carrying her shoes, slipped quickly down the stairs. In the cloakroom she exchanged her dressing gown for her coat. Then she unlocked the basement door, slid back the bolt and stepped outside. She locked the door and put the key in her handbag.

Once in the road Kristina experienced the elation of a newly escaped prisoner. Just to be out of Cabot House at night was exhilarating. Sitting in the bus, she put on some pink lipstick and a dab or two of perfume. How easy it had been to walk out! She must try to do it again in the summer term.

Alighting from the bus at the church, she slipped in at the front gate of the vicarage. The windows were shut, but dance music and voices could be heard from inside.

Her heart was beating wildly. Suddenly she felt self-conscious at the thought of appearing among the guests, and having to explain to the Wilsons how she'd escaped. As it was a dry night she decided to go and sit on the seat in the shrubbery for a moment, to compose herself before ringing at the back door.

By now she'd become used to the dark. Tip-toeing across the lawn and round some bushes, she was about to move towards the seat, when every muscle in her body tightened, and she stood, unable to move. A man and a woman were already sitting on it, and Kristina was sure the man had hastily removed his arm from around the woman.

She stared hard at the shocked faces of Pam and Eddy for what seemed like a whole minute, and then turned and ran, almost stumbling out of the gate. She continued to run, over the footbridge, past the old prison entrance, along Wapping Road and across the swing bridge. At the beginning of Prince Street she turned left into Narrow Quay on the river, and finally collapsed onto a bench to get her breath. There was no one about, and the silence of a Bristol Sunday night enveloped her.

What were they doing on the seat? How long had the affair been going on? How could Pam betray her husband with a student? As for Eddy, all those passionate sentiments, all those kisses and hugs had been a sham. Did Eddy "drop in" to the vicarage every day when Patrick was out and the children at school? Were they using the double bed she had slept in – or worse, the bed Patrick slept in? Were they laughing at her as they made love? It was Pam's fault, Pam, who had been so generous and understanding. No wonder Eddy had fallen under her spell and allowed himself to be seduced. Pam's kindness made the treachery all the worse. She, who had everything in life, had dared to snatch away Kristina's only happiness.

She couldn't get a grip on the thoughts racing through her mind. She was almost choking with hate, and for a wild few seconds the black water, glittering dimly in the light of a street lamp, tempted her. But no, she would fight, and get Eddy back. She rose and started the long walk up Park Street towards the Downs.

Kristina re-entered the basement, locked the door and stood in the dark on the stairs, listening intently. A car drew up outside Cabot House, and she heard a man's voice, and then a woman's. A door opened, and then another. Miss Deacon must be returning a day early. Kristina fled into the cloakroom. Twenty minutes passed, and all was quiet. Had the woman gone to her bedroom adjoining the study by now? Carrying her shoes and dressing gown, Kristina started up the long, steep flight of stairs. Halfway up, had she been old and feeble, she might well have suffered a heart attack, for Miss Deacon suddenly appeared at the top, like a grotesque ghost, clad in a shapeless white candlewick dressing gown. Her pale face and bulbous eyes were quite discernable in the dingy half light coming from the upstairs hall.

'You'd better come to my study, Kristina' was all she said.

The interrogation was short and to the point. Where had she been, and with whom?

Kristina had no intention of implicating the Wilsons, or naming names. She simply said she'd been meeting a friend, and refused to say more. Miss Deacon told her to go up to a small room next to the bathroom, in which a bed was kept for emergencies. 'You will stay there tonight, and in the morning I shall escort you to see Miss Craig.'

She sat on the bed in the room upstairs, aware that she would be expelled. She felt glad, even elated, but soon despair set in. She'd have to go to Hampstead and face her mother's fury, She'd be sent to another boarding school, far away from her friends. Life would continue to be intolerable. It was only towards dawn that she let herself dwell again on Eddy and Pam. Her father had hinted that Eddy might fall in love with someone at university – but not Pam, surely not Pam! How could an old married woman be more attractive to him than herself? It was unreasonable, impossible, and humiliating – the more so, since it was so unexpected. She couldn't imagine Pam in the role of seductress.

After a sleepless night, Kristina rose at six to wash and drink some water. She waited like a recaptured prisoner till she heard the breakfast bell and the rush downstairs, when she dared to venture to the dormitory to put on her uniform. She returned to the room until Matron appeared, bringing her coat, hat and outdoor shoes. The kitchen maid then entered with a bowl of porridge and mug of tea. There was no sugar or milk, but Kristina was so hungry she wolfed down the tasteless grey mess.

'You're to go to Miss Deacon's study at nine o'clock', announced Matron.

The walk to the main school beside the poker-faced, silent house-mother was distasteful in the extreme, but Kristina was in a state of utmost defiance. Since she was going to be expelled she'd nothing to lose.

'Do you know where your mother is?' Miss Craig snapped as Kristina stood before her desk.

'She's having a holiday in Kenya.'

'How annoying and irresponsible of her not to have notified Miss Deacon. Do you have the address?'

'It's at Cabot House.'

'Well, when you return, let Miss Deacon have it at once. We shall have to telegraph your mother. In the meantime you'll be kept in isolation at the sanatorium until arrangements can be made for you to leave. It hardly needs saying what a disgrace you've been to the school.'

Kristina suddenly found herself declaring in a loud voice, 'There's nothing I want more than to leave you and your horrible school. It's like a prison. I've hated every minute of my time here. I wonder you dare charge such huge fees for such awful education!'

For a fleeting second or two Kristina detected an expression of shocked astonishment on Miss Craig's face. She was a woman who'd never previously been challenged. Then, before Kristina could say another word, she was ordered to return to Cabot House, to collect all her belongings and pack her trunk, prior to going by taxi to the sanatorium. A prefect was waiting outside the door to escort her.

The dreaded word 'Sanatorium' galvanised Kristina's brain into action. It was three weeks until the end of term, when her mother was due to return from Kenya. Three weeks at the san would be a living hell. Even if Tessa came back earlier, Kristina was not going there, even for a night. She'd have to escape immediately to prevent it. As she and the prefect put on their coats in the cloakroom, she planned her route. She was thankful that her holidays with the Wilsons had enabled her to become familiar with Bristol and the area across the suspension bridge.

She walked down Stoke Hill in silence with the prefect, and then at the bottom made a dash for it across the Downs, running as she'd not run since sprinting along the beach at Manzanilla. She reached the bridge, planning to hide for a while once she'd crossed it. She dived into a thick copse of trees and bushes on the other side, and here she rested, sitting on her hat in the damp grass, wondering what action the school would take to find her. Would they leave her to it, or would they notify the police? What was the usual procedure if one defied the Dunbar Academy? She'd no idea. She wasn't a criminal, but she felt like one. She was 'on the run', like people she'd read about in books.

Emerging from her hiding place, where she was glad to abandon her battered hat, she proceeded along the road which joined Rownham Hill. Her aim was to reach Seaton, and this would only be possible if she was able to hitch a lift. Some of the older girls at school had tried hitchhiking. They made it sound easy, but she was very hesitant to start. It was safer, she'd been told, to hitch a lorry rather than a car. Lorry drivers had a reputation to keep up, and often liked to have a passenger to talk to on a long journey. Kristina supposed that once she reached the bottom of Rownham Hill there would be lorries travelling south towards Bridgwater. After waiting twenty minutes, during which no lorries passed, one did eventually come, on its way to Taunton.

The driver was a middle-aged, burly no-nonsense fellow, who remarked, 'A schoolgirl hitching a lift at this time of day! Are you running away, kid?'

'No, I've just been expelled. I want to get home to Seaton – it's in Devon.'

'Is that what they do, throw you out to find your own way home?'

'I wanted to get away quickly.'

'I'm not in the business of picking up schoolgirls. How old are you?'

'Sixteen', she lied. 'Couldn't you just take me a few miles out of Bristol?'

Kristina looked so pale and distressed that the driver helped her up onto the passenger seat, Her relief, after the events of the previous twelve hours, was so great that she burst into agonised tears, and once started she couldn't stop. The driver handed her a clean hanky, saying, 'That's right, my dear, just you have a good cry.' He produced another hanky, and slowly Kristina's sobs lessened.

He drove steadily along the road, only slowing down for a moment to offer Kristina a bag of barley sugar. 'Get some o' they inside you. Them'll perk you up.' The sweets and the rhythmic rumble of the engine soothed her, and by the time they'd been through Congresbury and turned off to join the main road to Bridgwater she felt better.

On reaching Taunton the driver pulled into a petrol station, and explained that he lived in Taunton, but was going on to Chard, and then Axminster. Since he was making good time, he'd go out of his way to take her to

Seaton first. He made it clear in his blunt fashion that he needed to be rid of her before making his deliveries.

'I'm so sorry to be a nuisance', said Kristina. 'I expect you're wondering why I've been expelled.'

'Ask no questions and you'll get told no lies is my motto. I'm glad to be of help.'

The journey continued. Together they finished off the barley sugars, saying little to each other. All too soon the lorry drew up at the top of Seaton Down Hill.

You'll know your way from here, I expect', said the driver.

'Yes', replied Kristina, quite overwhelmed with gratitude. 'Thanks very much for being so decent.'

'All in a day's work, my dear.'

She jumped down from her seat, and then watched the lorry turning and moving away. The driver hooted once in farewell, and she waved, feeling strangely forlorn.

She stood for a while, dazed by her luck, and the speed with which she'd reached Seaton. Her aunt had seemed so far away. Now she only had to make her way down the hill to Marlpit Lane and along the Beer Road to Seaton Hole Cottage to face the daunting task of accounting for her sudden arrival.

In the spring sunshine from the top of Seaton Down Hill she could see the stunning view of the wide blue bay, where the horizon always stood so high against the sky that it seemed the sea would topple over and engulf the town. In spite of her troubles, she experienced a sudden elation, the same sense of freedom she'd felt as a child on emerging from the trees onto the coast at Manzanilla. The immensity of the sea and sky lifted her out of the depression of her cloistered school life.

Chapter Sixteen

A s it happened, Kristina's arrival was by no means a surprise. Ruth had answered the phone soon after ten, to endure an angry ten-minute tirade from Miss Craig, during which she gathered her niece had been out at night, probably with a boy, which meant expulsion. Instead of waiting to be removed by her mother, she'd had the audacity to run away, and was now roaming the countryside. She was likely to come to Seaton, since she wasn't at the vicarage. If she didn't turn up at Seaton, the police would have to be rung, something she wished to avoid, in case the story got into the press. It was intolerable that the school's reputation should suffer on account of Kristina. To make things worse, her mother had gone off on holiday to Kenya without notifying the school. Since the girl had absconded without producing her mother's address, the matron had had to find it, and Miss Deacon was obliged to go to the Post Office to send a telegram, thereby missing one of her lessons. Where was Kristina's trunk to be sent to, and who would come to collect her suitcase? The whole sordid business of Kristina had been inconvenient and time-wasting. She'd proved to be nothing but a troublemaker since her arrival. In all her time as headmistress of the Dunbar Academy, Miss Craig concluded, she'd never come across such an immoral, negligent, discourteous and utterly irresponsible family. She bitterly regretted accepting Kristina as a pupil, and in fact had only done so, against her better judgment, on account of her father's being a clergyman.

Ruth scarcely had time to say she would ring if Kristina did or didn't turn up, before Miss Craig put down the receiver.

Ruth was stunned by this phone call. It wasn't surprising that Kristina had eventually fallen foul of the authorities, but the problem of John being in Trinidad and Tessa being in Kenya, meant that she and Peter would have to assume responsibility for Kristina in the meantime.

She rang her husband, who agreed to come home from school for a couple of hours to talk about the situation. Peter, as always, had no patience with boarding schools. He had always maintained it was useless incarcerating teenage girls in a strict nunnery and not expecting them to break out occasionally. At lunch he said, 'It beats me how Kristina managed to acquire a boy friend.'

'It's probably someone from Clifton Boys' College. It's very close to the Dunbar.'

They were discussing the likelihood of their niece, or even the possibility of Tessa, appearing at Seaton in the next day or two, when Kristina arrived, looking decidedly untidy and dejected. After giving her a hug, Ruth told her to have a wash, and then they'd give her a meal before going into explanations.

Kristina related the events already known to Ruth and Peter. She then added an emotional summary of her relationship with Eddy, leaving out the incident in the vicarage garden. She dreaded seeing Tessa, who would lock her up in another boarding school and refuse to let her see Eddy again. In any case her affair with him was over. Her life was ruined, and she wished she was dead.

Ruth rang the school and left a message for Miss Craig, saying her husband would come to Cabot House the following Saturday to collect Kristina's belongings. The next few days were full of worry. Peter spent the first evening trying to phone John, without success, and finally had to leave a message with the bishop. By the third day he was becoming distinctly annoyed. When alone with his wife, he grumbled about the utter lack of consideration on the part of Tessa, John and the school, in not communicating further. Tessa should have wired to say which day she was arriving in London. Likewise John should have telephoned. 'Is the girl to be left high and dry with us until her parents feel like doing something constructive? Tessa has treated us abominably, and yet she stays in Kenya while we feed and clothe and console her daughter.'

'It is very annoying', said Ruth, 'Yet in spite of everything, we must help the poor girl. We have to see this through.'

Peter calmed down and took care not to show Kristina how discomfited he was.

Kristina herself couldn't begin to feel settled, in spite of the relief at having escaped the Dunbar. She regretted having had to leave without saying goodbye to her friends, particularly Laura. And as always, there was the miserable thought of Eddy. Perhaps he would write – surely he would write? – but would his letter be sent on?

Anne and Penny were given an outline of what had happened, and once again were fascinated by Kristina's exploits.

'Now you'll have to live here and go to our school', said Penny.

But Kristina knew she'd have to live with her mother in Hampstead, and be sent to another boarding school. If Constance had her way it might even be to some kind of reform school.

On Saturday Peter duly arrived at Cabot House, and asked briskly for Kristina's things. Miss Deacon gave him the most frigid of greetings, but was polite enough.

'Have you heard from Kristina's mother?' he asked.

'Yes, she's written to the headmistress, disclaiming all responsibility for her daughter. Her father is to have custody and care of her in future. Miss Craig has written to her father, and sent a telegram. One would expect him to come to England as soon as possible to relieve your family of Kristina's presence.'

On his drive home Peter pondered over Tessa's astonishing decision, altering Kristina's life once more, and giving Ruth and himself a new problem. He found his wife sitting in the kitchen, re-reading a long letter from John. 'Listen to this', she said.

Tessa admits that she hasn't made a satisfactory relationship with her daughter, and has no time in her new life for the task of caring for such a wilful teenager. She's started a serious love affair in Kenya, and says she won't be returning to London in the near future. She's rented out her house at Hampstead, and suggests Kristina could spend the Easter holiday at Seaton. Constance will continue to pay the boarding school fees, and she herself will share all Kristina's other expenses as usual with me. Though I'm happy and relieved to have control of Kristina's education once more, I now have many problems, the most immediate being, could you possibly have Kristina for the Easter holidays? She can come to Trinidad in the summer ...

'Tessa obviously hadn't heard about the expulsion when she wrote that letter, and neither had John. It'll give him a much bigger problem, though at least he no longer has to contend with Tessa', said Peter. 'We might have guessed she'd embark on a new love affair and ditch Kristina, having messed up her life and given us great inconvenience.'

'In the long term we should be glad. But it's certainly left John in a fix.'

'He'll have to get leave immediately to sort out Kristina's future.'

'To my mind, the obvious answer to all this is for Kristina to live here and go to the Grammar School.'

'That means over three years with us.'

'I don't mind. We're all very fond of Kristina.'

'John might want to take her back to Trinidad permanently.'

'Possibly, but I doubt that would be the best solution.'

'Well, there's nothing we can do till we hear from John again, except to tell Kristina about her mother's decision.'

When Ruth told her niece about Tessa, Kristina found it very difficult to come to terms with the violence of her feelings. There was enormous relief, of course, at not having to face her mother again. But then came anger and bitter resentment at this final rejection after Tessa had snatched her away from Trinidad without caring anything for her happiness. At the same time she was struck by the irony that though she could now meet

Eddy quite openly – he could visit Seaton, and she could go to Bristol – he might not want to see her.

A week went by, during which the family became aware that Kristina had become ominously quiet, withdrawn and listless, markedly different from the high-spirited girl who'd first arrived at Seaton from Trinidad. The weather during these early spring days seemed to match Kristina's dark mood. On Sunday she woke at five to see grey clouds spread across the horizon like stiff cardboard cut-outs, resembling rugged mountains. Above the clouds the sky was a sickly duck-egg green, in the middle of which hovered a strange patch of angry black cloud. *That's me,* she thought. She dressed and ran the length of the almost deserted shingle to the harbour, crossing the bridge and continuing along the beach under Haven Cliff. There she sat panting on the pebbles, gazing at the smooth gun-metal sea. Looking up she saw the sky was now covered with a solid blanket of pale grey cloud.

All at once from behind came laughter and the calling of her name. She turned to see two small figures in red jumpers shinning up the steep cliff. Stumbling over the pebbles onto the grass, she shrieked, 'Come down, you'll fall!'

'No, we won't', shouted Penny. 'Why don't you come up?'

They were still kids – kids used to climbing high trees and cliffs without fear – she'd been so like them in Trinidad, and suddenly she wished desperately to be a carefree child again, racing along the beach with the Oropouche Gang. There was a danger of falling rocks and soil along this stretch of cliff. She was heavier than the twins, and unused to climbing. Nevertheless, she shouted 'OK, I'm coming!'

She kept snatching at small thorny bushes, which threatened to come away in her hands, and at one point felt herself sliding backwards. But finally she gained the top, and joined the twins. When she got her breath back, Kristina said, 'It's such a dangerous cliff! You shouldn't be climbing it.'

'We've climbed it hundreds of times', said Anne. 'But don't you dare tell Mum.'

The effort she'd expended on climbing had invigorated Kristina. She'd spent too much time recently sitting at a desk and walking along pavements.

'Look', said Penny, 'The cloud's breaking up.' And sure enough, over the next few minutes the sky cleared, and the sun rose in a fiery blaze of glory. Kristina felt a momentary rush of joy again, such as she had felt at the top of Seaton Down Hill. But this feeling vanished as swiftly as the sun disappeared behind a cloud.

'It's difficult for you', said Ruth after breakfast. 'Not knowing what's going to happen. At least now you can be sure it won't be another boarding school.'

Kristina was silent for a moment, then she said, 'I wish I belonged to a particular place, with a family of my own. I don't really belong anywhere. My mother took me away from my father, and then dropped me. I used to belong to Trinidad, but last summer I felt like a foreigner with my old school friends, and even with Dodo. Mrs Morrison and Pam and all of you here are sorry for me, but I'm not really wanted anywhere, am I? '

'I can assure you, Kristina, that Peter and I and the girls want you to live here very much. We never did like the thought of your being at boarding school.'

Kristina burst into dramatic tears, saying, 'The worst thing is, Eddy doesn't want me either.'

Ruth, unaware of all the implications concerning Eddy, said, 'I expect he'll contact you soon.'

'No, he won't. He's at university, and doesn't want a schoolgirl any more.'

'The first rejection is always the worst', said Ruth. 'You won't believe me when I say that by this time next year you'll have a new boy-friend. And who knows, it might be you who does the rejecting next time. That has its problems too.'

'I don't want a new boyfriend', said Kristina. 'I won't find anyone as wonderful as Eddy. Eddy's unique.'

Finally, on March 27th, when Peter and the twins had gone to school, a telegram arrived for Kristina from Port of Spain. *BE WITH YOU FRIDAY APRIL 7 LETTER FOLLOWING.* She could hardly believe it. For so long her father had been unable to come when she needed him most. Now, at last, he was moving quickly. Kristina's spirits began to revive a little, The twins, who'd always regarded their cousin as a romantic rebel, were now given a sensational account of her last days at the Dunbar.

Letters from John came at last – one to Ruth, and the other to Kristina, in which he wrote, *I've decided to leave Trinidad for good. I shall live and work in England. You've gone through some very difficult years, my poor Kristina, and I'm sorry the Dunbar turned out such a disaster. You'll be able to go to a day school, and I hope we can make up for lost time. I won't*

*write much more now, as there's a great deal to do before I leave.
My parishioners, as always, have been over-generous with gifts
and hospitality. It's very sad leaving after all these years, but I
don't think your coming to live at Morvant would be a good idea.
So I need to be in England, where I can see as much of you as
possible...*

To Ruth, John had written that the Bishop of
Trinidad had been most understanding. He was going to
use his influence with the Bishop of Exeter to find a
parish in Devon for her brother. Ruth explained the
situation to Kristina, saying, 'This is such good news.
Now your father will sort out your life in the best way
for you.'

John turned up at the cottage on a chilly, windy day,
shivering in an old pair of light trousers, a summer shirt
and sandals. His hair was now entirely grey. Ruth got out
the mac, tweed jacket, jumpers and shoes she'd always
stored for him, but suggested he buy some new clothes.
'You'll have to smarten yourself up, John. You could at
least have bought a sweater in Port of Spain.'

Kristina stared at her father with a mixture of
affection, guilt and mild irritation. In the bright sunlight
of Trinidad his old khaki shorts and much-darned white
shirts had looked passable, but now in England she
realised how scruffy he appeared. What could he have
been wearing the night he'd met her mother, who always
looked so immaculate? Perhaps his smile had attracted
Tessa – that benign but slightly amused smile, combined
with a kindliness which, Kristina began to suspect, often
led people to take advantage of him. Tessa had certainly
traded on his kindness. Kristina loved him for it, and so

did Ruth, but neither of them imagined he'd be easy to live with permanently.

John's most pressing problem was what to do with Kristina. For the first time she must be given a choice in the matter. She could live at Seaton. Peter had spoken to the Headmaster of the Grammar School, who was prepared to take her. Or she could live with him in his new parish. If she chose to make her permanent home at Seaton, then of course she would spend many weekends and holidays with him.

It was a hard choice to make. Kristina dreaded yet another unknown existence with new places, new people, and new domestic rituals and rules. She desperately needed security and continuity, and these she would get at Seaton, even allowing for the new school. She loved her father, but day-to-day life with him would be difficult. Morvant Rectory had shown her that. She sensed John was a loner who preferred living in his own eccentric way. He wouldn't be offended at her choice.

Ruth was pleased and very moved over her choice to make her home in Seaton.

'You're not going to have an easy time with Kristina', warned Peter. 'She's lost all confidence in herself. She'll be testing you all the time.'

'I realise that, but I'm glad we're going to have her. It's almost too late, but I'd like to give Kristina a sense of belonging unconditionally to our family. We must enable her to put down roots in Devon. Of course she'll be going to stay with John very often, and if we need a complete break we might even send the twins for a weekend!'

Kristina told her father the relationship with Eddy had come to an end. He pitied her, but wasn't surprised. Secretly he was relieved, though he did his best to console, without much success. The more unattainable Eddy became, the more obstinately Kristina wanted him. He would certainly write, she said, if only to say goodbye.

Other letters arrived, however. The first came from Tessa – a down-to-earth unsentimental letter, to the effect that it was a pity their relationship hadn't worked out, and she hoped Kristina would be more successful in her new life. Her mother's letters had always left Kristina feeling angry and resentful, but now, as she tore this one up, she felt satisfaction that the experiment was over for good.

Two letters arrived the same day, from Pam and from Miranda. Miranda wrote from her home in Sussex, in her usual exaggerated style: *Do, do tell me, how you outwitted Miss Craig, and everything else about that night. It must have been so romantic! The Toad summoned our dorm and tried to bully us into telling her who you were with. We all refused to talk, though she threatened us with the rack. Even Fiona kept her mouth shut. The expulsion was read out at assembly in Miss Craig's hushed, funereal tones, and we all kept a minute's silence pondering on the delicious wickedness of being out alone at night with a male creature. But seriously, we all miss you so much, and everyone sends masses of love.*

Kristina put Pam's letter under her pillow for a while before bringing herself to read it. *We are all,* she wrote, *very sorry indeed that you had to suffer years of misery at the Dunbar, ending up in expulsion.. Your aunt wrote to tell me you'll be living at Seaton, where I hope you'll be happy.*

I won't offer any excuse for my behaviour and Eddy's on the night of my party. I can only say that Eddy had become increasingly frustrated at not being able to visit you at school, or to see you alone during the holidays, except in secret. And it hasn't been easy, as you might imagine, for him to settle down in England and to put up with the prejudice he encounters. He began to confide in me and then thought he'd fallen in love. Perhaps I was too sympathetic. I can assure you, however, that I'm certainly not in love with him, though I was flattered for a while. There was nothing physical in our relationship other than his putting an arm round me after a few drinks on the night you saw us. He hasn't been to the Vicarage since then, and obviously we shan't be asking him.

We shall be sad if we never see you again. I can only say I'm very sorry for what's happened regarding Eddy. All the family have much enjoyed having you here. We shan't forget the good times we've spent together.

It was an immense relief to know Pam hadn't been in love with Eddy, and wouldn't be inviting him again. Kristina began to feel guilty for having hated Pam, and thought she might answer her letter – but not till she'd seen Eddy again. Whether or not Pam intended it, the letter gave her hope Eddy might revive his love for her once he knew she was no longer at boarding school or tied to her mother. When her father had settled, Eddy could be invited for a holiday in the summer. Kristina's hopes soared as she pictured the wonderful time they could have. She would write to him immediately and all would be well. It would be like those days in Trinidad again. But at the back of her mind there was a seed of doubt.

Kristina wrote to Laura, now on holiday in Torquay, and received a reply: *I'm so sorry you've left school, but it was inevitable they would find you out sooner or later. We could meet this holidays now you're living in Seaton...*

The girls arranged to meet at a café near the station in Exeter, where they spent an hour, and then another hour sitting on a bench in the park.

'I don't know how you're going to stick another three years or more at the Dunbar' said Kristina.

'Don't worry about me', replied Laura. 'For one thing, my housemistress isn't as bad as The Toad, and for another, I do have pleasant holidays in Cairo, and my grandparents always spoil me in Torquay.'

'I know some children have to go to a boarding school because their parents are abroad. But why do parents who live here send their children to a prison like the Dunbar? And why do they put up with it? Or am I just a freak?'

'No, you're just a natural rebel. Some children even enjoy being regimented. At a young age it's drummed into them by ambitious parents what a much better education they'll get at a public boarding school – with the most highly qualified teachers and the smallest classes, etcetera – and how they'll get into university more easily, and then into good jobs. Once girls start at the Dunbar, they don't want to upset their parents by asking to be taken away. They'd have to admit to being too weak to put up with the discipline, and it would mean buying a new uniform. So they begin to feel privileged, and think it shameful to be expelled. When someone like you gets kicked out, they pity you, but feel glad it wasn't them. The trouble is, children are brainwashed for years, just like those poor people in Russia today under Stalin.'

Kristina smiled. 'Surely you don't pity me?'

'No, you've been lucky. I'm glad you found a home and a day school. If I'd been expelled for being out at night with a boyfriend, my parents, especially my father, would have been livid. I'd have been packed off to another boarding school.'

'Wouldn't it be a wizard idea if all the girls at all the boarding schools went on strike to demand better conditions?'

'Yes. But who would organise and coordinate a strike?'

'I'd love to have tried if I'd had enough support.'

'You'd have had to be a sixth form prefect. The trouble is, once you're a prefect you become grateful for a few paltry privileges. You enjoy all the staff sucking up in the hope you'll get to Oxbridge, and you forget the horrors of boarding school. My father maintains the regime at his public school did him no end of good, even the canings. He says all children should be at state subsidised boarding schools learning to become responsible citizens.'

'If it means being like the Dunbar teachers. I don't want to become a responsible citizen.'

'Don't worry, no one will ever make you conform.'

'Are you always going to conform?'

'No, of course not. But instead of rushing at things like you, I've learned to be more subtle. If one starts a riot in prison, one only gets put in solitary or sent to a more secure place. I prefer to despise the Dunbar system quietly. The staff are perfectly aware of my views, but they can't punish me, because I don't break the rules.'

'The reason they leave you alone', pointed out Kristina, 'Is that you're so clever, and they can't miss the chance of getting an open scholarship out of you.'

'That's probably true. But the funny thing about it is that I shall refuse to stay on and sit the entrance exam.'

Kristina was impressed, but doubted she could ever quietly accept unjust authority as Laura was doing. Then she told her friend about Eddy's infatuation, and showed her Pam's letter.

'I'm not surprised', commented Laura in her forthright fashion. 'Eddy must have been most frustrated and unhappy. Don't blame Pam. She sounds like a person who's always ready to give sympathy and affection. Anyway, first love affairs usually come to a sticky end. You'll fall for someone else by Christmas.'

'I won't.'

'Has he written to you?'

'Not yet. I'm sure he will.'

'I wouldn't bank on it.'

'Why not?' asked Kristina desperately.

'I'm sure he's got the sense to realise he can't keep up a relationship with a schoolgirl he rarely sees. If he wrote, it might get you hoping.'

'He will write. I know he will! If I hadn't been at the Dunbar it wouldn't have gone wrong in the first place.'

'Yes it would. He's too old for you at the moment. Remember that night at the Colston Hall?'

'You don't understand. No one understands.'

'I do understand. Eddy still has years of study. You said he'll have to get a job each vac, so he won't be able to come to Seaton. And just as you're starting out on a career, he'll be returning to Trinidad. You admitted yourself you felt out of place in Port of Spain. And imagine how out of place Eddy would feel in Seaton. Besides, you hardly know him.'

'Of course I know him. We've spent hours talking.'

'You might have done in Trinidad. But here in Bristol you've hardly had the chance. The romance was doomed from the start.'

'You know nothing about being in love', said Kristina angrily.

'No, I don't, but I can imagine it. And if it turns people into idiots, then I'd rather not be in love!'

'If you think I'm an idiot, there's no point in being my friend.'

'Don't let's quarrel', said Laura. 'I'm going to miss you so much next term.'

'And I shall miss you too.'

'I don't think you'll go on being an idiot. I hope you'll put the Dunbar and Eddy behind you, and settle down at your day school, even though you'll probably find that quite restrictive. Let's look forward to the day we leave school. That will be the moment we actually start our education and make our own decisions. We grow up when we cast aside adolescence and begin to live in the real world. Then we can laugh at our so-called education.'

'Have you learnt anything of value at the Dunbar?'

'To parse and paraphrase, and how to write a good business letter!'

'I remember the terms of the Congress of Vienna. D'you think that's useful?'

'It all depends.'

'On what?'

'On whether you intend becoming a history teacher at the Dunbar!'

Kristina let out a loud, uninhibited laugh, and an elderly couple on a nearby seat stared in disapproval.

'You've got half an hour before your train departs', said Laura. 'Let's go back to the café, and I'll treat you to a knickerbocker glory.'

Linking arms, the two girls walked out of the park.